Margot

"Beautiful . . . Immediate and realistic, *Margot* brings Anne Frank and her sister to new life." —ERIKA ROBUCK, author of *Call Me Zelda* and *Hemingway's Girl*

"This is a haunting book—emotionally raw, beautifully written, and so close to the bone." —GWEN COOPER, *New York Times* bestselling author of *Homer's Odyssey* and *Love Saves the Day*

"The kind of story that will leave you breathless, both because of its ambitious subject matter and its deeply arresting story-telling. . . . *Margot* is the sort of book that remains with you long after the final page." —ILIE RUBY, author of *The Salt God's Daughter* and *The Language of Trees*

"Breathes life into a character we know only from her sister's famous diary. . . . *Margot* examines history versus story and how we cling to the fictions we tell ourselves." —T. GREENWOOD, author of *Two Rivers*, *Grace*, and *Bodies of Water*

PRAISE FOR

Margot

"[A] marvelously wrought 'what-if' story of the survival of Anne Frank's sister and her hidden identity in a new country. Psychologically subtle, satisfyingly suspenseful, and sensitively written."

—Margaret George, *New York Times* bestselling author of *Elizabeth I: The Novel*

"This beautifully told sister narrative is more than an intriguing what-if. It's a meditation on the nature of survivor guilt and the legacy of invisible wounds. *Margot* takes on big questions in an intimate story, and carefully considers whether it is possible to survive—and thrive—after unspeakable horror. A moving, affecting novel."

—Diana Abu-Jaber, author of *Crescent* and *Birds of Paradise*

"In this novel, a compassionate imagining of what might have happened had Anne Frank's sister, Margot, survived, Jillian Cantor provides more than a wistful what-if. She gives us a tour of the emotional nether land so often occupied by those who have survived the unimaginable and an example of extreme sibling competition—and love."

—Jenna Blum, *New York Times* bestselling author of *Those Who Save Us* and *The Stormchasers*

continued . . .

"Cantor brilliantly channels Anne Frank's sister, Margot, who survives the Holocaust horrors to hide yet again, in America, trying to forget the terrible secret that brought her here. A haunting meditation on who we really are versus who we wish we had been, regret, loss, and how we love in the face of sorrow. Glowing as a rare jewel, *Margot* is about discovering the truths of our lives, no matter what the cost."

—Caroline Leavitt, *New York Times* bestselling author
of *Pictures of You* and *Is This Tomorrow*

"Using historical facts and people we know and love, Cantor fills in the lost details of their lives with her imagination, and reaps a beautiful and redeeming new conclusion for a terrible chapter in history. Immediate and realistic, *Margot* brings Anne Frank and her sister to new life, while giving one of them a chance at a better future. The novel not only feels like a prayer for Margot and Anne, but for the many voiceless men and women whose memory deserves recognition."

—Erika Robuck, author of *Call Me Zelda* and
Hemingway's Girl

"This is a haunting book—emotionally raw, beautifully written, and so close to the bone that it's jarring to remember, when you come to the end, that Margot Frank isn't really alive and well and waiting somewhere in Philadelphia to answer all your questions. Even knowing this was a work of fiction, I was still moved to tears at seeing Margot finally get the happy ending we all wish she'd had."

—Gwen Cooper, *New York Times* bestselling author
of *Homer's Odyssey* and *Love Saves the Day*

"The kind of story that will leave you breathless, both because of its ambitious subject matter and its deeply arresting storytelling. Cantor has created a stunning reimagining of Anne Frank's sister, her journey to America, and the complex terrain that became her womanhood. Part love story, part family mystery, this singular, bold, and elegantly paced story is rich with historical imagery, but the ingenious plot is all Cantor's. *Margot* is the sort of book that remains with you long after the final page."

—Ilie Ruby, author of *The Salt God's Daughter* and *The Language of Trees*

"Breathes life into a character we know only from her sister's famous diary. *Margot* offers us the other teenaged girl who lived in hiding for two years in that annex. It honors the memory of a shadow, of a ghost, and boldly explores how icons are made and what is lost in this process. *Margot* examines history versus story and how we cling to the fictions we tell ourselves."

—T. Greenwood, author of *Two Rivers*, *Grace,* and *Bodies of Water*

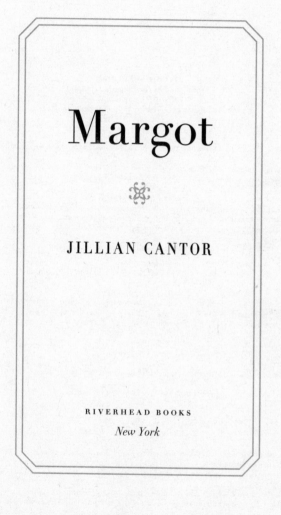

Margot

JILLIAN CANTOR

RIVERHEAD BOOKS

New York

RIVERHEAD BOOKS
Published by the Penguin Group
Penguin Group (USA)
375 Hudson Street, New York, New York 10014, USA

USA | Canada | UK | Ireland | Australia | New Zealand | India | South Africa | China

Penguin Books Ltd., Registered Offices: 80 Strand, London WC2R 0RL, England
For more information about the Penguin Group, visit penguin.com.

Library of Congress Cataloging-in-Publication Data

Cantor, Jillian.
Margot / Jillian Cantor.—First Riverhead trade paperback edition.
p. cm.
ISBN 978-1-59448-643-2
1. Holocaust survivors—Fiction.   2. Jewish refugees—Fiction.   3.   Holocaust,
Jewish (1939–1945)—Fiction.   4. Sisters—Fiction.   5. Frank, Anne, 1929–1945—Fiction.
6. Psychological fiction.   I. Title.
PS3603.A587C37 2013
813'.6—dc23
2013004959

First Riverhead trade paperback edition: September 2013

PRINTED IN THE UNITED STATES OF AMERICA

10   9   8   7   6   5   4   3

Book design by Kristin del Rosario

For my parents

And let us not forget Margot, who kept her own diary, which was never found.

—MIEP GIES

I want to go on living even after my death.

—ANNE FRANK

MARGOT

⁂ ⁂ ⁂

I should begin with the simplest of truths: I am alive.

You might wonder how this is possibly the simplest of truths, when you have thought me dead—when the entire world has thought me dead—for so very long. But this, I promise you, is really quite simple in light of all the rest of it. I breathe, and sometimes I eat and sometimes I sleep. But every morning, again, when I wake up, I find myself still breathing. Simple. Really, it is nothing more than science.

I can already picture you shaking your head. It is not simple at all, you are saying to yourself. Maybe your face is turning an angry red, and you are yelling that the Red Cross lists said I was dead. Maybe you are wondering where I have been, why I haven't found you yet. I've come this far. Why not just stay hidden forever?

But a person cannot really stay hidden forever. We both know that now, don't we?

The truth is, I have wanted to find you for a long time, but I have been afraid. Afraid of what you might think if I told you everything. Afraid of what you've become since I've seen you last. Afraid, even, of what you might think of what—and who—I've become. I am not a girl anymore. Neither am I a Jew. And I have done things that I can't understand or explain, even to myself.

But I promise you this, I am alive. There are simple truths about me. I live in Philadelphia, Pennsylvania, United States of America, where I am a legal secretary by the name of Margie Franklin. . . .

CHAPTER ONE

THE THIRD DAY OF APRIL 1959 SEEMS, AT FIRST, JUST LIKE any other Friday of my American life. I sit at my secretary's desk in the law office of Rosenstein, Greenberg and Moscowitz, typing out Joshua's schedule for the following week, gnawing carefully on an apple.

The office is quiet this afternoon, except for the sounds of the girls' fingers tapping against the typewriter keys and the hum of Shelby's radio coming from the desk across from me. Nearly all the lawyers have already left for the weekend, including my boss, Joshua Rosenstein, who has gone to Margate with his father, Ezra, who is Shelby's boss. Ezra Rosenstein is one of the partners in the law firm, so perhaps it is no surprise that he owns both a boat and a house by the ocean in New Jersey, which he and Joshua visit nearly every weekend, especially in the spring and summer.

By this particular Friday, I—Margie Franklin—have been

a resident of Philadelphia for nearly six years. I have been Joshua's secretary for three of those years, which means I have spent somewhere around 150 Friday afternoons like this one, typing at my desk, eating my apple, listening to Shelby's music.

This Friday, the Platters—Shelby's favorite—pour softly from her radio, crooning about how the smoke gets in their eyes, which is a song that always makes me think of Peter, even from the very first time I heard it, when I was with Shelby at Sullivan's Bar last month.

"We're leaving early today," Shelby announces to me just after she has devoured a ham sandwich she bought from the cart downstairs. "You're too thin," she had proclaimed in between bites. "Have half of my ham." She'd tried to force it across the desk.

"No thanks," I'd told her, pulling the apple from my satchel and then saying, "I don't really like ham."

"You're an odd duck, Margie." She'd shaken her head, but she'd smiled as she'd said it, so I knew she was saying it all in fun, that she had no idea why I would never bring myself to eat pork. And besides, that conversation, we'd already had it thousands of times. Or at least 150. Shelby often eats ham sandwiches, tries to offer me half, and insists I leave early with her when the Rosensteins are away.

Now Shelby switches off her radio and taps an unlit cigarette on the side of her metal desk. "You are going to leave early with me, aren't you, Margie?"

I shrug, though I know that she will pester me until I agree to do it. It's almost too warm today for my thin navy sweater, which I wear wrapped around my plaid dress, and I already feel the sweat building in pools under my arms, even in the office, but I resist the urge to fan myself with a file folder or even push up the sleeves.

"Good girl." Shelby laughs. "And one of these days, I may even get you to try one of these." She tosses the unlit cigarette in my direction, and then pulls a fresh one from her pack, teasing it between her lips.

"No thanks," I say, pushing it gently back across the desk. We have played this game many times before, and I know Shelby does not honestly expect me to smoke it. Many girls in the office smoke, but I do not. I still cannot stand what it reminds me of: another time, another place, one which I never wish to go back to in my mind. But these are things I'd never even dream of telling Shelby.

❈

Just past three, Shelby hangs on to my arm as we walk out of the office building and onto the sidewalk. The street is still fairly empty, as most people in the offices around us are still working, and the midafternoon sun glints off the low glass windows of the buildings on Market Street.

Shelby wears a short-sleeved white cotton blouse and full green skirt today, because it is April and the sun is warm enough to be without a sweater. But I still have my navy sweater on. I wear a sweater always, no matter what the temperature, so the dark ink on my forearm remains hidden, unseen.

"Any plans this weekend?" Shelby asks me, as if she doesn't know the answer, the same answer I give her every weekend.

"Studying," I tell her.

"Oh, good grief, Margie. All work and no play."

"Joshua thinks I'll make an excellent paralegal," I tell her. Joshua is tall, with an oval face and curly hair the color of warm chestnuts. Sometimes I have the urge to reach up and run my finger around a curl, and I have to hold my hands together, to stop them from moving.

"Oh, *Joshua* does, does he?" She laughs. Shelby's laugh is like water. Sometimes it's good, cleansing, even refreshing. Other times, I feel it might drown me. "Come on." She yanks my arm, turning me in the direction opposite my studio apartment. "I want to see a movie this afternoon. And I don't like to see a movie alone."

"What about Ron?" I ask her, referring to her beau, who I have no doubt she'll marry at a moment's notice if he ever asks, though some doubt he ever will. They have been dating for as long as I've known Shelby, which, as Shelby herself admits, is a long time for a girl to date a boy without any kind of promise.

"Ron is still working. Everyone else is still working. Come on," she wheedles.

Shelby is always wanting me to go somewhere with her after work. Mostly, it is to Sullivan's Bar to have a drink, and sometimes I do go with her even though I don't drink alcohol, but just because she is my friend and her laugh can be so much like water that I want to swim in it, to close my eyes and float away. But at least once a month or so, there is a movie she wants to see. And nearly always it is one that Ron is not able or willing to see with her.

Last month Shelby dragged me to see *Some Like It Hot* and then went on and on about Marilyn's curves and her butterscotch voice. I thought the movie was fine, but I did not laugh at the places Shelby did, at Tony Curtis and Jack Lemmon's antics dressed as women. I still do not fully understand the American sense of humor. Hiding is hiding is hiding. What's so funny about that?

"Come on," Shelby is still urging. "I've read the book and seen the play. The movie will complete the trifecta, and I don't want to see it alone. *The Diary of Anne Frank* is much too sad for that." She pulls her tiny pink lips in a pout, and all I can do is stare at her, not saying anything. I feel a tugging in my chest.

I saw a bit in the *Inquirer* a while back about the possibility of a movie being made, and something about non-Jewish actors being cast, but then I put it out of my mind. Perhaps if I didn't read the article or pay attention, it would simply go away? "I can't believe they've made a movie," I finally whisper.

"Oh, Margie, seriously, I swear it. Sometimes I really do think that apartment of yours is located under a rock." She shakes her head. "You've at least read Anne Frank's diary by now, haven't you? Oh, tell me you have!" All I can think is that she's saying it wrong—not "Frank," like the American version of hot dog with beans, a dish that Shelby seems rather fond of, but "Frank," rhymes with "conk," which is what I'd like to do right about now, conk Shelby over the head with my satchel if she doesn't stop talking. And she is *still* talking.

"I'm not feeling well," I interrupt her, and that is a gross understatement. I am sweating, and my hands shake. Black spots float in front of my eyes, and I close them, then open them again, which only makes the spots turn white. "I think I better go home," I whisper.

I disentangle my arm and take off briskly, hoping she won't follow me. "Margie," she calls after me. "Margie. It's the sweater. Take off the sweater. It's too darn hot outside."

But I don't stop running until I put the key in the lock, turn, and step inside my apartment.

CHAPTER TWO

In 1959, MY STUDIO APARTMENT IS IN A FIVE-STORY BRICK building with evenly spaced square windows on Ludlow Street, in Center City, Philadelphia. The building is much wider than the buildings on the Prinsengracht, but not any higher. Philadelphia, like the canal district of Amsterdam, is a city of lower buildings, surrounded by water. Shelby told me that because of a law in the city of Philadelphia, no building can rise higher than the statue of its founder, William Penn, which sits atop City Hall. He is like a beacon, this bronze man, watching over all the smaller buildings, and in a certain way that makes me feel protected here. It is a false kind of protection, but still, I feel it nonetheless.

My apartment is on the first floor, not far from the main entrance to the building, which is just the way I like it. It is a small studio, containing only a blue couch, a wooden table with two chairs, a single bed, and the tiniest of kitchens. But it is my own small studio, and in the three years I've lived in this apartment, it has come to feel like home.

Friday, after I have left Shelby calling for me on Market Street, I sit on the couch for a little while, letting Katze, my overweight orange tabby, knead his claws into the threads of my blue sweater, then my plaid dress. He cannot settle himself, my Katze. He can never decide exactly where he wants to sit, nor can he bring himself to chase the mice I sometimes hear scurrying in the walls. But I do not hold this against him. I cannot seem to settle myself now either, and I tap my pointy blue pump in an uneasy rhythm against the dark hardwood floorboards.

Friday nights, I always light a candle at sundown and say a silent prayer. *Barukh ata Adonai Eloheinu melekh ha'olam . . .*

Words repeat themselves in my brain, even though Margie Franklin, she is a Gentile. My Friday prayer, it is not religion, it's ritual.

But now it is not quite dusk yet, and the words repeating themselves in my brain, just after 4 P.M., are Shelby's: "*The Diary of Anne Frank* is much too sad for that," she'd said.

I push Katze aside and begin pacing across the room. It is tiny enough that I take only ten steps before I have to turn around and start all over again. Back and forth and back and forth.

Much too sad. I am certain Shelby cannot even fathom that kind of sad. Shelby was born in the United States, a Christian, and during the war she and her sister lived with their parents in a two-bedroom apartment that she describes as small. "There were rations," she told me once. "We didn't always have enough to eat. My shoes wore through, straight to the soles."

When she told me these things, I'd nodded, as if I were sympathetic to her plight. Then I bit my tongue to keep it from moving, from saying all the things I often think about my own time during the war, but never would dare utter out loud to Shelby.

You've at least read Anne Frank's diary by now, haven't you? She'd actually admonished me, standing there on Market Street.

I stop pacing for a moment by my bed, where my copy of the book sits atop the small shelf above my mattress. Its bright orange cover is tattered, the pages worn from too much use. *No,* I would tell Shelby, if she ever pressed me for an answer. *I haven't read it. I don't want to.*

And yet that, like so much else, would be a lie, as I know the words contained within the diary by heart.

I hold the book in my hand now, flipping through its dog-eared pages. My eyes skim through the mentions of Peter's name.

When I first came to America, before I discovered the book, I would often call the operator and ask for Peter, but it has been a long while since I have done that now. Sometimes, though, I still dream of walking into him on the street, by chance. He will look different, with shorter hair, and he will be older, of course, his body thicker, more of a man's, like Joshua's. But I will recognize him all the same—his face, or his eyes, blue and clear as the sea.

We promised each other we'd come here, when the war ended, or if we escaped. Peter picked the city of Philadelphia out of his world atlas. *The City of Brotherly Love,* he told me. *Surely, Jews cannot be in hiding there.*

Peter is dead, I remind myself now.

But then, so am I.

I put the book back on the shelf, and I reach for the phone on my small kitchen counter. I turn the dial to o, but I wait a moment, before letting my finger go.

"Operator," a woman's voice says on the other end.

I open my mouth to ask for him. *Peter Pelt,* I want to tell the operator. *I need to talk to Peter Pelt.*

There is a movie, Peter. A movie, for goodness' sake!

But it has been so long since I have called and asked for him under the new name we agreed on, and now I cannot bring myself to make a sound.

I look out the small square window behind my couch; it is nearly dark now.

I hang up the phone and reach underneath my kitchen counter for my Shabbat candle.

CHAPTER THREE

THE LAW OFFICE OF ROSENSTEIN, GREENBERG AND MOS-cowitz is on the seventh floor of a wide cement office building near the corners of Market and South Sixteenth streets in Center City, Philadelphia. It is close enough to walk to from my apartment, and also the courthouse, which makes it perfect both for the lawyers and for me.

Monday morning I am one of the first people to arrive at the office, at least according to the elevator attendant, a small brown-skinned man named Henry, who I find to have sympathetic brown eyes.

"Anyone else here yet?" I ask him, hopeful.

"Only Mr. Rosenstein," he says. "The younger one." I smile to myself as Henry ushers me through the elevator door. By Monday morning, both Shelby's voice and my call to the operator have dimmed. *So there is a movie,* I told myself on the walk to work this morning. *So what? It will be no different from the book.* Then I reveled in the fact that today it is Monday, and that means I will get to see Joshua again. That thought now turns my cheeks warm as I step off the elevator and walk into the large open center room of the law office.

My metal desk sits face-to-face with Shelby's in this center room, where all the lawyers' secretaries have their desks. We are surrounded by the lawyers' offices, which are behind closed doors all along the sides. Joshua's office is just to the right of our desks, and Ezra's office is the next one over. The other partners, Saul Greenberg and Jason Moscowitz, have offices on the other side of the room, closer to the elevator, but I suspect Ezra likes to be on this side so he can keep an eye on his son.

Joshua's office, like the others, has a small rectangular window by the door, and I watch him for a moment now, through the glass. He is sitting at his desk, studying something carefully. His forehead creases when he does this, as if concentration is either an art or a science. I can't decide. Joshua looks up from his desk, catches my eye, and smiles at me. I smile back before I walk to the break room and brew some coffee. I pour Joshua a cup with two sugars the way he likes it, and then I tread carefully back to his office and rap lightly on the door.

"Come in," he says. His voice floats, in a way that told me, even the very first time I met him, that he has never known anything like I have. Joshua's life in America has been charmed, I suspect, even when he was a teenager, during the war, with the rations. But I don't hold this against him. "Good morning, Margie." He smiles again. His smile is one of those warm American smiles where nothing is held back, where joy is uncontained. I hand him the coffee, and he thanks me. "How was your weekend?" he asks.

"It was fine, thank you," I say, even though I spent most of it cooped up nervously in my apartment. Saturdays, I always still keep as a day of rest, though this particular one had not felt very restful. Sundays, I normally take my correspondence work to Fairmount Park to study by the banks of the Schuylkill River, though this Sunday I walked to the Reading Terminal Market and perused the fruit instead, knowing I would be unable to concentrate on my studies. Across the street I'd spotted the cinema I have gone to with Shelby before, and I saw it there, on the marquee, in hideously assaulting red letters: *The Diary of Anne Frank*. I stared at the picture of the unfamiliar woman on the movie poster out front. I watched her face, her deep brown eyes, as if she too could stare back at me. *Look at you,* my sister said, laughing, in my head. *Living your American dream in a thick black sweater*. When I returned home, I thought about dialing the operator again. But something stopped me. Now I shake the thought away. "How was your weekend?" I ask Joshua.

He shrugs. "I've had better." Joshua and his father don't always get along. I learned this on my third day of work, when I heard their raised voices coming through the paper-thin walls of Joshua's office. Their disagreements have become, over the past three years, a fairly regular occurrence. Shelby says Ezra used to be nicer before his wife, Joshua's mother, died the year before they hired me. But this is something I would never ask Joshua about, though I feel a hole in the pit of my stomach for him, thinking about the empty space where his mother used to be. I wonder if she was the one who loved him better, the way it was with my mother and me. My sister was Father's. I was Mother's.

But all I allow myself to say now is, "I'm sorry to hear that."

He shrugs again. He is so casual about his family squabbles, the way all the Americans I've met seem to be. Once Shelby got into a fight with her mother, and they didn't speak for three months. Then, one weekend, they went out to lunch, and Shelby told me it was "water under the bridge." From the sound of her voice I understood that she was no longer angry, but I did not understand the reference to water and bridges, or how she could let go of her anger, just like that.

"Well." I stand. "I should get to work."

"Margie." He taps his fountain pen gently against his desk. "How are your paralegal studies coming?"

"Good," I say, feeling guilty now about having ignored them this weekend. Next weekend I will do double, I promise myself. "Two more correspondence classes left."

"Great. I'll talk to my father soon about finding a position for you when you're done," he says.

I smile at him, and I stop at the doorway for a moment.

He smiles back at me, his warm American smile again lighting up his face. "By the way, how's Mr. Katz?" he asks.

I laugh, the way I always do when he turns Katze, the orange tabby, into a Jewish-sounding man, most definitely a lawyer. It is doubly funny because there is a Mr. Katz who works in the district attorney's office, a portly man with a skinny black mustache who makes Joshua grimace whenever he has to go up against him in court.

"Mr. Katz is well," I tell Joshua. "Getting fatter by the day."

Joshua was the one who found him, right after I started work here. Katze was gaunt, crying in the back alley near the lot where Joshua parks his car. Joshua kept him for a month until he felt bad about leaving him all the time to go back and forth to Margate, and that was when I volunteered to take him home.

"I'll have to stop by to visit him sometime," Joshua says now.

I nod. He is always saying that, though he has never once actually stopped by to visit.

❉

I am still feeling warm from my conversation with Joshua when Shelby breezes in at five past nine, plunking her satchel down on her desk with a thud. "Well," she says, without even taking a breath. "The movie was fabulous. Of course. Millie Perkins was to die for. Absolutely perfect for the role, if you ask me."

"Who?" I ask, looking up from my typing. But the warmth, it is already gone, and for a moment I am chilled, even in my sweater.

"You do know who I'm talking about, don't you, Margie?" I shake my head. "All work and no play. Very dull."

"Who did she play?" I ask, my curiosity suddenly getting the better of me. Though as soon as the words are out of my mouth, I want to take them back.

"Who did she play?" Shelby laughs. "Anne Frank herself, of course. I read an interview with her in *McCall's* last month, and the darling girl—she was a model, didn't even want to be an actress, but she was so touched by Anne's story she took it on. And she was just fabulous. To see her and Peter . . . I nearly died I was crying so hard."

My stomach clenches at the sound of his name, in her voice. She is saying it wrong, of course. Not P*ee*ter, P*ay*ter.

"I'm telling you, Margie, you really missed out."

"I'm sure," I murmur. And Shelby looks at me and frowns as if she's caught on to something.

My lying is a second skin by now, so easy to forget it's there, so I don't always remember that lying is actually an art, and those who aren't meticulous about it are easily exposed.

I look up and Shelby is still frowning. "It's way too hot in here for that sweater, Margie." Today I am in a black sweater over a pale pink top and a high-waisted gray skirt.

"I'm rather comfortable," I say, but when she finally sits down at her desk and begins her typing, I lower my head and wipe carefully at the beads of sweat on my brow with a hand-kerchief.

CHAPTER FOUR

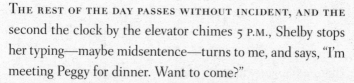

THE REST OF THE DAY PASSES WITHOUT INCIDENT, AND THE second the clock by the elevator chimes 5 P.M., Shelby stops her typing—maybe midsentence—turns to me, and says, "I'm meeting Peggy for dinner. Want to come?"

Peggy is Shelby's sister, and not just her sister, but her twin. They are fraternal twins, though, so they look surprisingly different. Peggy is tall and brown-haired, while Shelby is petite and blond. Peggy works as a nurse at the University of Pennsylvania Hospital, and mostly she must work odd hours and is not free to meet Shelby for dinner.

"I don't want to intrude," I say, though I have been to dinner with Shelby and Peggy many times in the last three years. Peggy is calmer than Shelby, and I imagine if I'd known them both together, Peggy and I would be more natural friends.

I glance through the glass window by Joshua's office, and I see he is still working hard, his head bent over at his desk.

Lately, I have been staying late, just in case Joshua might walk out of his office after everyone else has left and ask me if I would like to catch dinner, or a drink, as he did once before, in January, on the day Alaska became the forty-ninth state. "Do you know what we should celebrate tonight?" he'd said to me with a smile that nearly tumbled me out of my secretary's chair when he walked out of his office after six that night.

"I don't know. What should we celebrate?" I'd murmured, feeling warm and stunned, and thus completely missing the joke.

"Juneau," he said, laughing. "The capital of Alaska."

"Oh." I'd felt my cheeks turning red at my stupidity.

"I bet Ike's already back in Gettysburg toasting his new state. Or Mamie probably is anyway." He laughed again, and this time I got the joke, as Shelby was always telling me things she read about Mamie Eisenhower having a problem with drinking.

I laughed, and he turned his head to the side and looked at me. I am medium height and too thin. My dark brown hair tumbles past my pale cheeks, nearly to my shoulders, and I wear round glasses that hide my leather-colored eyes. I dress plainly, in conservative dresses and sweaters, the way any good secretary would. But the way Joshua was looking at me then, it made me wonder if he was seeing something else in me, something more than a secretary. It was just a moment, and then Ezra stormed out of his office, yelling at Joshua about something. Still, it is a moment I want to get back to, and so I often try to wait him out.

"Come on," Shelby is saying now. She pokes my forearm with her finger, hard enough so it hurts a little, even through the sweater. "It'll be fun. I promise. And Peggy thinks you're swell. She'd rather have dinner with you than me anyway." She laughs. And this time her laugh falls over me, like a stream.

I think about it for a moment, and I wonder if Shelby is finished talking about the movie. I've noticed Americans, Shelby included, have the ability to focus on something for only a little while, and then they move on to something else, so I am hopeful that the time has already passed for this. To Shelby, it is just a movie, after all. It is not real life.

I glance again through the window in Joshua's office. But I *want* to go eat with Shelby and Peggy. So I stand up and gather my things and follow Shelby to the elevator.

❈

Shelby and I walk down the city block, arms linked, our shadows stretching against the reflection of the office buildings and the soon-setting sun. We head toward Casteel's Diner, a short silvery building with wide square windows and a neon red sign, just down South Seventeenth Street. We walk inside, and it is loud and smells of grilled hamburger. It is crowded at this hour with men in suits and women in their work dresses, and the sound of something fast that I don't recognize pours from the jukebox. I spot Peggy still dressed in her starched white uniform, sitting in a red leather booth by one of the large windows, sipping on what looks like a tall chocolate malt. When she sees us, she stands up, waves, and then reaches for her sister.

She and Shelby, they hug, and then they kiss each other quickly on the cheek. I stand back, and suddenly my heart feels like it's bleeding out in my chest. When I see them together, the way they look when they hold on to each other, I remember again that something is missing from me, something that feels like the phantom weight of a stolen limb or internal organ, something so grossly essential that I'm not quite sure how I remember to keep breathing all the time without it.

I close my eyes, and I can still remember the feel of my sister's hip, resting against mine as we lay next to each other on her small bed, both writing in our diaries, our pens scrawling across the pages, nearly in unison.

My sister would sometimes put her diary down on her chest, put her head on my shoulder, and close her eyes. "You'll wake me, if anything exciting happens?" she'd whisper in my ear. Then she'd fall asleep, and I'd lie there, wide-awake, listening to the soft sounds of her breathing, her chest humming slowly as it moved up and down. She seemed so peaceful asleep, as if she was just back in her bed at home on the Merwedeplein, off in some distant dreamland where she forgot where and who we were. I always watched the door when she was sleeping, listening closely for even the softest of movements. I did not want her to be pulled out of her dreamland by the Green Police. I wanted to protect her. Which makes what happened, what I did, at the very end, feel even worse.

"Margie." I look up at the sound of Shelby's light voice.

Shelby and Peggy are both sitting there, next to each other now in the red booth, shoulders touching, staring at me. Two different sets of eyes, but really they could be one. Everything else about Shelby and Peggy is so different except for their eyes, rich brown, the color of milk chocolate.

"Come on," Peggy says to me. "Have a seat."

I slide across from them and pick up a thick plastic menu, but I do not actually read it. Instead, I listen to the sounds of their voices: back and forth and back and forth, like Ping-Pong. Are they arguing or are they chatting? It's hard to tell. Their words move so fast, thick with much emotion. I want to reach my hand out and capture them, to hold on to them and take them home with me to my apartment, to keep them there with me at night, when it is hard to find sleep. But Shelby and her sister, their words are like bubbles. Even if I could grab on to them, just for a moment, they would pop and disappear.

Can I read your diary? I hear my sister's voice in my head. She asked me that once, as we lay there together, hip to hip. Her voice was still light then, much the way Shelby's is now.

If I can read yours, I told her, and then we switched books. Because why not? There was no privacy anymore. And besides, maybe I'd wanted her to know exactly how I felt about Peter, so I could claim him for my own. Not that that was the way things ever worked between us.

"Peg," I hear Margie saying now. "You must go see the movie. Peeter is so dreamy."

Oh, the movie. Clearly, I have underestimated her; Shelby is not done talking about it.

Peggy laughs and shakes her head. "Only you would see that movie as a romance, Shel."

"That's not true," Shelby says, picking up her own thick plastic menu and hiding behind it with mock offense. "He's dreamy. That's a bona fide fact." She lowers her menu and stares pointedly at me. "See," she says, wagging her forefinger at me. "You should've come with me, Margie, so you could back me up on this."

"What makes him so dreamy?" I ask, and the sound of my own voice startles me, as if the question has popped out of my mouth, without my permission. Immediately, I want to take it back.

"The way he hangs on to Anne and kisses her, just as they're about to be ripped out of the annex . . ." She shakes her head. "You have to see it."

"That didn't happen," I say softly.

"How do you know?" Shelby asks, and I realize I have said too much. I feel my brow breaking into a sweat, and I am ready to stand and run. *The way he hangs on to Anne and kisses her . . .*

"Of course, Margie's right, Shel," I hear Peggy saying, though her voice sounds very far away. "It was just a movie. Do you really think hiding from the Nazis was romantic?"

"I don't know," Shelby says. "Maybe. All cooped up like that, with nowhere to go."

Peggy rolls her eyes in my direction, but I cast my gaze down, toward the table. My stomach turns, and I stare at the menu, as if I am trying very hard to decide what I should eat, though now I am no longer hungry in the least. I breathe deeply, fighting the urge to stand up and run out of the diner. For a few moments I concentrate on my breath, in and out and in and out, until I hear the conversation turn, and Peggy and Shelby start bickering over which sandwich to share for dinner.

"Fine," Shelby is saying now. "If you don't want hot turkey then Margie will split with me instead, won't you, Margie?" I look up and nod slowly, carefully.

Peggy rolls her eyes again. "Everything is always so difficult with you, Shel." But she says it lightly and with a smile, so I know she is teasing.

Shelby elbows her sister and laughs. The sound of it now, once again, falling over me like a stream.

CHAPTER FIVE

BACK IN MY APARTMENT, LATER THAT EVENING, I lie on the blue couch with Katze and think about what Shelby said. *The way he hangs on to Anne and kisses her . . .*

That is ridiculous, not at all what happened. Not even close.

I stare at the phone. I have not called to look for him for so long. But now I wonder again, for maybe the millionth time: what is true and what is not? If the movie is filled with such outrageous stories like the one Shelby spoke of, well . . .

I kept a diary before my sister even started hers, before the annex even. In 1941, I wrote about a boy named Johann, who had straw-colored hair and pale blue eyes and who lived around the block from us on the Merwedeplein. I wanted him to notice me so badly it made my stomach hurt.

Once, before the annex, my sister had picked the diary up off my dressing stand and read it without asking me.

"Who's Johann?" she asked me.

"That's private," I told her.

"You tell *Maria,* but you won't tell me." She put her hands on her hips, honestly offended, as if Maria were a real person whom I loved more than I loved her. Maria was just the name I called my diary, only further evidence of her snooping.

"Johann is not a real person. He's just a character," I lied.

"Oh." Her eyes lit up then. "You're telling stories."

I remind myself of this moment so often, every time I look through the book. Every time I read the words she has written about Peter. And again now, having heard Shelby's description of the movie.

You're telling stories.

I stand up and reach for the phone on my kitchen counter; I pull the dial to o again, and this time, I quickly let it go before I lose my nerve.

"Operator," the woman's voice says.

"I need the address and number for a Peter Pelt, Philadelphia," I tell her. The words shake in my throat. *Peter Pelt.* That was the name he told me he would go by, in Philadelphia. *I will no longer be a Jew,* he'd whispered to me as we were lying on the divan in his room, more than once. *I will leave everything behind. Hiding who you are, it'll be so much easier than hiding where you are.* He would be Peter Pelt, and I would be Margie Franklin. We would come to Philadelphia, and we would be Gentiles together, safe together.

"Just a moment," the operator says now.

I hold my breath and close my eyes. According to the Red Cross, Peter died in 1945, after a death march to Mauthausen. But also, my sister and I both died of typhus in Bergen-Belsen.

"Miss." The operator comes back, and I am waiting for her to say it again: that he doesn't exist. *Peter van Pels died, near Mauthausen, fifteen years ago, almost.* "Here you go," she says instead. "I've got a P. Pelt, at 2217 Olney Avenue, Apartment 4A . . ." She is still talking, but my ears buzz so loud, I almost cannot understand what she is saying.

I have not called to ask for him for so long. How long has this listing been there? *Peter died, near Mauthausen.*

After the war, we will go to Philadelphia, he told me, so many times. *We will find each other in the City of Brotherly Love.*

But Peter is dead.

Or he isn't.

I can never be entirely sure what is real and what is not.

CHAPTER SIX

THE NEXT MORNING AT WORK, I SIT AT MY DESK AND HOLD
tight to the yellow piece of paper on which I wrote down P. Pelt's
information. I stare at it so hard that the letters swim before my
eyes, becoming something unreal. I force my eyes away, and
then they catch on something else. There, through the glass,
working at his desk, is Joshua. He concentrates hard, reading
something carefully, so from this angle I can see only the arch
of his broad shoulders and the top of his chestnut curls. I wonder how late he stayed last night, and if I had stayed too, if he
would've walked out of his office and invited me for a drink
again. But it feels wrong to imagine that now, and I quickly look
away. I finger the yellow paper between my hands until it starts
to crumble. *P* could mean a lot of things, I tell myself: Paul,
Patrick, Peter. *Peter Pelt.*

Shelby steps off the elevator, and I hastily fold the yellow paper up into the smallest of squares and tuck it in the bottom of my satchel before she can ask me about it.

But when she reaches her desk, I see her eyes are red and puffy, and she does not seem to notice what I am or am not doing in the least, which is not at all like her.

"Everything okay?" I whisper across the desks. She nods, then shakes her head. "Do you want to talk about it?" She opens her mouth, then closes it again, and I guess that whatever happened has something to do with Ron, as he seems to be the only thing that can shake Shelby's normally happy disposition. It occurs to me that whatever it is, it might have taken her mind off her new favorite topic, the movie, and I feel a little guilty for feeling relieved. Though Shelby sometimes pesters me, I don't ever want her to get hurt.

"Margie." Joshua buzzes me through the intercom, and Shelby sits down at her desk and pulls the beige cover off her typewriter.

"Yes, Mr. Rosenstein," I say.

"I'm leaving for court in five minutes. Can you get my Zimmerman files ready?"

"Of course," I say. I look to Shelby, who shrugs, and then Joshua bursts out of his office, dressed to the nines in a navy-blue three-piece suit. His body hums with nervous energy, the way it always seems to before court, and I notice, as he straightens his striped tie and reaches for his hat off the rack, that his hands shake just a little bit.

"Good luck," I say, handing him the stack of files he'd asked for. Zimmerman, I remember, is a man who'd embezzled money from the Franklin, a Jewish social organization where he'd once been treasurer.

Joshua nods and smiles at me, a smile tinged with nervousness, but still, a Joshua smile nonetheless, so I cannot help but smile back, even as I now think guiltily of the yellow square tucked in my satchel.

I watch Joshua walk to the elevator, and then I turn back to Shelby. Her face is pale and small, her blond hair a little mussed. She is listening carefully to instructions from Ezra now, through her intercom.

"Yes," she is saying. "Yes, of course. Right away, Mr. Rosenstein."

In a way, I think, looking at her now, thinking about the way her voice sounded last night as she insisted the annex was romantic, Shelby reminds me of my sister. She is alive and stubborn and kind and terribly emotional. If it had been her and Peggy in the annex, I am sure, she would be the one the world is in love with now, while most everyone else wouldn't even remember that Peggy had ever existed or, for that matter, kept a diary. And Peggy, like me, she would probably be happy about that.

For the longest time, I have lived in fear of walking by Robin's Books and seeing my own face staring back at me as well as my sister's. I have been full of fear, wondering what would happen if everyone knew, if my father knew, that I am still here. At first, I became Margie Franklin, the Gentile, because it was Peter's plan, but then it became about survival, all over again. I did not want people to know that in so many ways I was that girl too: that Jew trapped like a rat, deeply in love, stolen away by the Green Police. That I *am* that girl. That Jew.

About a year into my life in Philadelphia, I began to notice articles in the *Inquirer* about terrible things that had been done to Jews. A gang of hoodlums went after Jewish children in a very "Jewish section of the city," my sponsor, Ilsa, informed me. Then a few weeks later, a flaming flare was nailed to a house nearby, just because a Jewish woman was thought to live there. With the flare, the Nazis left a message that said *der Jude,* the German word for Jew, and *Deutschland über alles.*

Ilsa looked over my shoulder as I read the articles and clucked her tongue. "It is terrible," she said to me. "And with the firebomb thrown into that synagogue last fall."

"Firebomb in the synagogue?" I asked, the words feeling like rubber on my tongue. Synagogues being bombed, in the city of Philadelphia? Jewish children being attacked?

It was late spring 1954. The air had just begun to grow warm and heavy. I put my sweater on. And I have worn it, tightly, ever since.

CHAPTER SEVEN

"I think Ron has another girl on the side." Shelby whispers this to me, across the desks. It is Friday again, and by now, I have almost forgotten about both her teary entrance on Tuesday and her talk of the movie, which she has dropped in favor of a new concern over Rock Hudson and Doris Day: are they an item or no? Shelby believes they are, especially because she saw the poster for their new movie, *Pillow Talk,* coming out in the fall, and she thinks they just *look* like an item.

"A girl can always tell these things," she told me as I'd nodded and half listened, thinking instead about the tiniest square of paper still folded inside my satchel. It was one thing to know Peter might be here, but another thing altogether, to actually call the number. After all this time.

Now Shelby's voice has taken on an unusually serious tone, and her normal smile is gone from her face as she mentions that she thinks Ron is not being faithful to her.

"Why do you think that?" I ask her, looking up from my typing.

"He's been lying to me. Telling me he's working late, when really he's not," Shelby says.

This Friday morning Joshua has come in for a few hours before heading to Margate, but Ezra is already gone and Joshua doesn't mind when Shelby plays her radio softly. I hear the strains of Mr. Frankie Avalon's "Venus" floating across the desks. Frankie croons, and I glance through the glass window at Joshua, who is talking on the phone and scribbling something at his desk. He runs his fingers through his chestnut curls and smiles as he says something to the caller. He is hunched over his desk, but still, his shoulders look wide and strong in his dark brown suit, a near exact color match to his curls. For a moment I think about Peter, about whether he wears a suit to work now, like Joshua, and whether his shoulders now are just as broad. And then I quickly look away from the window, from Joshua.

"Perhaps you're mistaken?" I murmur, and I notice now Shelby is chewing on her fingernails, the way she always does when she is distressed about something.

She shakes her head. "No," she says. "Peg saw him, on the way home from Casteel's the other night. She said he was walking down Chestnut with some . . . hussy." She bites her lip now, as if she is holding back tears.

"I'm sorry," I say. "But maybe it isn't what you think? Sometimes things, people, they are not as they appear to be."

"What else could it be?" she asks.

I shrug, because I honestly don't know, though I also know

Shelby has sat across from me for three years, and she neither knows nor seems to suspect nearly anything real about me. She has an American blind trust in the people around her. "His sister?" I finally say.

"He doesn't have a sister."

"Cousin?" I ask. She shrugs. "Maybe you should just ask him?" I tell her, thinking how ironic it is that I am giving her advice about getting the truth.

She considers it for a moment, as I find my eyes drawn back to Joshua again, through the glass. He hangs up the phone, moves toward the door, and I quickly avert my eyes and hands back to my typewriter.

He walks out of his office, grabs his brown hat off the hat rack by my desk, and places it atop his chestnut curls in one swift motion. Shelby turns the music down so it is barely audible. "Don't do that on my account," Joshua says, smiling at me. I remember my image of Peter, broad-shouldered and in a suit, wondering if this might make me immune to Joshua's smile now, but apparently it does not. I smile back. "Margie," he says. "I have a new client coming in Monday afternoon, and I want you to sit in on the meeting."

"Me?" Though Joshua has encouraged me on the paralegal front, he has never offered me more than secretarial duties.

"You speak Polish, right?"

I nod, and my smile falls away in an instant as I swallow back the lie I tell everyone when they ask me about my accent. It is only a hint of an accent by now, but still, Americans seem to have the ability to detect even the slightest bit of foreignness in a person. Yet, of course, they cannot tell the difference between German and Polish accents. And I cannot say the truth, that my accent is German. There is so much hatred still for Germans in America, especially among Jews.

"It has been a long while," I tell Joshua now. "I barely remember my Polish."

"That's all right," Joshua tells me. "She speaks English. But heavily accented. So I might need your help understanding."

I know many languages: French, Hebrew, German, English, Dutch. Some Latin. Polish is not one of them.

"Well, have a nice weekend, ladies," Joshua says, tipping his hat in my direction as he floats toward the elevator. The doors shut behind him. Shelby turns up her music louder, and for a moment Frankie seems to be shouting at us. *Surely the things I ask can't be too great a task . . .*

"Maybe you're right," I hear Shelby saying. "I should just ask Ron."

But now all my words are gone, and all I can do is sit there and cling tightly to my sweater against my chest.

CHAPTER EIGHT

THE WEEKEND PASSES IN A BLUR OF RESTLESS NIGHTS, AS I pace my apartment, staring at my paralegal work without absorbing any of it, and folding and unfolding the yellow square from my satchel, though now I have memorized both the address and the number by heart. *P. Pelt. It cannot be him,* I think, and yet, maybe it is. But Sunday afternoon I become more consumed with what is waiting for me at work on Monday, and I find myself at the Free Public Library of Philadelphia, browsing through a Polish dictionary.

I am quite good at learning. In the annex, through correspondence, I learned English, French, Latin, mathematics, physics, literature, and English shorthand, which is something that helped me get the job with Joshua. And so I try to cram as much Polish into my brain as I can within the space of a few hours.

But by Monday afternoon as I sit at my desk, nervously

awaiting the Polish woman's arrival, the only Polish words I can seem to remember are the two I have known for a very long time. *Jestes diablem*. You are the devil. They rattle in my brain, as if they are still being screamed there by an old and helpless woman. They will be useless words in whatever business Joshua is conducting, I'm certain. But still, I cannot turn them off.

Joshua is in his office, on the phone, and though I am supposed to be typing addresses on billing envelopes and preparing his schedule for the rest of the week, I find myself, instead, furtively watching the elevator and nodding my head as Shelby wonders off and on if she *should* ask Ron about the hussy. They had such a nice weekend together, feeding the ducks in Fairmount Park and having a picnic. Maybe she shouldn't . . . ?

"I don't know," I murmur, wondering if Ron is anything like me, and if it will even matter if she asks or not, if he will dare tell her the truth. But maybe he will. If she asks enough, maybe he will be forced to.

Lying can be a second skin, but when you are called out on a lie, it becomes all too easy for that skin to start to peel away. I have been called out before, in my life in America, but never here. Not with Shelby or Joshua. Before, it was my sponsor, Ilsa, as she looked over my shoulder when I filled out my job application.

"You list Poland as your country of birth?" she asked. I nodded. "I thought you were born in Germany?"

"I lived in Germany as a child," I said, and that was not a lie. I *did* live in Germany as a child. Ilsa frowned, but she didn't question me any further. Even if she had, I would not have told her the truth, that I *was* born in Germany, but in my American life, I want nothing to do with Germany. And even though I lived there for many years, I did not dare write Holland, for it is the country everyone most closely associates with my sister. I settled on Poland for my lie because it seemed a believable explanation for my accent. And I was there, once, a place west of Kraków. I did not know it at the time, but that is where I was. I died there. Afterward, I was born again. A new person. A Gentile.

Jestes diablem.

In my head now, these words, they drown out the sound of Shelby's voice.

Fifteen minutes past three, I watch her step off the elevator, cautiously, reading the signs above her as if she's not quite sure she's in the right place. True Americans, like Shelby and Joshua, always walk with a particular sense of confidence. This woman, I can tell, just from her walk, is not a born American. She is like me.

I look at her carefully as she approaches my desk. I think she is older than me, though it is hard to tell. Her black hair is streaked with gray and pulled back into a tight bun at the nape of her neck. She wears a black half-sleeved dress and looks nothing in the slightest like the clients who usually step off the elevator, most of whom are men, dressed in richly layered three-piece suits.

"*Czesc*," I say to her. *Hello*. The Polish word, learned

yesterday at the library, finds me again as she approaches my desk, and I smile in relief. My studies, they will not fail me, even if they were hastily done.

She narrows her brown eyes at me. "Bryda Korzynski," she says. "I speak English." I nod. "I have appointment," she tells me.

"Have a seat." I point to the chairs off to the side of my desk. "I'll buzz Mr. Rosenstein to let him know you're here."

She turns, and when she does, I catch something by the lip of her sleeve, on her left forearm, just a trace of dark blue ink, the familiar echo of the letter *A*.

I blink, and then the image, it is gone. The sleeve has gone back, and she is sitting in the chair across from my desk. I open my mouth, but then no sound comes out. Since coming to America, I have not seen a tattoo like this on anyone else, and the idea of it now, here, in the safety of the office where I work, it unnerves me. Perhaps it was something else, I tell myself. Perhaps the movie being so fresh, my thoughts of Poland, they are making me crazy, making me see things that aren't even here.

"Is there problem?" Bryda asks, frowning at me, and I realize I am still staring.

"No." I quickly shake my head and depress the intercom button to let Joshua know she's here.

❖

Inside Joshua's office, Bryda Korzynski lifts up her sleeve and thrusts her arm in Joshua's direction.

I sit in a side chair, observing, as Joshua has asked, though

I am not sure if he asks me to interpret I will be able to speak at all. Not because of the Polish but because of the tattooed number, right there, on her arm, in Joshua's face. I wasn't mistaken.

Joshua shakes his head. "Miss Korzynski, I'm so sorry. I can't even imagine." His face turns for a moment, darkens in a way I have rarely seen from him, and I think it's because he is a Jew. I suppose that's why Bryda is here in his office, thrusting her arm in his face. If I were her friend, I would tell her that American Jews are different, that they don't understand what it was like to wear a yellow star, to not be allowed to ride your bike or even the bus. They will think they understand, because religion is religion, and Jews have always been a persecuted people. But you cannot understand what you cannot really imagine, and they cannot really imagine it. No matter how much they think they can or how many books they've read or movies they've seen. In America the Jews still prosper. They are lawyers with houses in Margate and also on the Main Line. I cannot bring myself to hate Joshua for this, though, as it is not his fault, where he was born, what he was born into.

"So," Joshua says, "let's talk more about what we discussed on the phone. You said you have a Jewish problem that you want me to handle because I am a Jewish lawyer, right?"

She nods and she thrusts her arm in his face again. "You see this? I already suffer at hands of Nazi. My mother, she gassed immediately after we arrive to Auschwitz. Dominik, my brother, he sent to work and he die in Mauthausen after death march. My father, he die of cholera in Neuengamme. I only one to survive it."

The names of the camps fall in my brain, in her thick Polish accent. Her words hurt; they are sharp. Needles. Mauthausen, where Peter was said to have died, and I think uneasily of the tiniest of squares that has sat in the bottom of my satchel for nearly a week now.

I look up, and I realize Joshua has said something to me. "I'm sorry." I shake my head and pull my sweater tighter around my body. "What did you say?"

"I was telling Miss Korzynski that you are also from Poland. But you were lucky that you weren't there, during the war, right?"

I nod, hanging on to the lie. It was one of the first things he'd asked me, at my job interview, and I'd forced myself to smile then as I'd told Joshua I had gotten the American version of wartime, like him.

Bryda Korzynski stares at me, as if she can see through me. Her eyes are hard brown stones. I wrap my sweater tighter around my body.

When she turns back to look at Joshua, I exhale, not even realizing I've been holding my breath. "Anyway," she says, "the Nazi take everything from me. My family. My life. My country. I don't even sleep without the nightmares anymore." She pauses and shakes her head, as if she's thinking about them. The nightmares. I know them so well, the way screams torture you in the dark. Voices of your family crying for help you cannot give. My sister holding on to my hand with all her remaining strength. The sounds of gunshots breaking my ears.

"I'm very sorry," Joshua says, "But I still don't understand how I can help you."

"My boss is Nazi too," she says. "And now after the war and now that Anne Frank movie so popular, everybody know you cannot be Nazi anymore. Not in America."

I bite my lip, drowning in the mention of my sister's name, said correctly, in Bryda's thick Polish accent. And then I wonder if Bryda has missed the articles in the paper about the hatred against Jews in Philadelphia. And not just in 1954, but even still, now, my eyes catch on something, all too often. Swastikas painted on synagogues. This was the latest I'd seen, a few weeks earlier.

"Your boss?" Joshua is saying now, and he frowns.

"Mr. Robertson," she says.

"Robert Robertson?" Joshua raises his eyebrows. It is a name I recognize. Robert Robertson is a prominent local businessman who owns several clothing factories, and who has once or twice brought some business to the firm. "I don't even think he's German," Joshua says kindly. I could not form the words to speak, to tell him that not all anti-Semites are German, even if I wanted to.

She shakes her head. "My friend, she nice Christian girl."

"Like Miss Franklin here?" Joshua smiles in my direction, and Bryda narrows her eyes at me, so I am forced to look away.

"Anyway," she says. "She work same hours as me and make two dollar more a week."

"Has she worked there longer?" Joshua asks.

Bryda shakes her head again. "No, I work there two year more than her."

"And you think this is because you're a Jew?" Joshua asks.

She nods. "All the Jews, we make less money. But everyone afraid to complain. President say there hard times. Who else will hire us?"

"I'm sorry," Joshua says. "That's really awful."

"You no be sorry, Mr. Rosenstein. You help me." She pauses. "My English, it not so good. So maybe I confuse you little bit."

"I think I'm understanding you," Joshua says. "You want your boss to pay you what he pays your friend."

"I want him to pay, yes," she says. "But not just money. Understand what I say?"

"I understand," Joshua says. But I wonder if he really does. In German, the way to say it would be *Jedem das Seine*. But I am not exactly sure what the right word would be in American English.

Bryda sighs. "For so many years I suffer as Jew. Why I still have to suffer, here, in America?"

Joshua nods slowly. "Well, on your own I'm not sure we really have a case but . . ." He rubs his chin the way I've seen his father, Ezra, who has a thick white beard, do. Only Joshua's chin is smooth, like a boy's. "If we get others. A group litigation."

Bryda frowns, clearly confused, but from my studying I know exactly what a group litigation is. But I cannot speak, even if I might want to. I am frozen, Bryda's words about the suffering of Jews echoing in my head.

"That means we'll get other people from Robertson's factories, like you, to join in on the suit," Joshua explains. "If we have more people, we'll have more power to fight." He rubs his chin again. "I'll tell you what, let me talk this over with my father. His name is the one you see on the sign out front." She nods. "And in the meantime, can you do something for me? Can you make a list of everyone you know who might be interested in joining you?"

"Yes," Bryda says, and her eyes follow Joshua's face in the way mine so often do. Suddenly Joshua is her Jewish American hero.

CHAPTER NINE

Even after Bryda leaves the office, I cannot concentrate on my work because I cannot erase the image of her number, right there, so horrible and obvious, on her forearm. I want to forget about it. But I cannot.

I stare at my typewriter for a while after she leaves. I cannot exactly remember the look of Bryda's face. But the look of the numbers, the way they were preceded by a sharp dark blue *A*, I can remember without hesitation.

I know it's because I *was* in Poland during the war, just like Bryda. I did not want to be there; I did not really know it at the time. But I was.

In 1944, Mother, my sister, and I waited in line after we were unloaded from the cargo train by thick black-booted men. They had pulled our arms, throwing us off the train as if we really were cargo, laughing, joking with one another in German as they did it, cigarettes hanging loosely from their mouths, thick rings of smoke swirling above their heads. We'd just been transported from Westerbork camp in Holland to Auschwitz in German-occupied Poland. It was the beginning of September, a month after we'd been ripped from the annex. The sun was shining. To walk in it, it actually still hurt my skin, as if its rays were overexposing me, after so much time hidden away.

We stood in line, and I held on tightly to my sister with one hand, my mother, with the other. Mrs. van Pels was somewhere behind us.

"We'll be killed," my sister whispered to me as we waited there for what felt like forever, the soles of our feet beginning to burn from standing still. It was warm outside, and we were sweating, thirsty. Even my sister's whisper sounded hoarse.

"Shhh," I told her. "No, we will not." I felt I was lying to her then, but it seemed a necessary lie. I was terrified she would hear the pounding of my own heart in my chest. "Just do what they tell you," I whispered slowly. "Don't struggle."

The woman in front of us in line was an older lady, older than Mother by twenty years at least, and her back was already hunched; her arms fell frail around her sides. The guards yelled at us in German to undress, and when she was naked, her flesh hung off her bones, loose, wrinkly. It seemed she was too old to be so naked.

Then the guards came to shave us, and she began shouting. *"Jestes diablem. Jestes diablem."* She shouted it, over and over again. So loud, her voice hurt my ears.

"You are the devil," Mother whispered, translating. "It's Polish." Mother knew a little Polish from a childhood friend.

My sister's almond eyes opened wide, the way they often did. "She's so brave," she whispered.

"Don't even think it," I whispered to her, because it seemed they must have had a way of knowing then, even our thoughts. When you are stripped naked, shaved bare, nothing is yours anymore, nothing is left.

We stood in line again for a long time, and her words, they began to hurt my ears. My bare flesh turned numb. My ears felt like they were bleeding. *Jestes diablem*. The Polish woman screamed and she screamed.

The guard held her down as he tattooed her arm, and then he shoved her roughly and yelled at her in German to shut up. She was still screaming.

Finally another guard came and pulled her away into the other line, made up of people, I would later learn, who were immediately gassed, instead of put to work. They were not supposed to tattoo you if you were to be gassed right away, but with her, they made an exception.

My sister was standing just in front of me watching all of this. I saw her open her mouth, and I covered it with my hand and pushed her back behind me so I could be tattooed before her. I wanted her to see that it wouldn't be so bad.

"It's only a little ink, just a number. Don't scream," I whispered to her. "Don't struggle. Just be quiet and do what they ask."

Her almond eyes stared back at me, so wide they could burst. She opened her mouth again but no sound came out.

I held out my arm, closed my eyes. My skin singed and cried out in pain, but I did not say a word. I bit my lip.

I opened my eyes again, and there it was, thick dark ink on my forearm: The letter *A*, followed by five seemingly random numbers.

My sister went just after me, and her number was one digit higher than mine.

"It doesn't mean anything," Mother said afterward. "It is nothing. It cannot mean something. We cannot make nothing mean something, girls."

"When we go home, it'll be a badge of honor," my sister said.

"Margie." Shelby interrupts my thoughts. "Are you okay? You look like you've seen a ghost."

"Yes," I whisper. So many ghosts. Everywhere, all the time. I am one myself, am I not?

"Your face is so flushed," Shelby says. "It's warm in here. Take your sweater off. It's 1959, for goodness' sakes. A girl can show a little skin." She laughs and holds out her own bare pale freckled arms, which radiate from her blue cotton short-sleeved dress.

But I shake my head. I will not take my sweater off. I will never take it off.

CHAPTER TEN

WHEN I WALK OUTSIDE AT 5 P.M., MY ARM THROUGH
Shelby's, who is trying to convince me to go get a drink with
her, I see Bryda Korzynski sitting on the bench outside the
office building, and then I think my heart may stop.

She stares right at me: brown eyes, hard like stones. So I
know she has been waiting there, just for me.

"You go on ahead," I murmur to Shelby. "I should study
tonight." But I'm wondering whether I can outrun Bryda. I am
a fast runner. I outran a train, once; outran the men who I
thought were chasing after me. When my life depends on it,
I can run.

"Oh, Margie," Shelby says. "One of these days I'll loosen
you up a little bit." *Paragon of virtue,* my sister taunts in my
head, the way she always did when she teased me about being
too good. But Shelby goes on without me, without any more
of a fuss, because, as she mentioned in the elevator on the

way down, Ron has agreed to leave work early for once and meet her there.

"Miss Franklin," Bryda says. She doesn't stand, but I stop by the bench. Mainly because she is Joshua's client and I don't want her to tell him I am rude. Without that, I'm pretty sure I would be running right now.

"Yes," I say to her. "Can I help you with something?"

"You not from Poland," she says.

"What?" I let out a laugh that catches in my throat, so it's possible it's not a laugh at all, but a scream. "It's been a long time. But I am," I say. Lying is a second skin. It suits me better than the first one, maybe. It is not the kind of skin a paragon of virtue wears, is it?

"Where in Poland?" she asks, her eyes narrowing to slits.

"Kraków," I say, too quickly.

"You not from Kraków," she says. "Austria, maybe. Germany?"

I shake my head. "But I am," I say meekly. "It's just been so long."

"Why you wear sweater when it so warm today?" she asks.

"I'm cold," I say, wrapping the sweater tighter around myself.

"You one of us," she says. I'm still shaking my head, back and forth, back and forth. I want her to stop. I want it to stop. It never stops. *Nothing can't mean something,* Mother said. She was wrong; nothing could mean everything. "Your eyes," Bryda says. "They like eyes of dead person."

"You're mistaken," I whisper.

And then I do run, as fast as I can, the clicking of my small heels on the pavement not nearly enough to drown out the sound of Bryda Korzynski's voice echoing in my ears. *You one of us.*

❦

You cannot understand what it is like to hide until you have done it yourself. And I do not mean the kind of hiding my sister and I did as girls on the Merwedeplein, where we'd play hide-and-run around the thick oak trees before we'd catch each other and start all over again, counting off in German: *Eins, zwei, drei* . . . But real hiding, where your life depends on being squirreled away, being somewhere or someone else—that's entirely different. That was what we did, of course: my family, the van Pelses, and the dentist. We were not the only Jews who hid this way, but now we are the most well known. From 1942 to 1944, the seven of us inhabited the five small rooms in the annex above my father's office on the Prinsengracht, Amsterdam.

You cannot understand the fear that courses through you at the sound of every noise, every rat or howl of wind creaking the attic, wondering if it is someone coming for you. The fear of discovery, it is the kind of fear that makes your heart feel always full, pounding too fast. It is the kind of fear that keeps your eyes pried wide open at night amid the dark and the snores of your parents, even if you haven't slept in days. And, it is a fear that does not go away, even now, even fifteen years removed, in a new city, with a new name, a new religion, a thick sweater.

You not Polish. Bryda Korzynski said. *You one of us.*

That night, after Bryda has confronted me on the sidewalk, I lie in bed, for a long time fully awake, listening, listening, waiting. It feels peculiar, that the only sound I hear is the sound of Katze scratching against the furniture with his claws.

After a little while I get out of bed, and even though it is late, already past nine, I pull the smallest folded square from my satchel, unfold it, and stare at the address and phone number again. *P. Pelt.* 2217 *Olney Avenue.*

Peter told me that he would be Pete in his American life. "I'll be Pete, and you'll be Margie," he'd said. "Good American names." Is that what the operator had said? *Pete Pelt.* Did I hear her wrong?

I feel my breath tightening in my chest, and I can see his face, right there, so clearly, the way it was when he was afraid, when he too feared discovery. I think about the time in the middle of the night. 1943 or 1944—it all falls together now. There was a crash, then a clanging in the office below us. The next morning we would learn that someone burglarized the office, but in the middle of the night I did not know at first if they were burglars or the Green Police. I prayed they were burglars. People who stole things felt so much safer than people who stole people.

"Margot," Peter whispered in the dark, his voice tracing a circle in the air in my parents' room, where I slept on a foldout after the dentist arrived a few months into our stay. Mother and Father were both still sleeping. I heard Mother's soft breathing, and Pim's—that was our pet name for Father—snore. I was afraid to move.

I could barely see Peter in the darkness, only the outline

of his hand holding on to something. "I will use this," he whispered. "I will slash their throats."

Then I realized it must be the knife, the one we had used to prepare potatoes that night for dinner.

"Don't move," I whispered. "They'll hear you."

"I will use this," he repeated. "I will slash their throats."

"Oh, Peter," I whispered. We both knew he wouldn't do it, but I guessed he felt safer holding on to it, feeling he had something, some way to stop them. Peter was seventeen then, not yet a man, but almost. He was independent, more so than me and my sister, more detached from his parents, certainly. And he was brave, but he was not stupid. If the Green Police had charged in and saw Peter holding on to a knife, they would've shot him faster than he could move. They would've shot all of us.

The noises stopped, and we waited in silence. I heard the tick of Pim's clock. It was a tick that often could rock me to sleep, gentle and regular. We waited, perfectly still.

Peter lowered the knife, and it was then my eyes grew focused enough in the dark to see he was shaking. "Margot," he whispered. "Do you want to come up to my room?"

※

Now my hand traces a circle on the phone dial, shaking, the way Peter was that night. I turn the numbers, one at a time, unsteadily going through each one, until all the numbers have been turned, and then I am waiting for the sound of ringing in my ear. I do not consider what I will say, other than hello. I do not consider that even if it is him, he might not remember me, the way I remember him. I shut off my brain and listen to the ringing. Once. Twice. Three times. Four.

"Hello," a voice says on the other end of the line. It is high and sweet and mellow, the voice of a woman, not at all unlike the way I might imagine my sister's voice to sound today, had she lived. "Hello," she says again. "Anyone there?"

Quickly, I press the button on the phone to disconnect the call.

CHAPTER ELEVEN

I OFTEN REPLAY THIS FANTASY IN MY AMERICAN LIFE, A story of my own, if you will. In my head I picture a sweet little American family living in a tidy tract house not too far from Ilsa in Levittown. They are Margie and Pete Pelt, who have two children, a girl named Edie and a boy named Herman, after Margot's mother and Peter's father. Margie worries about things like curtains and wallpaper for the children's rooms and Pete takes the train into the city, where he works.

At night, Pete takes the train home again, and when he arrives, it is already dark and Margie has already tucked the children safely into their beds. She has a roast chicken waiting in the oven and a candle lit on the table.

Pete walks in the door, a brown suit coat hugging his broad shoulders. His eyes find Margie, right away, so blue, blue like the sea. Then he finds her mouth with his, and they kiss, a long kiss that is still imbued with passion, even after so many years, so many secrets.

"How was your day?" Margie asks.

Pete takes off his coat and hat. "It was good," he says. "Are the children asleep?"

"Not yet," she answers, and he smiles, a bright American smile, like Joshua's, so that Margie cannot help but smile back. Then he rushes back to the children's bedrooms to tuck them in and kiss them good night.

Later, after dinner, when it seems the world is pitched with blackness, Margie and Pete crawl into their bed together and cling to each other. The moonlight shines in through the bedroom's large picture window, just enough to illuminate Pete's face as he kisses Margie good night and they both fall into a deep and dreamless slumber.

❖

I am thinking about this fantasy the next morning as I walk to work. Wondering about the woman's voice who answered the phone last night. Maybe she was a housekeeper, I think. A friend. She cannot really be someone important, another woman who could slip right into my fantasy, just like that. Could she?

When I arrive at work, Shelby is already there, sitting at her desk holding the phone to her ear, but she isn't speaking into it. This is Shelby's ruse, what she does when she wants to eavesdrop on something and doesn't want anyone to know.

"Good morning," I say to her. She holds a finger to her lips, then points in the direction of Joshua's office.

I'm not trying to eavesdrop like Shelby, but I cannot help but hear Ezra Rosenstein's booming voice, his words breaking like claps of thunder. "How many times do I have to tell you?" he says. "We don't take clients who can't pay our retainer . . . I don't care. And I've played golf with Robertson before."

"So," Joshua says. "That doesn't mean he isn't an anti-Semite. Half the men at the club are."

I sigh, realizing they are arguing about Bryda. I slump down in my chair and lean my head on my arms against my desk, not even bothering to cling to Shelby's ruse. I am exhausted this morning, barely having slept at all last night, my dreams filled with Bryda Korzynski, who morphed into the disembodied woman's voice on the other end of the telephone line last night, who quickly morphed into Peter's mother, Mrs. van Pels, yelling about having to sell her rabbit fur so the van Pelses would have the money to pay for food in the annex. "She's so materialistic," Peter told me once, hanging his head in shame. He did not love his mother the way I loved mine, and for that reason, I always felt sorry for her, even if she was, as Peter said, materialistic.

"She just wants to hold on to something," I told him then. "Just one thing to remind her of who she used to be."

Now I think of her in the camp. She did not have her rabbit fur then, of course. Neither did she seem to have her voice. She was so much smaller, naked and bald, her flesh pale as snow. Suddenly all she had—all we all had—was indelible ink.

A badge of honor, my sister said.

Shelby hisses my name across the desk, and I lift my head.

"But she is one of our people," I hear Joshua saying now, through the paper walls. Joshua's words feel kind and stupid all at once, his thinking that his people and Bryda's people are the same. Though underneath, really, are they so different? Joshua was luckier than Peter. Had Ezra Rosenstein practiced law in Germany, Joshua might have marched to his death in Mauthausen. The thought makes me cringe.

"What are they arguing about?" Shelby whispers. I shrug, as if I am as stumped as she is. "I think the Zimmerman verdict came back," Shelby whispers. "But that doesn't seem to be it."

I nod, guessing this probably means Joshua lost the case, and that Ezra's anger over Bryda is really, doubly, anger about that.

"Not everything is about money," I hear Joshua saying now. His voice is softer than his father's, but it's louder than usual and infused with anger.

The door flies open and Ezra storms out, slamming the door behind him hard enough for the wall by my desk to shake.

I quickly pick up the phone, borrowing Shelby's trick, but he doesn't even glance my way as he passes.

"Miss McKinney," Ezra barks, and Shelby says a pretend good-bye into her pretend phone call. "Where's my schedule for the day?"

"I'll have it right on your desk," Shelby says quickly.

❖

Ezra Rosenstein is a businessman at heart, who does not seem to appreciate Joshua even though he is smart and kind and filled with goodness. I do not understand why Ezra cannot look at him and see the wonderful man that I do, and for this reason, I hate Ezra, even though he'll be the one keeping Bryda Korzynski away.

After Shelby takes Ezra's schedule into his office, I walk to the break room, pour Joshua a cup of coffee, black with two sugars, and bring it to his office.

"Oh, Margie," he says, taking the cup and having a sip. "You always know just what to do, don't you?" He smiles and runs his hand through his curls.

I nod and turn to leave, shining a bit with his compliment and keeping my hands taut at my side, but then Joshua invites me to have a seat across from his desk, so I do.

He doesn't say anything for a moment, so I say, "The Zimmerman verdict came back?"

He nods, then shrugs. "You can't win them all." He is in a black suit today, with a white shirt and straight black tie, and somehow, as I am sitting closer to him now, he appears smaller than when I watch him through the glass. Is it that the suit is too big, and he is like a boy trying on his father's clothes, or that Ezra's harsh words have somehow shrunk him?

"I'm sorry," I tell him.

He shakes his head, opens his mouth to say something, and then, as if he has thought better of it, he takes a sip of his coffee. "Margie," he says, when he is finished. "Can I ask you something?"

"Of course." I nod.

"What did you think of Miss Korzynski yesterday?"

"Me?" I fix my eyes on the bronze placard at the front of his large oak desk that reads *Joshua S. Rosenstein, Esquire.* The S stands for Samuel, I know, who was Ezra's father, Joshua's grandfather, one of the original founders of this firm. For some reason, I think of Samuel in the Bible, the great uniter against the Philistines. But wasn't it Joshua, in the Bible, who led the Israelites into the Promised Land? Or was that Peter? No, I remember. Peter was the fisherman, who for a moment walked on water, until he lost his faith and he began to sink.

"Yes," Joshua is saying now. "I'd like your opinion."

I don't know why Joshua is suddenly so keen to have my opinion, but it could be because he knows I will not yell at him as his father just did. "Well," I say, choosing my words very carefully. "Her story was very sad . . ." I have a but. *But, there are many people with sad stories,* I would say. *And they cannot all be helped.* My sister knew this about me, used to tease me about it even. *There is always a but with you, Margola!* Joshua doesn't know me well enough to ask, or if he does, he doesn't actually want to hear it.

"Yes," he says. "It was very sad, wasn't it? I should help her, shouldn't I? I mean, I owe her something, don't I?" He seems to be talking more to himself than to me.

"Why is that?" I ask.

"Because," he says, but I know what he really means is because he is also a Jew but he hasn't suffered for it, not the way that she has, or the way Margot had. Also, Joshua likes to help people. "Anyway." He clears his throat. "Bring my schedule in for the day, will you?" I nod, and as I turn to walk out, I hear the sound of Joshua's giant sigh, floating past me.

As I reach my desk, I sigh too.

Bryda Korzynski, I think, she is just like that night in the annex, that burglar. For a moment Peter held on to the knife, tracing a circle in the air with his voice. And then the moment passed. And once again we were safe.

At least, for a little while longer.

CHAPTER TWELVE

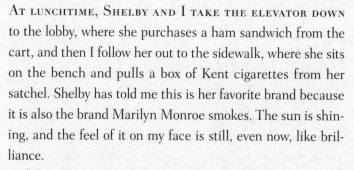

At lunchtime, Shelby and I take the elevator down to the lobby, where she purchases a ham sandwich from the cart, and then I follow her out to the sidewalk, where she sits on the bench and pulls a box of Kent cigarettes from her satchel. Shelby has told me this is her favorite brand because it is also the brand Marilyn Monroe smokes. The sun is shining, and the feel of it on my face is still, even now, like brilliance.

"Here." Shelby hands a cigarette to me, and I roll it around in my fingers. Another time, another place, one that I do not like to go back to.

I hand the cigarette back to her. She shrugs, lights her own, takes a puff, and leans back against the bench and closes her eyes as if she is dreaming. "You know what I don't get," she says to me, holding her pale freckled arm out with the cigarette dangling loosely from her fingers, as if wishing to catch the rays of late-April sunlight and smoke them.

"What's that?" I ask.

"Joshua and Ezra."

"What's not to get?" I say.

She shrugs. "I mean, I would never work for my father if he treated me like that. Why doesn't Joshua just go work for some other law firm?"

"I don't know," I say, but I am thinking that it is not as easy as Shelby thinks, that Shelby's missing sense of duty to her father might not be an American thing, but a Gentile one. "Who can you trust if you can't trust your own father?" I swallow the words as I say them, worried they might choke me.

She shrugs. "Did I tell you I'm missing a glove?" she asks. And there she goes, with the attention span the size of a pinhead.

"A glove?" I murmur.

But I am thinking about the way Ezra yelled at Joshua, not so dissimilar to the way my mother and sister used to yell at each other. You have to love someone to yell at them so intensely; you have to care so unbelievably much that your anger explodes and burns across the sky like the Soviet's *Sputnik* I've read so much about. My sister always thought they fought because Mother hated her, but I knew better.

"I think Ron took the glove," Shelby is saying now.

"What?" I shake my head. "Why would he do that? To give to his hussy?"

She laughs. "No. To find my ring size, silly." She holds the cigarette in her left hand, out in the sunlight, as if admiring a diamond. "And besides that. What you said about trusting one's father, it reminded me." I'm surprised that she has brought the conversation back full circle—I have misjudged her attention span after all.

"Reminded you of what?" I ask.

"My father is acting funny. I think he knows something. I think Ron has already asked him if he can marry me."

"But what about his hussy?" I ask her.

She shrugs. "I'm sure it was just all a big mistake." She smiles and takes a drag on her cigarette, but I wonder, how can she be so sure? She seems so excited about her missing glove, and I do not want to burst her delicate bubble, so I do not press her further. Instead I find myself thinking again about the woman's voice on the phone last night, and in the sunlight, now, I wonder if she might be a mistake as well. Did I simply dial wrong?

Shelby crushes her cigarette with her foot and grabs on to my hand. "Can you imagine it?" she asks me. "Me as somebody's wife?"

"No," I say. "I cannot." I smile at her, so she will know I am teasing. Because in truth, I can see Shelby as someone's wife. I believe Shelby would be much like that Donna Reed, who Ilsa had me watch on TV with her one evening when I was there at her house for dinner, bright and charming and hospitable and capable of running a busy household. Much like the Margie Pelt of my fantasy world.

"Oh, hush," Shelby says, but she smiles too, so I understand she is not really cross. She stands and throws the remains of her sandwich in the trash. I do the same with my apple core. And then Shelby takes my arm so we can walk back inside the building together.

❈

My father is a good businessman, just like Ezra Rosenstein. Even now, I imagine him in Switzerland with his new wife, spending his days drowning in correspondence from the book he edited and put out into the world, and which, I imagine, has made him a millionaire several times over.

Even before the war, we always lived well, and after we were hiding, he worried about his business, Opekta, a company that distributed pectin used to make jams. One time there was an important meeting down in the office below us, and he wanted nothing more than to attend. "Why don't you listen at the floor?" I suggested, and his wide smile was my reward. The space was too tight for him, though; he grew cramped, so I offered to listen for him. Of course, my sister insisted on coming along. She fought so much with Mother, but Father was hers; she couldn't give him to me, even for a moment.

I strained my ears and forced myself to record the conversation, boring as it was. All the talk about the price of pectin and importing and such. I recorded it in shorthand in a notebook.

My sister fell asleep, her head lounging against my knee, and I dared not move for fear I'd startle her awake, she'd make a noise, and we'd be discovered. Finally she awoke and sat up, and she immediately grabbed the notebook, and off she went to find him.

"Pim," she said cheerily. "Oh, Pim, we have conducted

business on your behalf today." Father kissed and hugged her and read the notes, that he seemed to assume were her notes, and I thought they meant a lot to him because he mumbled things to himself and took down some notes of his own to tell Mr. Kuglar the next time he came up.

"Did I do well, Pim?" my sister asked.

"Indeed you did," he told her, smiling at her, and only her, as if he had forgotten that I was even in the room. He kissed the top of her head. "Indeed you did, my little Anna."

❧

I think of that moment even now, when I think about my father, as I often find myself doing. I have written him a letter in my head many times in the past few years. He is my father, the only piece of my family left, and when I realized he was alive after I discovered my sister's book, I had the urge to reach across the ocean and pull him back to me. But whenever I sit down and try to write the words I think, I find myself looking through my sister's book again, and I cannot bring myself to commit a single word to paper.

The problem is this: I am not his daughter anymore. I am not even a Jew. And if he were to know I am still here, I would not go back. I could not. I do not want the world to know me, as they know him, and my sister.

And also, there is something else. I think of how he looked right past me that morning, just at her and her only. Father and I did not fight. We did not yell. But still, it was so clear to me, even then, how he felt about my sister.

I am still afraid of many things in my American life, but what I am most afraid of now is how my father might look at me if he were to know what I have done. If he were to know the truth about what happened with the two of us, me and my sister, just before the very end.

CHAPTER THIRTEEN

✤

On Thursday morning, Joshua buzzes me into his office
and asks me to shut the door behind me. "I want you to do
something for me, Margie," he says. "But you can't mention it
to anyone else here, especially not my father, or Miss Mc-
Kinney."

"Okay," I say slowly, not sure yet whether to be excited or
upset about what he is going to ask of me. My brain is foggy
again, since I'd stayed up late last night, then fallen into restless sleep after dialing P. Pelt's number once more, just to
make sure I had not, indeed, made a mistake dialing. The
same woman answered, and I'd hung up. Then I'd called the
operator back to double-check I'd written the number down
right. I had. *It still could be a mistake,* I'd been telling myself
as I'd been tossing and turning in bed all night. Though what
kind of mistake, I cannot wrap my brain around now.

"I'm going to write down the address," Joshua is saying now, and I realize I have missed a bit of his instructions.

"The address?" I ask.

"Miss Korzynski's address," he says, and my heart falls into my stomach, a place it is so often used to tumbling. "I want you to stop by and see her after work today. Find out how many others she thinks will join her suit. Get their names and contact information and bring them back to me, okay?"

"But your father . . ." I say, my voice breaking.

"Don't worry about my father," he says quickly. He picks up his pen, writes Bryda's address on the yellow legal pad on his desk, tears the sheet off, and then holds it out to me.

I hesitate before taking it, because I do not want to seek out Bryda Korzynski, to watch the way her brown eyes call me a liar by looking through me. Maybe she looks at everyone that way. Maybe her eyes are dead too.

"Couldn't we just call her instead?" I finally say.

He shakes his head. "Let's keep this all out of the office, all right?" He pauses. "And besides, it's always better to do these things in person." He thrusts the paper closer to me, and I have no choice but to take it from him. "I'd like to get the ball rolling. Leave a little early this afternoon so you're not working any later than usual, all right?" My whole body tells me to say no, to run out of his office, to quit my job and move back to the safety of Ilsa's house in Levittown. But I love working here, in this office, for Joshua, and I cannot really imagine leaving it all behind just because of one crazy woman. I have survived worse, hidden from worse. So I breathe deeply, and I tell myself to stay.

"I know it's a lot to ask," Joshua says. "But you understand how important this is, don't you? Please, Margie. This is really a very big deal for me. And I need your help here." His gray-green eyes, they plead with me in their softness. And I think guiltily of the way Bryda's voice shook as she called her boss a Nazi. This is a good thing that Joshua is trying to do, an honorable thing. And what will Joshua think about me if I refuse to help him?

"Okay," I finally agree.

"Thank you," he says. I nod and stand. "And remember," he says, before I open the door, "not a word to anyone."

❖

"What was that all about?" Shelby whispers, when I'm back at my desk.

"What?" I say, innocently enough.

"I was watching through the glass. It looked . . . steamy."

"Steamy?" I say, my voice uneasy. I shake my head. "No. It was nothing, really."

"He didn't tell you what they were fighting about, did he? Ezra's still miffed about it."

"That's not my place," I say.

She rolls her eyes at me. For a second I think she might call me a paragon of virtue. But then she says, "If you find out, you tell me. I'm dying to know."

"Of course," I say. But Joshua needn't worry. I am good at

keeping secrets. I am wrapped in them now, the way I am wrapped in lies, like my sweater, clinging tightly to my skin, even on the hottest of days.

�֎

When the big clock by the elevator strikes four o'clock, I lie to Shelby and tell her I have a doctor's appointment and have to leave early.

"Everything all right?" she asks. I nod and stare past her, in through the glass window by Joshua's office. He has the phone slung between his shoulder and his ear, and his brow is ripe with concentration as he's talking. He notices me gathering my things, and he waves me toward the elevator and shoots me his uniquely Joshua smile. I smile back.

But in the elevator, I am no longer smiling. I hold tightly to the yellow paper with Bryda's address in my hand. *I can lie about this,* I think, the way I have lied about so much else already. I can tell Joshua I went and not go. I can crumple up the paper in my hand and walk my usual route down Market Street toward home.

But I also know that Joshua is a meticulous lawyer, and that he will almost certainly follow up with Bryda with a phone call, and that tomorrow, also, he will expect a list of names and numbers from me.

I have a choice, I think as the elevator doors open into the lobby and Henry tells me to have a good afternoon. I can do as Joshua asks. Or I can walk out the door of this office building and not come back. There would be other jobs, and there is always Ilsa's house.

I think about the way Joshua just smiled at me, the way he is filled with so much goodness, and I know I will do what he asks. I do not want another job. And besides, I think as I step out onto the sidewalk, Ezra will never let Joshua take this any further.

CHAPTER FOURTEEN

I HAVE TO TAKE TWO CITY BUSES TO GET TO BRYDA'S apartment, and the whole way there I think about what I will say to her. If she accuses me again, I will tell her that she knows nothing about me. I will be strong, and I will be firm, which are both things I am used to, and quite good at, being.

I lean back against the hard bus seat and take a few deep breaths. I am glad to be sitting now, because my legs, they already feel unsteady.

In Amsterdam, before we went into hiding, Jews were no longer allowed on buses, so we walked everywhere, even in the heat of the summer, even with packages to carry. We walked and we walked, our yellow star across our hearts, right there, like a target.

In Philadelphia, it is easy to take a bus, and for this I am grateful. There are so many, you just have to read the map to know which one and pay a little money to be able to navigate around the city.

I have never been to Bryda's part of town before, and as the bus pulls closer, I can see why. The buildings are shabby row houses with crumbling striped awnings and low brick apartments, flanked by beggars on the street. I think of Jodenbreestraat, the street in the center of Amsterdam where Jews lived, that began to crumble just before we went into hiding. So many Jews taken away. There was no one left to take care of the street any longer.

As the bus comes to a stop, I look out the window and consider not getting off at all. There are beggars here too, even at the bus stop. I could stay on the bus until it loops back again closer to Center City, I think.

But I find myself standing slowly, walking toward the door and then onto the street, where I find myself staring into the face of a wan beggar.

She is a young girl, her hair pulled in a messy braid, her face streaked with dirt. She holds out a cup and looks at me with wounded brown eyes. She is too thin. Her dirty plaid dress falls over her.

I reach into my satchel, pull out a shiny nickel, and drop it in her cup.

❋

Sometimes I am haunted by my sister's eyes. It's hard to remember them the way they were, when we were girls, living on the Merwedeplein, or even when we lay next to each other quietly in the annex, writing in our diaries. I cannot remember their inflections of joy, or the way they darkened with jealousy when she asked if she could read my diary and she read how I felt about Peter, or even the way they fell when she cried, as she did so often. All I can remember is the way they looked, at the very end. She was skin and bones by then, her face barely even a shape, her eyes sunken and huge. They were brown, the color of almonds, with small green flecks. They were too big for her face. They begged me to help her.

I try to shake the thought away as I walk to the stairwell in Bryda's brick apartment building, then up three flights to her floor. The smell of garbage in the stairs overtakes me, a smell like rotting putrid rats, and I gag, because suddenly I am there, again, hauling trash with my sister. Her eyes. Like saucers. Begging me to carry her.

I take a deep breath once I'm in the hallway, practicing in my head what I will say to Bryda, how I will keep the conversation all business, only about Joshua. But the smell in the hallway is not much better than in the stairwell. The air is stagnant and I fight the urge to vomit as I wrap my sweater tighter around my chest.

I reach my hand up to knock on her door. Apartment 3C in the north section of Philadelphia, Pennsylvania, United States of America. It is a long way from Auschwitz, Poland. But as I knock, I understand it is not as far as you might think.

❧

"You," Bryda says, when she opens the door, her voice thick with disgust.

"Hello," I say, as cordially as I can, given the circumstances, and then quickly spit out what I have just rehearsed in my head. "Mr. Rosenstein asked me to stop by and talk. Can I come in?" I don't want to come in. Every bone in my body is telling me to run. *Run.* Take two buses back to Market Street. Then run again, to my neighborhood, where the rats stay hidden—or at least Katze sometimes keeps them at bay when he feels like it, and the smells are of blooming spring flowers and taxicab fumes.

She opens the door a little wider, and I step inside. The room is tidy, but smaller than mine by at least half, a little box room without a trace of a kitchen, only a hot plate on a table, next to a wooden chair. There is a cot in the corner, where I imagine she sleeps.

Even in the annex, at the height of the war, we had more than this.

"So," Bryda says. "What you want?"

Her hair has tumbled out of the bun, after what I imagine was a long day of sewing for her, and today she wears a blue Robertson's Finery uniform, with a sleeve long enough to cover her number. For this, I am grateful. Though I notice the way *Robertson's Finery* is stitched in yellow, just across her heart—it is so much like the color and placement of the yellow star we once wore.

I clear my throat. "Mr. Rosenstein asked me to come over and visit with you and gather up the names and contact information for any people you found to join you."

"Group litigation?" she says. I nod. "So he really do help me?"

"Maybe," I say, because I am still entirely unconvinced about Joshua's being able to go anywhere with this case after the screaming match in his office with Ezra, and also because I don't want to get Bryda's hopes up. Perhaps she deserves a lot. The war is over; the Nazis are done. But it is still quite hard to be a Jew, even here, in America, and also to live openly without fear. I have considered before what might happen if I were to walk down Ludlow in the summer, wearing a sleeveless dress without my sweater, my Jewishness right there, so obvious, out in the open, for everyone to see. I imagine the terrible way people might look at me, as if they knew everything.

"I have two names," I realize Bryda is saying now, and I swallow hard, trying to erase the bitter taste in my mouth that comes with fear. "I tell them to you, you write them down."

"Okay," I say, pulling the yellow legal pad that I took from the supply closet at work out of my satchel.

"I do not write anymore," she says. She holds out her right hand, which I did not notice before is missing the forefinger. I turn away at the sight, not wanting to imagine how she received that horror. "It not what you think," she says.

"Okay," I say again, because, of course, I am thinking it was the Nazis' doing, that it happened in the camp. But I don't ask her what really happened—I don't want to know, and besides, I am suddenly having trouble speaking. Bile rises in my throat. The air is too warm; it's suffocating, drowning me under the weight of my second skin, and the sweater. She tells me the names, and I scribble them quickly down.

When I look up, she is staring directly at me, squinting

until she reminds me of a hawk, perched at the edge of a cliff, searching for prey. "What?" I finally say to her, and somehow I think I am able to disguise the fear in my voice as annoyance.

"You know what worse than Gestapo?" She pauses and clucks her tongue. "Snake," she finally says.

I run down the steps in Bryda's building, to the street. I run so fast that it is hard to breathe. I run past the bus stop I came from, to the next street over. And it is only here that I slow my pace and attempt to take slow deep breaths. Even now, so many years later, the memory of the camps, of staying hidden, it is a muscle memory, one that neither time nor distance can completely erase, and it takes so little for me to slide back into my fear. Over and over again. Bryda, her voice, the smells of her terrible apartment, our shared horror, they are everything about my past that I am running from, all the things I try to avoid in my American life. And now I understand that these terrible things, they are only a bus ride away from the safety of the Jewish law firm, which in so many ways reminds me of the comforts of my childhood, before the war. This is perhaps the most terrifying thought of all.

It takes me a few moments to catch my breath on the street, and when I do, I look around. Here, on this street, the buildings look even worse. One has been ravaged by fire, and the bricks are black and ashy, the glass of the windows blown away. I hear a child crying from somewhere in the near distance, and my head begins to ache as I remember a similar sound from the camp. It is a particular wail of pain or hunger or desperation. I confuse them now.

I hear footsteps behind me. Heavy. The gait of boots. The Green Police or the NSB. I do not turn to face them, but I run again, faster, farther, up the street to where I see a city bus pulling into a different stop. I have no idea where the bus is going, if it will take me anywhere near to the right place, but I do not even care. I run up the steps, hand my coin to the driver, and fling my body into a seat.

Even when I am sitting there, against the hard seat, my eyes peering out the dirty window as the bus drives away and the broken buildings fall from my reach, I do not feel even the smallest sense of safety. I have no idea where the bus is headed.

This is no escape plan, I think.

�֎

In 1944, when we were held against our will in Poland, Mother had a plan. She always had a plan. Even when we were girls and we first moved from Frankfurt to the Merwedeplein and she fed us books in Dutch to integrate us into our new world, or when she filled our soup with extra chicken fat in an attempt to get us to gain weight when my sister and I grew sickly in the new world of Holland.

I believe, even now, that the plan she had in the camp, she had worked out for a long time, before we even needed it, just like Father did, with the annex. When I received my call-up notice from the Germans, he was ready. But the difference was, Father never believed we'd be found in the annex. Mother, I suspect, did.

Mother whispered her plan to me in pieces, late at night, after the others in the camp were asleep, once our heads were already shaved, our arms marked, our bodies falling apart. She was sick by then, and her voice came out of her in gasps. There had been whispers that they'd be moving us soon, to another camp, but not Mother. She was too sick. I did not want to leave her behind, but I was in no position to protest, and I knew she would never let me, anyway.

"When they put you on the train, you run," she whispered to me. "You grab your sister and you run. Wait until the train is moving, but not too fast. Wait until he is watching. He will not shoot you."

I knew who she meant, the one guard, who I vaguely remembered from our life in Germany. A neighbor. A Nazi. His name was Schmidt—I could not remember his first name, and I did not want to. I could still picture watching him out our front window in Frankfurt, watching as he watered his grass with a long green hose. Once, when I was a very young girl, not even in school yet, I walked across the yard and played with his shepherd puppy. Schmidt smiled at me then while he tossed the puppy treats and cooed sweet things at her. Schmidt was a different man in his Nazi uniform, his arm wound tightly with the red swastika. His face had grown hard, unyielding.

"He will not shoot you," Mother repeated.

I nodded, not because I thought she was right, but because

by then, I was not afraid of being shot. It sounded like an easy way to die, almost a relief.

"You run," she told me, "and you take your sister." She paused. "And when you are free, you find Eduard, in Frankfurt. He will help you."

I nodded again, the rhythm of her whisper tickling in my ear. It was like she was telling me a bedtime story, lulling me to sleep, winging on a fantasy.

"Promise me," she said again.

"I promise," I finally said, my throat so parched that the words barely formed.

CHAPTER FIFTEEN

FRIDAY MORNING EZRA ROSENSTEIN IS NOT AT WORK, HAV-ing already departed for Margate, but Joshua comes into the office and announces to me and Shelby that he will not be heading to Margate this weekend.

"This fight must be serious," Shelby whispers to me after he goes into his office and shuts the door. She is frowning, I think because she knows Joshua's presence means she won't be able to start her weekend early.

"Maybe," I say. "Or maybe he just has a lot of work to do."

Shelby shakes her head. "He's a lawyer," she says. "And he's rich. It's not about the work."

Joshua buzzes me, just as I am beginning to wonder if Shelby is right, if their fight is the reason why he's here. "Yes, Mr. Rosenstein," I say.

"Margie," he says, "did you get me those papers I asked for?"

"Papers?" I ask.

"After work yesterday . . ."

"Oh yes," I say, thinking of the four different city buses it took me to finally make my way home. "Yes, I did."

"Good," he says. "Let's discuss them over lunch today, all right? We'll walk down to Isaac's Delicatessen at noon."

"We?" I hear myself saying, though I know it is a stupid thing to say even as the word escapes my lips.

"Unless you have other plans," he says.

"No, no. Of course not," I say. "Lunch will be perfectly fine."

I hang up the phone, and Shelby is staring at me with raised eyebrows, her lips in the shape of an O, but I ignore her and begin typing. And then I smile to myself as I wonder if Ezra is not the reason why Joshua is here today. If the reason why is me.

❈

As I wait for Joshua to come out of his office, just before noon, my cheeks grow warm at the notion of our upcoming lunch, just the two of us. Then I find myself thinking, *That was how it began with Peter and me, lunch.* And it is confusing how my mind wanders to Peter, when I am so eagerly awaiting the time with Joshua. But I cannot push the thought away. Peter is there, always there. And the woman's voice from the phone sounded so much like my sister, though, of course, it could not be.

My sister's voice and Peter. They go together in my head now, though, don't they? Even when things first began between Peter and me, it was because of her. My sister and I had been lying on her bed together that day, writing in our diaries and studying, just the two of us, as we did often.

Sometimes my sister slept, and I watched the door. Other times, that day, she could not sit still. It was so small in the annex, and there were so many of us, and we weren't supposed to talk above a whisper during the day when the office was filled with workers below us.

This was the hardest for my sister. She enjoyed the sound of her own voice hanging in the air. She was inquisitive. She always wanted to know things, to analyze them out loud. She whispered to me, all the time, about everything. There was no room to think.

"Can't you just stop?" I finally said to her, in something that verged on louder than a whisper that day.

"Just stop what?" she asked, chewing on the edge of the fountain pen she was writing with.

"Talking," I said.

"I'm just asking you how you feel about the weather," she huffed. We could hear the gentle sound of rain against the rooftop.

"The weather?" I fumed. "Who cares about the weather? We're trapped in here. And you're always talking, always so cheerful."

"So I shouldn't say a word, and what? Be a paragon of virtue like you? A silent and gloomy and determined-to-become-smarter-with-all-your-studies-while-you're-here bore?" She glared at me, and I got off the bed, and I stormed out of the room, or my best attempt at it while also tiptoeing in my stockinged feet. Right in the hallway, I nearly bumped into Peter.

He stood there, holding on to his cat, Mouschi, and a few

pieces of bread. Peter was tall, with blue eyes the color of the sea. I'd noticed him at school before, but he'd never once seemed to notice me before that moment; even in our closeness in the annex, we'd barely spoken.

"You can sit in our room with us," he said then, referring to himself and Mouschi. "It's quiet. And we'll share our lunch with you."

�֍

"Margie." Joshua's voice interrupts my thoughts, and I glance at the clock and see that it is exactly noon now. "You ready to go to lunch?" He taps his hand easily against the edge of my desk before reaching up for his hat. Shelby is typing. I hear the clickety-click of the keys, but I also feel her eyes on me, burning steadily through my skin. She will ask me many questions about this when I get back.

"Yes," I tell him, standing and picking up my satchel. "I'm ready."

✖

Isaac's Delicatessen is at the end of the block, at the corner of South Sixteenth Street and Market, a mere twenty steps or so from the front entrance of our office building. But I have never been in Joshua's presence outside the office before, so it feels strange, stepping out into the sunshine, next to him, keeping up with his long strides on the sidewalk.

"I hope you don't mind that I asked you to come out to lunch with me today," he says as soon as our feet hit the pavement.

Joshua's long black shoes turn my small black pumps into dwarves.

"Not at all," I say.

"I know Miss McKinney can be a bit of a gossip, and I don't want what we're doing here to get back to my father. At least until I have a plan."

"Of course," I say. I am surprised by the fact that he seems to have some understanding of Shelby, but more, I am pleased that he has used the word "we're." Joshua and I. We're doing something together. Then I remember what that thing is, and I cling tighter to my sweater around my chest.

Isaac's sits in a small glass-covered storefront, underneath a low brick office building. Joshua pulls open the heavy glass door and holds it back, motioning for me to pass in front of him. "Order whatever you want," he says as he strolls up to the counter. "I'm buying."

I order an apple and a cup of chicken soup, and I carry my tray to a small table by the window, which is one of the only ones still open. There are twenty or so tables crammed into the small space, but most of them are already occupied by men in dark-colored suits like Joshua's. A haze of smoke hangs in the air from their lunchtime cigarettes, but Joshua, he does not smoke. Or at least, not at the office.

Joshua sits down across from me, so we're facing one another. It's loud in here, men's laughter bellowing across the room, but when Joshua looks at me, I no longer hear it. His eyes are a gray green, closer to the color of winter grass than the sea. I spoon my soup carefully into my mouth while Joshua takes a bite of his chopped liver, which looks just the way Mother used to make it before the war, when there was still food to be had, and when everyone still had an appetite.

"Are you sure that's enough food, Margie?" Joshua asks, looking at me, in between bites.

I nod. "Yes," I say. Joshua raises his eyebrows, but then the moment passes and he takes another bite. I could tell him that once you have come close to starving, it still feels impossible to eat in abundance, these many years later, but of course, I don't. We weighed ourselves in the annex once, and I was 132 pounds. After the camp, I was flesh and bone, and now I am only marginally better. The last time I stepped on the scale, at Ilsa's urging, I was just around 110 pounds. But I try to avoid weighing myself now, the same way I have stopped checking my face in the mirror. Though my face is rounder than my sister's, my nose a bit wider, my eyes a bit more circular, there is still something there that bears a similarity to her. And without my glasses on, my face appears blurry in the mirror, an apparition. My sister's face staring back at me.

"So tell me," Joshua is saying now. "How was Miss Korzynski yesterday?"

I swallow some soup and will myself to also swallow away the image of my sister's ghost. But even as I put down my spoon and pull the thin yellow paper with the two names on it out of my satchel, her face stays in my mind. *Paragon of virtue,* she whispers. *Living your great American life hiding in your thick sweater. What do you think you're doing here, now, at lunch with your boss? And what of that other yellow paper folded in your satchel?*

I glance down to check that this yellow paper is the right one before handing it across the table to Joshua. It is. He takes it from me, and for just a second the tips of our fingers touch before I pull back quickly. But Joshua seems not to notice, as he is already staring at the paper and frowning. "Two isn't enough," he says. I nod, because I have already come to this realization myself. "We need fifty names. Maybe a hundred."

"A hundred?" I say, focusing my full attention on him now, on the way he looks so different when he's frowning, older, more like Ezra. "I don't think she'll ever get you that many names."

"You may be right, Margie. And yet I know they're out there. Robertson has three factories in Philly and another four across the river. And many of his workers are Jewish immigrants, like Miss Korzynski." He sighs. "I'm sorry I've wasted your lunch hour with all this."

"You haven't," I say. "I was glad to leave the office for a little while."

He nods. "You should leave the office more at lunch. It's good to get out of there sometimes."

"Okay," I say.

"Sometimes I think I'll suffocate in that place." He shakes his head. "My father always seems to think greatness and money are the same thing, but you know what I think greatness is?"

"What?" I ask.

"Being brave, like Miss Korzynski. Doing something that

no one else has dared to do before you. Finding something that terrifies you and then doing it anyway. Does that make sense, Margie?"

"Yes," I say. "It does."

I stare at Joshua, and for the moment before he stands, his gray-green eyes flicker with something that I can't exactly put my finger on. And then, quickly, he smiles, and he is glowing again, like the Joshua I am used to.

※

Peter's eyes, they were a blue so deep you might have thought they were in a painting, a van Gogh or a Cézanne. His eyes held on to me when we spoke.

At first, we shared lunch. Every day for a week. Or maybe two. Time had an odd quality in the annex, hours into days, days into weeks, weeks into months, then years. It was hard to remember the days, to keep track.

But for some time, Peter and I sat on the divan tossing bread crumbs at Mouschi and talking about the people we knew from school, wondering what had happened to them. Who had been taken? Who was in hiding? Later, when we wanted to become a secret, Peter and I would be together only at night, after everyone else was sleeping. But at first, we shared bread and whispers as the sunlight poured in through the high glass window in Peter's room.

After that week, or maybe those two weeks, Mouschi decided he liked me and came onto my lap, which Peter said was strange, because Mouschi normally only liked him and him only. "He knows that you are special," Peter said as he stroked back Mouschi's fur. His hand bumped against my leg, unintentionally, but it warmed my skin, even through the cloth of my skirt.

"I can't believe your parents let you bring your cat," I said, wondering what had become of our own poor Moortje. Had the neighbors found her, or had she escaped and become one of those fierce alley cats? Father had said bringing her was too dangerous.

"They didn't have a choice really," he said. "I told them I wasn't coming here without him."

"You did?" I stared at him, at the way his blue eyes held steady. "Were you serious?" He nodded. "You were ready to die for a cat?"

"It's different for you," he said. "You have a sister."

"But you have your parents," I pointed out. "They have to mean more than a cat."

He shook his head. "Nah, they probably would've left me there and come into hiding without me. But they were too busy worrying about themselves to argue with me over a cat." His voice sounded small as he said it, and watching the way they alternated between yelling at him and ignoring him in the annex, I was almost inclined to believe him.

He held on to me then, with his blue eyes, as if we were the only two.

"Oh, Peter," I said. "They wouldn't have left you behind. How could they have? You're their son." He shrugged, and I reached my hand up to touch his cheek. It was smooth, a boy's cheek still, or perhaps an almost-man's. "I would never leave you behind," I whispered.

He smiled at me and stroked Mouschi's fur. His hand grazed my thigh, and stayed there a second longer than if it were an accident. "I know that," he whispered back. "And I would never leave you behind either."

CHAPTER SIXTEEN

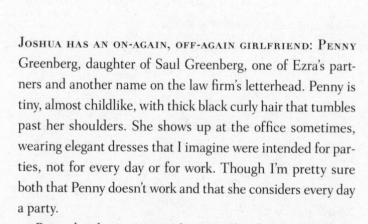

Joshua has an on-again, off-again girlfriend: Penny
Greenberg, daughter of Saul Greenberg, one of Ezra's partners and another name on the law firm's letterhead. Penny is
tiny, almost childlike, with thick black curly hair that tumbles
past her shoulders. She shows up at the office sometimes,
wearing elegant dresses that I imagine were intended for par-
ties, not for every day or for work. Though I'm pretty sure
both that Penny doesn't work and that she considers every day
a party.

Penny has been stopping by to see her father a lot lately,
but mainly I suspect she is at the office to see Joshua, using
her father as an excuse. I also suspect that she likes Joshua a
whole lot more than he likes her. More than once, Joshua has
asked me to lie about him being in a meeting or on an important phone call when she has shown up.

This afternoon, though, she saunters in, draped in a dress

the color of a ripe tomato, with a hat to match, her hair twisted underneath in some kind of fashionable up-do that seems impossible to create oneself. I wonder if she has paid someone to do it for her.

"Hello, Margie," she says. "Josh is expecting me."

She walks past my desk, sashaying her hips. "Hold on a second," I call after her. "I'll buzz him. He may be in the middle of something."

"Oh, that won't be necessary."

I press the button on the phone to buzz him, but she is already past me, in his office. She doesn't shut the door all the way behind her, and after a moment I hear the sound of her giggle and Joshua's ebullient laughter.

Five minutes later, he walks out with Penny draped on his arm. "Margie," he says to me, tipping his hat on the way past. "I'm leaving for the day."

"Okay," I say.

He winks at me, and then he says, "Have a nice weekend."

✸

Shelby stops typing as soon as the elevator door shuts behind Joshua and Penny.

"Now this," she says, smirking, "is an interesting development."

"What's that?" I ask, finding nothing about Penny's quick escape with Joshua in the least bit interesting.

"I thought he didn't go to Margate because he and his father are in a fight. But maybe he didn't go because of her."

"Why would you say that?" I ask, my face turning red,

thinking about how I considered our lunch might have been the reason.

"His father is away for the weekend. They can have his father's big Main Line house all to themselves."

"But Joshua has his own house," I say. I have ridden the bus past it before, a duplex near Broad and Olney, on a corner filled with flower boxes, a location I find divine but that I imagine feels way too bourgeois to Ezra Rosenstein.

Shelby waves a hand in the air. "But a girl like Penny. She'd be impressed by the fancy house. Heck, I'd be impressed by the fancy house."

"You'd be impressed by anything." I can't stifle my annoyance.

"I'm just saying," she says. "The cat's away, and the mice will play."

"That's such a stupid expression," I say. "It doesn't even make sense."

She laughs. "Come on, Margie. It's the weekend. Let's get out of here and get a drink."

I shake my head, because even with all of Shelby's talk about Penny and Joshua, I am still thinking about what Joshua said to me at lunch. That greatness is in bravery. Have I forgotten how to be brave, even in the smallest way? Is that why I hold so tightly to my sweater, my new name? Is that why I have not written the letter to my father that I have composed in my head a thousand times? Why I have not tried to find Peter, for so very long? Why I have tucked the woman's voice away, in the back of my head these past few days, denied it, excused it? Am I a coward now?

"No," I tell Shelby. "I can't. I have something else I need to do."

"It'll keep till Monday," she says.

"No," I say. "It won't."

❊

I leave Shelby on Market Street and then walk in the opposite direction from my apartment toward the bus stop at the corners of Market and Seventeenth. After I turn the corner, out of Shelby's line of sight, I pull the tiniest of squares from my satchel. I unfold it, read the address again, though I have already committed it to memory: *P. Pelt, 2217 Olney Avenue, Apartment 4A.*

Once I am sitting on the bus, I still clutch tightly to the fading scrap of paper. My fingers ache and tremble, and I do not feel brave in the slightest.

When I first came to Philadelphia in 1953, I tried desperately to look for Peter. I called the operator every day from Ilsa's telephone and asked her for Peter Pelt. "No listings under that name," she always told me.

"Try van Pels," I'd say, just in case he'd decided not to change his name after all.

"No. No listing for that either."

But then, nearly a year into my American life, I saw it for the first time. My sister's diary, in the window of Robin's Books. It caught my eye as I walked by, the echo of her face. I walked past it, then slowed down, then stopped, then walked back, though I am not certain how my legs moved.

They were numb, and I suddenly couldn't breathe. I gasped at the air and reminded myself to inhale, exhale. My heart pounded so hard in my chest I thought it might explode.

I stopped at the window and pressed my nose against the glass. And there she was, preserved the way she'd been ten years earlier, maybe more, before she'd been stripped and shaved, tattooed, and broken.

I walked inside the store, like walking inside a dream. The air was fog and silt and clung to my sweater. It was springtime, but I was shivering. Somewhere a bell clanged on the door. A man asked if he could help me. I pointed to the book, my sister's face. Or I picked it up. I don't remember paying for it, though I'm sure I did.

The next thing I remember is being back in Levittown, at Ilsa's house.

I sat down in her front room, on a hard-backed chair, and I opened the book. It was nothing like the orange-checked book I'd seen my sister write in, so often, in the annex. It was a brighter orange, almost a red, and my sister's name was written in big letters on the front. Such big letters. Her name—it was shouting at me.

Dear Kitty. The words swam across my eyes, as if I'd imagined them there.

"I'm calling my diary Kitty," my sister told me, after she got the diary for her birthday.

"Kitty?" I'd raised my eyebrows. "Do you want a friend or a pet?"

"I'll have you know that Kitty is a very American name."

I blinked and looked again. *Dear Kitty.* And then I screamed and dropped the book on the hardwood floor, where it landed with a terrifying thud.

"Margie," Ilsa said, running in. "You look like you've seen a ghost, my dear."

I nodded. But I couldn't speak.

She picked up the book, looked at the cover, and then handed it back to me. She clucked her tongue, the same way she had when she'd looked over my shoulder as I'd read the article about the Jewish children being attacked. "I've heard about this," she said. She pulled over a chair and sat down next to me. "Maybe for you," she said, "who lived through the war over there, it is better not to read these things." Ilsa seemed to understand vaguely that wartime had been horrific for me, for Jews, in Europe, though she did not ever ask me for specifics. Not that I would have told her, even if she had.

That afternoon, I simply closed the book in my lap and nodded.

After Ilsa and her husband, Bertram, went to sleep that night, I traced the letters of my sister's name with my fingers. Then, on the inside page, I did the same with my father's. *My Pim,* I thought. *He is still alive.* I was flooded with joy, and then quickly, uneasiness. *He did this,* I thought. He published this. *For her.* And then I felt like I might vomit as I imagined it in my head again and again and again, like always: the last time I saw my sister, on the train. What I did to her.

Maybe for you, Ilsa said, *it is better not to read these things . . .*

But I took a deep breath and read the entire book from cover to cover that night. Twice.

According to the book, she was the one Peter kissed. She was the one Peter loved.

For a long while after I found the published book, I did not try to find Peter.

❧

I get off the bus at the corners of Olney and Broad streets, not too far from Joshua's home, but far enough so I cannot see it from here. I think about what Shelby said, about Penny and Joshua spending the weekend at his father's house, and I wonder if she is right. The thought of it, the two of them together, annoys me. I know it shouldn't, but it does. But I am not here for Joshua, I remind myself. I'm here for Peter. And in my mind I again conjure up the exact color of his eyes: deep and blue and clear as the sea. Then I walk down Olney for a little while, until the numbers turn into the 2000s.

2217 Olney Avenue, Apartment 4A, is in a group of tiny brick connected houses. They are European in their styling, not even all that dissimilar from the outside of the Prinsengracht. "I will never come back here," Peter said to me as we lay there together on his divan. "After the war, we will go to Philadelphia, City of Brotherly Love. We will be different people, no longer Jews."

Peter promised me we would come here together, though once, when I asked him what if . . . ? What if we could not? What if we were captured? Separated? All things we did not like to speak of.

"Shhh," he'd whispered into my hair. "Do not worry so much. I will find you. I will always find you."

Peter said he would find me, and I do not think it would be hard to do this in Philadelphia, if he were looking. Margie Franklin's phone number is listed, and there have been a few times when I have answered a call, only to hear the sound of heavy breathing on the other end, followed by a slow click. Always, a part of me has wondered if he is here, trying to find me, just like he said he would. But also, I understand now, I can find him. I could've found him all this time. And if not for my sister's diary, I know I would've. Or at least, I would've been trying. Now I am ashamed that I have not. That I have been such a coward, for so very long. *Greatness is in bravery,* Joshua told me. *Doing something that terrifies you.*

I walk up the cement steps to 4A, slowly. There are six steps, and I count them in my head, the numbers making an easy rhythm, calming my quickly beating heart.

By the front door, there is a square green mailbox with one word painted on it: *Pelt.*

I am in the right place.

I take a deep breath and press my finger to the doorbell. I ring it once, and I wait. Then I ring it again, and I wait some more.

I rap softly on the green door, and notice the paint is peeling, in ripples.

I do not hear footsteps or even see shadows moving against the curtains. Then I notice the drive is empty of cars.

No one is home.

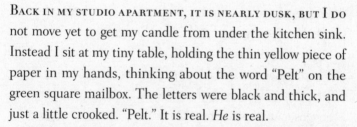

CHAPTER SEVENTEEN

BACK IN MY STUDIO APARTMENT, IT IS NEARLY DUSK, BUT I DO not move yet to get my candle from under the kitchen sink. Instead I sit at my tiny table, holding the thin yellow piece of paper in my hands, thinking about the word "Pelt" on the green square mailbox. The letters were black and thick, and just a little crooked. "Pelt." It is real. *He* is real.

Sitting there, I think about the last time I saw Peter, the morning the Green Police came for us. August 1944. Two years we had been in the annex by then. But the war would be over soon, we knew it. We crouched around the radio at night after dinner, and there was a burgeoning sense that things were beginning to go our way. Only two weeks earlier there'd been an attempt on Hitler's life, and by a German count. We were not the only ones fed up with the war. "The tide is turning," Father had said, smiling gently at Mother.

Peter and I whispered about it at night in his room after

everyone else was asleep. Each night, I waited in my parents' room until I heard the soft sound of Pim's snore and Mother's breath rattling in her chest, and then I would tiptoe, ever so carefully, up the stairs, to Peter's.

Once, all our talk about after the war had felt almost like talking about a story, something that could never happen to us. But by this point, it had begun to feel real, like the idea of the sun on our faces, the feel of August rain against my cheek. I would feel these things again. We both would.

Peter and I had spent many nights whispering furtively in the dark about the future and what it might hold. But that night, what would be our last night in the annex, Peter lay waiting for me on the divan. I sat down next to him, and he pulled me close and put his finger to my lips before I could speak. "Let's not talk tonight," he whispered.

I watched the turn of his face, his blue, blue eyes reflecting in the sheerness of the moonlight as he traced his finger from my lips, slowly, across my cheek. And then he leaned in even closer and kissed me.

I kissed him back, my lips moving against his as if they belonged there, as if we belonged like that, together. We held on tightly to each other as we kissed, and my hands trembled a little against the warmth of his back.

"Tell me again," I whispered. I could hear the sound of his breath moving against his chest, so close, it was almost as if it were my own. "Tell me what we'll do when we leave here."

"We'll move to America," he whispered, tracing the outline of my cheekbone with his thumb. "Philadelphia. City of Brotherly Love. We'll be married, and we will no longer be Jews."

"You won't forget about me," I whispered.

"Never," he whispered back.

And then, for the first time, there in Peter's room, in the darkness, I actually fell asleep, Peter's warm body tucked against the folds of mine, my hands still resting against his back.

The next morning, just before the Green Police came, I awoke to the heavy sound of Peter's door swinging open. My sister stood there, at the entrance to Peter's room, her big brown eyes holding on to us like the eyes of a wounded animal. I expected her to yell at me, to gasp at our indecency, to call for Father. But she did none of those things. Instead her eyes turned to him.

"Peter?" she said softly.

Then the door by the staircase was breaking open, and Mrs. van Pels was screaming, louder than I'd ever heard her. "No," she was screaming. "No. No."

Peter locked eyes with me. Blue, blue eyes like the sea. They were there, so close to mine I could touch them.

And then they were gone.

My phone rings, and the sound of it startles me. It barely ever rings, unless it is Ilsa calling to check up on me from time to time, but she would not call me on a Friday night. Ilsa does not know my true identity, but she knows more than anyone else in Philadelphia; that once I was a Jew, that on Friday nights I still light my Shabbat candle.

"Hello," I say, expecting a breath, followed by a click. *Peter?*

"Margie. It's Joshua Rosenstein." My mouth is open, but I have nothing to say. "I hate to bother you, at home like this on a Friday night. I called the office first but you'd already left."

"I'm sorry," I say. "I finished my work before leaving."

"Oh, no. Don't worry about that. It's just . . . I had an idea. About Miss Korzynski's case, but I need your help."

"My help?" I know I sound like an idiot, but I am still dazed by the fact that Joshua is calling me, at home, asking me to help him.

"Are you free now? Can we meet for a drink and we'll discuss it?"

"A drink?" I say, compounding my idiocy. I am wondering what has happened to Penny, or why Joshua can't tell me his plan on the phone, but of course I don't have the courage to ask him any of that. I stare at my unlit candle, at the skies darkening outside of my window. Joshua is a liberal Jew, and I'm sure he does not observe the Shabbat. Margie Franklin is not a Jew either, I remind myself. And Margot, who is a Jew? She is dead. I stare once more at the piece of paper in my hand. *Peter Pelt.* "Of course," I finally say. "Of course I can meet you."

❊

O'Malley's, the bar where Joshua has asked me to meet him, is back on Sixteenth Street, near the office, and I walk out of my apartment building and head in that direction. It is dark outside now, and the streets are quieter than during the day, or the five o'clock hour when everyone is bustling home.

It occurs to me that it might not be safe for a woman, even

a Gentile one, to walk on Ludlow Street after dark, all alone. I do not usually go out after dark. Never on a Friday.

I hear the sound of footsteps behind me. They are heavy, the gait of boots. Surely, NSB footsteps. The Green Police.

I cannot help it. I quicken my pace, until I am almost running.

CHAPTER EIGHTEEN

JOSHUA IS ALREADY AT O'MALLEY'S WHEN I ARRIVE, AND I spot him sitting on a bar stool by the long rectangular bar in the back. The place is small and dim inside, with high-topped tables filled with businessmen in suits and their dates dressed in shiny full dresses, all of which block my path to Joshua. I look around and I realize that this is not the kind of bar I've been to before with Shelby and Ron, where the men and women dance too close and holler on a checkered floor after everyone has had one too many drinks. Of course, I only watched in those bars. But here, in O'Malley's, I feel even more out of place, in my plain gray cotton work dress, covered with a simple navy sweater.

I make my way through the haze of smoke, well-dressed bodies, and the bright sound of laughter. The stool next to Joshua is one of the only empty seats in the bar, and I realize, staring at it for a moment, that it is meant for me, that maybe he has saved it for me.

"Hello," I say, sitting down next to him.

"Margie." He smiles, and I smile back, suddenly so happy that he called, that I am sitting here next to him. Then I think uneasily about the green mailbox on Olney Avenue, and I feel a tiny surge of guilt. "Can I buy you a drink?" Joshua asks. His drink is in a half-size glass: something brown that he takes a sip of, grimaces, and then takes another, bigger sip.

"No thank you," I say. "I don't really drink much." Or at all.

"How about a club soda, then, with a twist of lime?"

"Okay," I say, and he beckons to the young man in the white-collared shirt and red bow tie who is standing behind the counter. Joshua orders my drink, and then he turns back to look at me. He is still dressed in his work suit, but his black tie is loose around his collar and the top button of his shirt is undone.

"So it's official," he says. He takes another swig of his drink and smiles again. "I must be the world's worst boss, dragging you out here on a Friday night."

"No, you're not," I say.

"After I called you, it occurred to me that you might have had another . . . obligation."

I shake my head. "I don't mind, really."

"Really?"

I nod. I do not let myself think about the Shabbat, the unlit candle in my apartment. I do not let myself think about Bryda Korzynski, or even the crooked black letters on the Pelt mailbox again. Instead I think that Joshua is close enough to me that if I swing my stool, just a little, our knees might touch, and that his arm rests easily across the bar counter, just inches from my own. "You're working on a Friday night too," I say timidly. "I thought you had a date."

"Oh, that," he says. "Penny and I just went to see a movie. *Diary of Anne Frank*. Have you seen it?" I shake my head and hold my breath. "Penny thought we should go together." He doesn't elaborate on why, and I'm not sure whether it's because Penny is his girlfriend again or because they are both Jews. I don't ask.

"Did you like it?" I ask instead, though I regret the question as soon as I say the words. The bartender sets my drink down on a small square napkin in front of me, and I pick it up and take a sip. The club soda burns my throat, and I wonder if it is not club soda at all, but a clear alcohol the bartender poured by mistake. It makes my head warm, but it's a feeling that I like, so I drink a little more.

"It's not really a movie you can like, is it?" Joshua is saying. "It's more like school. Where you know you have to go and learn. Or going to the doctor. You know it's good for you. That you *should* do it. But you don't exactly enjoy it."

"I guess so," I murmur. But then, I always quite enjoyed school. I was a star pupil at the Jewish Lyceum. It is hard for me to consider what I might have done, had we continued our lives in Amsterdam, had I been able to go on to college.

"It does make you stop and think," he's saying now. "How your life might have been different had you been born somewhere else in the world." He pauses and finishes off his drink.

"My father would've been the type to take us in hiding. Although," he adds, "it would've been someplace we wouldn't have been found, I'm sure. He'd be very good at hiding, at pretending not to be a Jew."

I nod, though I begin to feel annoyed with Joshua for the first time. I know he cannot help it that he is an American Jew, that he cannot really understand the way it was. I am sure already, from Shelby's description, that the movie has put a glamorous sheen of Hollywood on all our experience. Maybe it made Father look weak, the annex cozy, though none of that is true, of course. But then again, how is Joshua to know?

"Anyway," Joshua says, "it just made me think more about Miss Korzynski, and how I really do want to help her. So I had an idea." I take another, bigger swallow of my drink, and though I am now fully convinced it is not club soda, I don't care. *Who's a paragon of virtue now?* I think, inching myself just a little bit closer to Joshua so I am almost close enough for him to whisper, even in the crowded bar. "This is what we can do," Joshua is saying. His breath is warm, and it brushes against my cheek as he speaks. "I want to put an ad in the *Inquirer*. We'll ask people to call us to join the suit. This way, we can collect a group of them, without Miss Korzynski having to do all the work, and this way we can reach all of the factories. Make sense?" I nod slowly, even though Joshua's words, and his face, are swimming before me. "But I can't put the law office's name or number or even my own in the ad. My father will know. Once we have the suit together, I'll tell him. I'll show him how important this is, but until then we need to work furtively."

I finish off my drink, and my stomach turns. Joshua's gray-green eyes go in blurry swirls, around and around.

"So, Margie, what I want to do is this. We'll put an ad in the *Inquirer* that says something to the effect of: 'Jews who work for Robertson's unite against anti-Semitism.' And then we'll put your number underneath it. The people will call you, at home; you'll take down their names, numbers, information, and then bring them to me." Joshua pauses and stares at me. "I know it's a lot to ask," he says. "So I'll pay you extra. Five dollars more a week."

I cannot imagine it, listening to their surely sad stories of being a Jew and being punished for it. Or even, other Brydas yelling at me through the phone, calling me a liar. Joshua's face swims in front of me, his eyes swirl faster, until I am not sure anymore whether they are green or blue, whether it is him or Peter sitting there, asking something impossible of me. *Peter van Pels. Peter Pelt.* 2217 *Olney Avenue . . .*

"Okay," he says. "Seven dollars more a week."

I think about the way I felt, there in the annex, lying on the divan, kissing Peter, the way I wanted to be close to him. I hear my mother's voice, my sister's, the voice of the girl I was before the annex. *What are you doing, Margot, paragon of virtue?*

"I don't know, Peter," I say now, only maybe I don't say Peter's name. Maybe I just think it.

"Margie." I hear Joshua's voice, although it sounds like it is coming from somewhere very far away, not right next to me. "Your face is so red. Are you feeling okay . . . ? Are you too warm?"

I shake my head, even though I feel myself falling just a

little bit off the side of the bar stool, and then I feel Joshua's hands, steadying me, tugging at the sleeves of my sweater.

❁

Peter's eyes were blue, like the sea. So blue that they made me remember swimming and sky. They held me; they swallowed me; they kept me alive.

"Margot," Peter whispered in my ear. "It's like you and I are the only two people here,"

I knew what he meant. There was nothing else but me and him, in the middle of the quiet night, in the darkness. We were no longer trapped rats there, hiding, terrified for our lives.

We were alone, but we were together. Some nights, I wished we would be able to stay there, in the annex, forever.

"Who's Peter?" Joshua asks me now. We are standing on the sidewalk, in front of O'Malley's, and after the noise of the bar, the quiet is almost alarming. Joshua is still holding on to my arm, steadying me with his large hands. "Would you like me to call him for you?" he's asking now.

"Peter?" I say, and I realize I must have actually said his name, inside the bar, when I was thinking it. I shake my head. Then I say, "I don't think that was a club soda."

He nods. I notice the sleeves of my black sweater are pushed up slightly, and I tug at them quickly, to pull them back down. "I thought you were going to pass out," Joshua says. "Come on." He tugs gently on my arm. "Let me walk you home."

"You don't have to," I say meekly.

"Yes," he says, and his voice is curling with what sounds like guilt. "I do."

❈

Joshua is still holding on to my arm as we walk down South Sixteenth, and then Ludlow. For a moment I pretend that it is because he wants to touch me, not because he thinks he needs to hold me up. The air is cooler now, and it calms my cheeks. I inhale deeply, taking in the scent of a Friday night outdoors. On Ludlow Street, that scent is roses, city bus exhaust, a hint of garbage, and something else, a little sweeter, that I think is Joshua's cologne because it is slightly familiar, something I have smelled before.

"Margie," Joshua says. "I hope I didn't upset you, with my idea."

I don't say anything because, for once, I am not sure how to lie without also telling the truth.

"I just want you to understand, how important this is to me. Being a Jew." I think about the fact that Ezra, he is also a Jew and does not feel compelled to help. I wonder if it is not just a money thing, but also a matter of his reputation. Though the partners at the firm are all Jews, many of the clients are wealthy businessmen who are not. "I cannot imagine what it must have been like," Joshua is saying now. "To have been treated like that, tortured, and then even now . . ." He pauses. "Did you notice Miss Korzynski is missing a finger?"

I nod, but I remember what she said: *It's not what you think*. Maybe it wasn't the war. Maybe it was an accident in the factory or something that happened to her as a child, in Poland.

"I can't give her back her finger, or her family. But she should be treated the right way, in America, after all." He pauses. "You know what scares me the most?"

"What?" I whisper.

"That people will forget, and it will happen again. Another Hitler, more camps. If Jews aren't seen as equal, then when will it ever stop?" Something clenches hard in my chest, so hard that for a moment I cannot breathe. What if Joshua's right? What if it could happen to me again? *But Margie Franklin is not a Jew,* I remind myself. *And it could not happen in America. Maybe a few terrible incidents, but not another Hitler. More camps.*

We stop at the entrance to my building, and I turn and look at Joshua. In the soft shadow of the moonlight, he tilts his head, and he looks younger than he does at work, sitting there at his desk, his brow stretched with concentration. Now I can see Joshua as a younger man, a teenager, like the Peter I remember. He is vulnerable, in the moonlight, pondering about the fate of humanity. I want to reach up and touch his cheek, but I clasp my hands together, not only because Joshua might think it strange if I touched him, but also because the feeling of Peter and me there, that last night on the divan, it is so fresh in my mind now. It feels wrong that I should like Joshua so much. A betrayal.

Joshua lets go of my arm, and he looks at me. I blink, until Peter's face disappears. In the moonlight Joshua's gray-green eyes take on a yellowish cast. *You know what scares me most . . . When will it ever stop?*

"Okay," I say to him now.

"Okay?"

"I will help you."

He smiles at me and puts his hand on my shoulder, a gesture of kindness, or maybe it is just to make sure I am steady on my feet. We are standing close now, close enough that I could feel his breath almost against my cheek as he spoke. His eyes trace my face, as if he is seeing something the way he did that day in January when Alaska became a state and he invited me for a drink.

He begins to say something else, then stops and hesitates for a moment, and he takes a step back.

"What is it?" I ask.

"I was just thinking I could walk you up, say hi to Mr. Katz." My heart pounds so hard and loud in my chest that I am certain that Joshua can hear it, or possibly even see it pulsing through my sweater. Joshua wants to walk up, come inside my apartment? I try to remember if I put the yellow paper back in my satchel, my sister's book back on the shelf, my pile of freshly laundered sweaters back in the drawer . . . "But it's getting late," Joshua says. He shrugs. "I probably shouldn't."

"Another time," I say, and the boldness of my words surprises me.

"Another time," he repeats. He smiles at me, and takes another step back, so he is walking away now, slowly, but away nonetheless. I turn to walk into my building. "Margie," he calls out, and his voice echoes against the empty night sidewalk. I turn back around to look at him. "I'm lucky to have you, you know that?"

He smiles at me and waves, and then he turns and takes off walking quickly back toward Sixteenth Street as I walk inside, still light-headed.

CHAPTER NINETEEN

WHEN I FIRST CAME TO WORK FOR JOSHUA IN JANUARY OF 1956, I did not realize he was the kind of lawyer who defends criminals, or that later on he would become the kind of lawyer who would convince me to help him with a case like Bryda's.

I'm thinking about this Monday morning as Joshua's new client, Charles Bakerfield, a rich man accused of killing his wife, is sitting in the chair by my desk, waiting for Joshua to arrive for their ten o'clock appointment. Charles is tall, with green eyes that chill me a little when he stares at me too hard as I am typing.

Joshua is running late this morning. At five minutes to ten, he has not even stepped foot in the office yet, and I am filled with a nervous sort of anticipation, not only because of Charles Bakerfield's intense stare, but also at the thought of seeing Joshua again, this morning. *I'm lucky to have you, you know that?*

I'm lucky to be here, I think.

I saw Joshua's advertisement in the *Inquirer* for a legal secretary the week before Christmas, 1955, over a lunch with Ilsa of ginger tea and ham sandwiches, in which I'd cautiously removed the ham and eaten only the bread and cheese. Just before lunch, I had helped Ilsa string garlands and tinsel around the thick evergreen tree that rested in front of their fireplace, where Ilsa had hung an extra stocking, just for me. Ilsa had asked me to climb the ladder and place the yellow star on top of the tree. Not the Star of David. The Star of Death. But a star that seemed all wrong, so unfamiliar that to me, it barely looked like a star at all.

"After lunch, we'll unpack the baby Jesus," Ilsa said to me as she chewed delicately on her ham. My days with Ilsa were spent alongside her as she shopped and decorated. She taught me to sew curtains and make dolls. She consulted me on matters of color and materials, dinner recipes and grocery lists. I knew she was trying so hard to be kind, to include me in her life, so I would never tell her that decorating made my brain feel dull, that her ham and her baby Jesus and her star, they all made me feel more than a little uneasy, even if I had already told her that I no longer planned on being Jewish in America.

Then I saw it, there in the paper, Joshua's notice: *Rosenstein, Greenberg and Moscowitz.* Their Jewishness, it was right there, so obvious.

I couldn't help it. I had to apply. There is this wayward sort of homesickness that eats Margie Franklin, the Gentile, at her core. In the law office often, even now, it is the place where I feel most at home.

❊

Joshua arrives promptly at ten and ushers Charles Bakerfield right back into his office. He runs in quickly, without even so much a glance at me, and I am overcome with a sense of disappointment. I'm not sure what I was expecting, really, but it wasn't that.

I watch them now through the glass window, Joshua and Charles. Charles seems much taller than Joshua even just sitting across the desk from him. It's possible Charles is innocent, though more likely, I think, he is not. The majority of the law firm's clients are not who I would count among the good people of the world, but the ones who are accused murderers, they make me the most uneasy. Shelby says that someone has to defend them, that it is only fair and right under American law that a person is innocent until proven guilty, but still, I wish it didn't have to be Joshua.

This is a case Ezra has insisted Joshua take on. Shelby and I had listened last week as Ezra had yelled at Joshua about it through the paper walls, talking about redemption and bringing in some money for the firm. Joshua either hadn't responded to Ezra's rant, or had kept his voice low enough so Shelby and I hadn't heard his reply.

So I suppose I can understand it, then, why Joshua wants

to help Bryda so badly. Why he is asking so much of me, more than he knows. *Money is not greatness,* he told me. *Bravery is greatness.* Still, sitting there at my desk, watching the two of them through the glass, watching Joshua pull at the nonexistent beard on his chin, I realize that helping Joshua with Bryda's case, it will not be the same at all as helping him type notes and compile documents for a trial, not even a murder trial.

This will be no different, I tell myself. *No different from all the other lies I've told.* Yet somehow it feels different.

⁂

Joshua's meeting lasts nearly two hours, and when Charles Bakerfield exits, with an almost eerily contemptuous nod in my direction, Joshua walks out of his office right behind, looking browbeaten.

"Lunch?" he says to me, quietly, tapping the corner of my metal desk with his forefinger. He grabs his hat from the rack, and tosses it atop his curls.

Shelby stops typing, and her jaw nearly plummets to the floor. I can almost see the wheels of her brain turning, wondering about his weekend with Penny, and about the fact that Joshua and I went to lunch together on Friday. And she does not even know about the drink on Friday night. I think again about him standing there, on Ludlow Street, the way his voice floated and his eyes traced my face, and I have the strangest feeling that we share something now, something more than work, a thought which makes me smile.

Joshua turns and looks at Shelby, and she nods at him and continues her typing. I stand up, grab my satchel, and follow him to the elevator.

❊

"You have to eat more than an apple and a cup of soup," Joshua says as we stand in line at Isaac's counter. "Really, don't be shy about it, Margie."

"I'm not a big lunch person," I say. Or dinner. Or breakfast.

"All right." Joshua shrugs. "As long as it's not on my account." I shake my head. "But really, Margie, you're thin as a bird. I worry about you, and I say that as a friend not as your boss."

"I'm fine," I say, because lies, they are so easy now. And really, what I'm thinking about is that Joshua has called me a friend, that my thought back in the office was right: somehow we are connected now, more than we were. Bryda Korzynski, her case, it has made Joshua begin to see me. *I'm lucky to have you . . .* This is a thought that both thrills and terrifies me.

"So I wanted to tell you what I've done," Joshua says, after we are seated at the same table by the window. I gnaw carefully on my apple. I nod, and he continues. "I stopped at the *Inquirer* offices this morning before work. That's why I was so late. Anyway, the ad will begin running tomorrow. It has your phone number, with a note to call between the hours of five and six only. This way, it will only be an extra hour you will be bothered with work, and you can leave a little early to make it home by five, all right?"

"All right," I say, though secretly, I am already hoping that no one calls. I think Joshua is overestimating. He does not really understand it, as much as he may want to, the continued need to hide and to stay hidden. Bryda Korzynski cannot be the only one who feels she deserves more than she is getting at the factory, but how many others will truly come forward to complain openly as she has done?

"Let's have lunch again at the end of the week, and you bring the list of callers with you. Then we'll see where we are."

"Okay," I say. His eyes seem greener in the daylight, and because we are sitting by the large picture window, sunlight streams past me and onto his face. I smile at him.

But he shakes his head, as if his mind is off somewhere else, perhaps contemplating the fate of humanity once more.

"You know that man who was in my office all morning?" he finally says. I nod. "He's guilty as sin," Joshua whispers. "And I'm going to keep him out of jail."

"That's your job," I tell him, though it seems little consolation.

"Yeah," he says, and his voice is thick with something I don't recognize from him. Joshua, whose voice is usually so easy, so filled with that American happiness. Now there is a layer of something like gloom, or sadness. "That's my job," he repeats, and then I realize what it is. Joshua is bitter. Joshua dislikes his job.

How is it that I have worked for him for three years, this whole time, watching him through the glass by his office door as his brow furrowed in concentration, his gray-green eyes dancing with laughter, and I have not understood before now, how unhappy Joshua is with his work?

Maybe Joshua is as good at lying as I am.

CHAPTER TWENTY

MY FIRST TELEPHONE CALL COMES ON WEDNESDAY NIGHT, after the ad has run for two full days. But it is not a call from anyone who might join in Bryda's lawsuit. It is a call from Ilsa.

"Margie," she says right away when I pick up, and I sigh with relief at the sound of her voice. Two days I've left work early, avoiding Shelby's questioning looks, and I've run home to stare at the telephone, where I've willed it not to ring the entire hour.

"Oh, Ilsa," I say. "I'm glad it's you."

"My dear," she says, and I can picture her on the other end of the line, shaking her petite blond head. "Why on earth is your telephone number in the *Inquirer*?"

"Oh." I draw in my breath. I have not considered the possibility that Ilsa, the one person who knows my number other than Joshua, might see the ad and find it perplexing. "Well . . ." I say, though I am not sure what I should say next. Lying is a second skin, but it is failing me now. The first skin feels warm, ripened, ready to break to the surface.

"Spit it out, my dear," Ilsa says. Ilsa is not my sister, nor my mother. She is the American cousin of my mother's German friend Eduard. After I told Eduard I needed to come to America, he persuaded Ilsa to sponsor me and take me in. Our relationship is a strange one because it is not quite a friendship. She holds a power over me, and not because she means to, or necessarily even wants to. But still, she does. When Ilsa asks me for the truth, sometimes I am compelled to give it.

"I am helping my boss with something," I say. "With a case."

"Involving anti-Semitism?" she says, sounding skeptical. I imagine her pulling at her earlobe a little, the way she does when something her husband, Bertram, tells her makes her nervous.

"Sort of," I say, "But it is very top secret. He's asked me not to discuss it."

She hesitates, and I hear the short sound of her breath on the other end of the line. "I don't like the sound of that," she finally says. She doesn't say anything for a moment. "You know you can always give the job up, move back in with us."

"I like my job," I say. And also, now, I cannot imagine not seeing Joshua every day. *I tell you as a friend, Margie,* he'd said to me. *A friend.*

"Well, at the very least, you'll come for dinner tomorrow," she says. "We haven't seen you in a while. We worry about you. Are you eating?"

"Of course I'm eating," I lie.

"Well, good," she says. "Tomorrow night. Bertram will drive over to pick you up so you don't have to take the bus."

I agree, we hang up, and my phone doesn't ring again that night.

※

The next night, Ilsa's husband, Bertram, pulls up outside the sidewalk by my apartment building in his blue Ford Fairlane. He honks once, and I walk outside to find him waiting for me in the car. He is a tall, quiet man, who hides his face behind a thick copper beard and mustache.

"Margie," he says, after I slip into the passenger seat. "It's been a while."

"Yes." I nod. "It has."

"Are you well?" he asks.

I nod. "And you?"

"Fine," he says.

We don't talk anymore as he drives us slowly toward the home he shares with Ilsa in Levittown, Pennsylvania, United States of America. But it is not because Bertram and I don't get along; it is because Bertram is a quiet man, and also because I think he is used to being with Ilsa, who talks so very much that it's possible he now has nothing left to say.

※

Ilsa and Bertram live on Oak Lane, in a quiet suburban neighborhood where all the houses—and the streets beginning with the letter O—look nearly identical. In fact you probably could not tell Ilsa's house from all the others on the block from the outside alone, but on the inside, the house is uniquely decorated with Ilsa's hand-sewn curtains and dolls.

Ilsa is robust in every way that Bertram is not, and after the quiet ride, she greets me at the door to their familiar tract house with a hug, then pulls back and looks at me. "My dear," she says, shaking her head, so her blond curls tumble against her shoulders. "You are too thin. Come in. Eat."

Even now, when I look at Ilsa, I see the face of the woman who came to pick me up in New York City, New York, just after my boat arrived. Eduard had shown me a picture of her, her wedding photo with Bertram. She was a tiny woman, nearly childlike in size next to Bertram, who is tall and a little burly. In the black-and-white photo all I could tell was that her hair was lighter than Bertram's, and that her smile was enormous. In person, her hair is nearly the color of snow, and her smile, it is even bigger.

That first time I saw her she was waiting for me at the New York Harbor, her tiny arms pushing through the crowd to get to me. Eduard had made sure I'd had a first-class ticket from Bremerhaven, so my experience in getting off the boat in America would be an easy one, so I would not be subject to poking and prodding and questioning at Ellis Island. After a cursory glance at me, my shoulder-length curls, the nice brown dress Eduard had purchased for me for just this occasion, the doctor had signed my paper, and I'd disembarked.

It was warm, nearly summer, and there was a crowd. Mostly men, mostly in suits. The men in tattered clothes, I imagined, they waited at the exit from Ellis Island where the third-class passengers entered into America, if they were lucky.

"Margot?" Ilsa said my name. I did not see her at first, amid all the men, but once I heard her voice, I turned, and there were her arms, pushing through the swarm of men. Her arms reached me, and she stared at me for a moment, as if she wasn't sure it was really me, or perhaps she was wondering if she'd made a giant mistake in agreeing to sponsor me, to take me into her home.

"Why would she even take me?" I had said to Eduard when he told me of her. "I am a perfect stranger." Or more rightly so, an imperfect one.

"I know my cousin," Eduard had said. "She will take you. In fact, she will love you."

That first time I saw her, she put her arms on mine, and she said, for the first of many times, "My dear, you are so thin. You are flesh and bones. I will have to fix that, Margot." She clung to me, and her high voice rose above the din of the crowd.

"Margie," I told her, when I found my voice. "Everybody calls me Margie." Nobody had ever called me Margie, except for Peter. But I was in America. I was going to be Margie.

"Okay then, Margie," Ilsa said. "Come. Come with me, my dear. Let's try to catch the train so we are home in time for dinner. I will fatten you up in no time."

In six years, not so very much has changed.

❖

"So," Ilsa says as she cuts her meat loaf into delicate pieces and watches with the eyes of a hawk to see how much I am eating. "Tell me about this boss of yours who is making you take after-hours phone calls at your home."

I shrug and chew carefully. "He's not making me do anything," I say. "And he's paying me seven dollars extra a week."

"A raise," Bertram says, lifting his thick copper eyebrows.
"Good for you, Margie." That's the nice thing about Bertram—
when the time is right, he figures out the most decent thing
to say. I smile at him.

"Hmm," Ilsa says as she tugs on her earlobe a little.

"It's really not a big deal," I tell her. I feel so comfortable
telling her this lie that it barely feels like a lie at all. "And
besides, no one has even called yet aside from you."

She shakes her head. "Still," she says. "I don't like it. A
woman living all alone in the city with her phone number
published in the paper."

"Illie," Bertram says, his voice hanging lightly on his pet
name for his wife. "Margie is a big girl."

Ilsa smiles at me. "You know I only worry out of love, my
dear."

"I know," I say, and I do. Ilsa and Bertram were unable to
have any children, and in a way, I suppose, I have helped her
as much as she has helped me. She told me once that before
I arrived, there were mornings when it was hard for her to get
out of bed, and that once, in the bathtub, she put her head
under the water and thought about not coming up. "What is
one's life if she doesn't have a purpose?" Ilsa had asked me
then.

I'd nodded as if I'd understood, though really, what I
understood was that American sorrows are so, so much different from my own.

"Just don't take any calls from men," she tells me now. I

nod, but she is still frowning. "And certainly, don't give anyone your address."

"Of course not," I say. "Now really, stop worrying."

She relents, for now, and we eat the rest of our dinner,
making small talk. Bertram talks about his own job in the
city, where he runs an accounting firm and Ilsa talks about
the curtains she has decided to make for the bedroom: blue
lace. Before I came—and after I left—this has been Ilsa's
purpose in life: decorating. I nod politely through the dinner,
and in a way I miss this: family, dinnertime, easy conversa-
tions. In another way, I am very ready to leave by dessert.
Quiet is my solace. And I am relieved when Ilsa begins to
clear the dishes and Bertram grabs his hat.

"Oh," Ilsa says, wiping her hands on her blue-checkered
apron as I am walking toward the front door. "I almost forgot.
I was going to tell you that Bertie and I are planning a trip to
Germany for some time next year." I nod, though I do not like
at all where this is going. "I would like to visit Eduard and
show Bertie the city of my birth," she says.

"But Eduard is dead," I say. He died of cancer, just before I
began working at the law firm three years ago. Ilsa did not go
to the funeral then because it was too far, too hard to get there.
And I, well, I could never go back. Not even for Eduard.

She nods. "But I would like to visit his grave. And it is getting cheaper and easier to travel overseas now. We could all
take an airplane. It would be a grand adventure." She smiles
at me, revealing her tiny white teeth.

"I don't think so," I say.

She leans in and kisses my cheek. "Think about it," she

whispers in my ear. "Sometimes you can go home again, you know. The war has been over for many years, my dear." She holds on to me tightly, gives my shoulder one last squeeze, and then, at last, she lets me go.

As Bertram drives me back to my apartment in silence, I find myself staring at the darkness out the car window, imagining home again, and not even Frankfurt, but the Prinsengracht. There is a reason why I could not go home again. Why I did not. Why I do not, even now. It is the same reason why I cannot commit any words to paper to send to my father. Ilsa would never understand it, even if I tried to tell her. But then, she knows nothing of my sister. And perhaps, even if she did, she would not understand, with her purely American sensibilities. But there is another reason why I haven't told her the entire truth. If I am being honest with myself, I know it is because I fear if she knows it, all of it, she will hate me.

"Margie," Bertram says with a nod when he pulls up by the sidewalk on Ludlow Street.

"Thank you for the ride," I tell him. "And please thank Ilsa again for the dinner." He nods, opens his mouth as if to speak, then closes it again.

"What is it?" I ask him.

He stares at me, hesitates for a moment, and then says, "You know, if you should ever need anything, Ilsa and I, we always want to help you . . ." His voice trails off, as if, suddenly, he is out of words again.

"Yes," I say. "Of course. Thank you, Bertram."

He nods and pats my shoulder in what is meant to be a sweet gesture, but comes off awkward instead. I smile at him and get out of the car, but for a moment, as I walk back into my apartment building, I wonder if Ilsa and Bertram are right. If, by myself, in this city, working on Joshua's case, hiding, hiding, hiding, if by doing all this, I am somehow teetering on the brink of something terrible.

CHAPTER TWENTY-ONE

IT TAKES ME A LONG TIME TO FALL ASLEEP AFTER I RETURN home from Ilsa and Bertram's. I lie there for hours in the darkness, thinking about Frankfurt, wondering if by now it has been put back together, the way it once was, before the war, and what Ilsa might see where I last saw broken glass and red swastikas. Then my thoughts turn to my father in Switzerland, and I wonder if he has as much trouble sleeping at night as I do. Do so many terrible memories still haunt him, or does he instead fall into an easy sleep brought on by thoughts of everybody reading the book? Perhaps his dreams are pleasant, bursting with the knowledge that because of him, the entire world knows my sister, loves her. Or thinks they do. *But what of me?* I wonder now. Does he ever still think of me, of the diary I kept? The life I once lived?

When I finally do fall asleep, my night is filled with black and tumultuous dreams. In them, I replay a memory, the way

I so often do. This time, I am lying on the parched earth. I am a sack of flesh and brittle bones in German-occupied Poland, not too far from the train tracks. I am too tired to run any longer; I expect to die, and I welcome it. And then, there is a hand on my shoulder.

I squint and in my eyes there are only shadows, a nun's coif, the sounds of German. But not Nazi German; her German has a softness that reminds me of when I was a little girl.

"Steh auf, komm schnell." Get up, come quickly. She's whispering, in my ear. Or maybe she is shouting. My ears hurt and ring, and it is so hard to hear. *"Komm mit mir bevor sie dich finden." Come with me before they find you.*

I am so thirsty; I can't move my mouth to speak or barely even breathe.

She holds on to my arm, dragging me along, as if I am a sack of potatoes. My bare feet scrape against the ground, but I do not feel them being scratched. I feel nothing.

Her black Beetle is parked off to the side of the road, and she opens the door and pushes the front seat forward, revealing the tiniest of spaces in the back. Her hands find my back and push me inside the car. *"Runter, niedrige." Get down, low.* I crouch into a ball on the floor of the backseat.

Only then can I get my lips to move. *"Meine schwester?"* I whisper. *My sister?*

"Ja," the nun says.

"Meine schwester?" I whisper again.

"Ich bin Schwester Brigitta," the nun says. *I am Sister Brigitta.* She reaches down to touch my forearm, a bone with

indelible ink, and then she whispers in my ear. *"Ich werde dir nichts tun, Kind."*

I will not hurt you, child.

❊

I wake up to the sound of a clock ringing, and I am sweating, German words echoing in my head: *Meine schwester? Meine schwester?*

That morning was the closest I ever came to telling Brigitta about my sister and what happened to the two of us just before she found me that day. Brigitta hid me in the nunnery until the end of the war, and then let me stay for a while after I searched the Red Cross lists for my family . . . for Peter. But even at the very end, when she dropped me at Eduard's in Frankfurt, I did not tell her the truth.

I hear the sound again, and I wonder if I am still dreaming. It sounds like the alarm clock in Eduard's guest room, and suddenly I see his face. After the war, when Brigitta dropped me on his doorstep, his face was warm and ebullient. Only now, in my half sleep, I see it shriveled from the effects of his cancer, and instead, he is Eduard the skeleton.

I open my eyes, and I realize it is not a clock ringing at all, but the telephone in my apartment. *The telephone.* And it is still ringing. Over and over again. The clock on my nightstand reads 5:01 A.M.

I get out of bed, put on my slippers, and fumble in the darkness to the other side of the room where the phone sits, on the counter by the icebox. "Hello." I pick up, expecting

Ilsa's voice, saying, maybe, she is still worrying about me, or plotting to take me home with her, even in her dreams.

"Hello," a voice says. It is a man's voice. And for a moment I think, *Peter! I have found him, and he has found me. He knows about the movie too.* Then the voice says, "I call number, from advertisement." He speaks in broken English, in a voice I do not recognize, and I realize he is not Peter at all but a stranger who has gotten my number from Joshua's ad.

"Now?" I say, and I sigh.

"Advertisement say between five and six only."

This man is clearly confused, as am I, in my half-sleep state. Though it is, in fact, between five and six. Joshua must not have specified P.M. Americans would assume this to be the case, but for a new immigrant, a factory worker, a man who is used to early mornings, perhaps the implication is lost. "Yes," I finally say. "I guess it does."

"Advertisement say, Jews who work for Robertson's unite against anti-Semitism," the man says.

"Yes." I nod, and Ilsa's words echo in my head. *Do not talk to any men.* I push the warning aside. There is no harm in merely talking to anyone, and Joshua has asked me for this much.

"You are Jew?" the man asks me.

I draw my breath in, because no one has ever asked me this, so directly, in my American life. "No," I finally lie, and I explain to him about Joshua and Bryda Korzynski and the lawsuit.

"Group litigation?" The words sound funny in his voice, as if he's talking about a child's game.

"Yes," I tell him, trying to make my voice sound reassuring. But it is hard, when you are half asleep, and when you are sweating because you sense that even through the phone, this man, like Bryda Korzynski, is enough like you to recognize your secret.

"I don't know," he finally says. "I thought I just meet other people. Like me. America is lonely place, no?"

"Yes," I say, and suddenly I feel I am biting back tears. "It is."

❦

A few hours later, though my hands are moving on the type-writer, I can feel the particular slant of Shelby's eyes on my face. Finally, I stop typing and look up.

"Okay," she says. "Spill, Margie."

"What have I spilled?" I ask her, shaking my head, not understanding. My brain still falls underneath a heavy fog of sleeplessness, the weight of my half dream/half memory of Brigitta. Then there is the sound of Ilsa's voice last night, still echoing in my head, telling me that I can go home again. And the lonely voice from the phone this morning. "Gustav Grossman," he told me, when I pressed him to give me his information for Joshua.

"What is going on, with you and . . . ?" Shelby nods her head meaningfully in the direction of Joshua's office.

"Nothing," I say, putting on my best secret keeper's face, which is to say, keeping my expression entirely blank. A skill I learned specifically in the camp: a skill of survival. But then I remember it is Friday today, and Joshua had said we would meet again at the end of the week, a thought that fills me with happiness. "Nothing is going on," I repeat, keeping my voice calm, for Shelby's sake.

"He's been staring at you," she whispers. "Through the window, all morning."

I feel my cheeks turning warm at the thought of Joshua watching me, the way I have so often watched him. What does he see now when he looks at me? Does he see the tired, too-thin woman with the thick brown curls, the tortoiseshell circle glasses, the sweater? Or does he see something different, something else, something no one has seen except for Peter? I put my hand to my face, as if to wipe away the embarrassment. "You must be mistaken," I say.

"Nope," she says. "Oh . . . don't look now, but here comes Papa and he doesn't look happy."

I pound my fingers noisily against the keys and see, out of the corner of my eye, Ezra, stomping past us. Can he know? About the advertisement? If he does, surely he will fire me. He is Joshua's boss, which makes him my boss too. My heart explodes against the walls of my chest, and I draw in my breath.

I hear their angry voices slip through the paper-thin walls. I hear some of the words. "Penny" . . . "Margate" . . . and "good son."

Shelby picks up the phone but doesn't talk, and casts her eyes in my direction, brows raised.

After a few minutes they both walk out, Joshua trailing behind Ezra, head down as if he is a wounded animal or a little boy who's just been scolded. He stops in front of my desk for a moment, tips his hat. "Monday," he says to me. The word sounds like a promise, and I nod, understanding, that on Monday we will convene again to discuss our secret case.

"Have a nice weekend," I say to him.

He smiles at me, and then he runs to catch up with his father on the elevator.

"Somebody's in trouble," Shelby says to me in a singsong voice, after the elevator doors shut. She shakes her head. "Now, that Penny, she's a girl I wouldn't mess with."

"What do you mean?" I ask.

"Clearly she's got her hooks in Joshua, and she is used to getting what she wants."

"I don't think so," I say.

"Maybe you, Margie, are a sweet little fling, but Penny, she's the girl a guy like Joshua marries."

"I am not Joshua's fling," I say, exasperation leaking into my voice.

"I'm just saying, Margie. Be careful. I don't want you to get hurt."

Why is everyone always telling me this, as if I am a delicate girl, made of glass? I wrap my sweater tighter around myself, holding on to my left forearm with my right hand, tightly, tight enough so my arm begins to hurt.

CHAPTER TWENTY-TWO

THE SECOND THE BIG CLOCK BY THE ELEVATOR CHIMES 3 P.M.,
Shelby switches off her radio, stands, and begins gathering
her things. "Let's get a drink," she says. "And today, I'm not
taking no for an answer, Margie."

"Maybe I wasn't going to say no," I tell her, and I stand and
gather my own things, relieved for once to get out of the office
early. I remember what Joshua said about feeling suffocated
here, and right now I can understand that feeling.

Ron is still working, so it is only Shelby and I who walk
across the street and take a seat at a table at Sullivan's Bar. This
is the place I've been to with Shelby before, where the dance
floor is checkered, and where the office girls, like us, sometimes
hike up their skirts a little too far to dance after they've drunk
a little too much. Not me, though sometimes I wonder what it
might feel like to let yourself go like that, to be so free.

Shelby and I sit at a low round table, just next to the checkered dance floor, though it is too early now for anyone to be on it, for the loud music to be playing, or even for the place to be crowded. Only one other table is taken, on the other side of the bar, with two girls looking not all that dissimilar to Shelby and me in their plain cotton dresses, so I guess they work for rich men who leave early on Fridays too. And there are a few young men sitting by the bar, dressed in suits, who are either conducting a business meeting or pretending to, I think.

Shelby orders a vodka tonic, and I order a club soda with a twist of lime. When our drinks arrive, I am surprised to find myself mildly disappointed when I take a sip and it does not burn my throat. Perhaps I should've ordered what Shelby is having. Maybe next time I will.

"Okay, Margie," Shelby says. "You know what I think?" I shake my head. "I think it is time for us to find you a man."

"A man?" I laugh a little, into my club soda.

"Yes," she says. "Preferably a good-looking one with a decent job." She scans the room with her eyes.

"Oh, stop," I say.

"You're not getting any younger," she tells me. "Before you know it, you'll be thirty, and being unmarried and thirty is like death in this city. You may as well just buy a few cats and call yourself a spinster."

Really, I am thirty-three, but Shelby, like everyone else who knows Margie Franklin, believes her to be twenty-seven. So I don't tell her now, of course, that I am already well past thirty. "I don't even want to get married," I say instead. "And I like cats."

She gasps, as if I've just said something blasphemous. "Of course you want to get married," she says. "Don't you want to fall in love?"

"I've been in love," I tell her.

"And not with Joshua." She shakes her head. "That doesn't count."

"I told you," I say, biting back my annoyance. Though it is not, truly, annoyance with her. At the moment I feel more annoyed with Penny, with just the idea of her in her frivolous, tomato-colored dress. "Nothing's going on with me and Joshua." I pause. "And I wasn't talking about Joshua."

"So what's his name?" she asks me.

"Peter," I say, and I surprise myself with my honesty. But in some instances, you are so hidden that even the truth is safe. I know Shelby will never connect the pieces between the movie she has seen and a Polish American girl named Margie Franklin. She would never even imagine that my Payter is the Peeter she saw on the silver screen, the Peter who was kissing that Millie Perkins Shelby is so fond of.

"Peter," she says, arching those eyebrows. "And where is this Peter now?"

"I knew him when I was a girl." Then I add, for good measure, "In Poland."

"Well, Margie," she says, waving her hand in the air and polishing off her drink. "That doesn't even count. We need to get you an American man."

"That does count," I insist. "And who knows," I say, "perhaps now he is an American man." I think of the tiny square, folded, folded, folded again in the bottom of my satchel, the mailbox reading *Pelt*.

"No," she says. "I mean a real American man. How about him?" She points to one of the men at the bar. He is tall with wire glasses and the face of a boy, and he wears a brown suit that swims on his lanky frame.

I shake my head. "I know you are trying to help," I tell her. "But really, Shelby. I'm not interested." Then, to change the subject, I quickly say, "Whatever happened with Ron and his hussy? Did you ask him about her?"

"Shhh." She leans into the table and looks around the room to see if anyone has heard me. "You can't just go shouting that word in public, Margie."

I am not sure why not, as she was the one who used it first, and in the office no less, but I offer an apologetic shrug, then take another sip of my drink.

"Now don't laugh at me," she whispers, and leans in close, as if she is about to reveal the grandest of secrets. I nod. "Last Friday he said he was working late. So Peggy and I, well, Peg did it actually, we tried to call the office to check if he was there. But no one answers, right? Because it's after hours. The girls have all gone home."

I nod and hang on to her words. "So then what did you do?" I whisper back.

"Peg and I, we took the bus to his house, and the whole house was dark, so we knew he wasn't home. Then we waited on the street, hiding behind the big oak tree when we saw his car."

"And . . . ?"

"And nothing." She shrugs. "He got out by himself, carrying his attaché, and he walked into the house. He really was working late, just like he said."

I think about the fact that Shelby does not really know where Ron was before he drove home, that he could have been off with his hussy then, but I am not going to point this out to her. "What about the huss—woman Peggy saw him with before?"

Shelby shrugs and takes a sip of her drink. "Maybe it was a mistake." She rolls her eyes. "Peg is forever forgetting to put her glasses on. Maybe she wasn't wearing them, and it wasn't even Ron."

"Maybe," I say. I do not really believe that Peggy would've made such a dramatic mistake. But then I remember the way my own face changes in the mirror, without my glasses on. The way I so easily see myself as a ghost.

"Now, enough about me," Shelby says. "I'm serious about finding you a man, Margie." Her eyes scan the room once more.

I finish my drink, and I stand up. "It is time for me to go home," I say.

"Oh, come on," she says. "Don't be like that. The night is just getting started."

I shake my head again. I want to leave plenty of time to make it home before nightfall.

I have missed one Shabbat. It is not the end of the world, I know it, but still the guilt bubbles up inside my chest when I remember last Friday night, at O'Malley's with Joshua. Father was a liberal Jew and couldn't care less about rituals. Mother, however, she always believed. "Religion is breath, Margot," she told me once.

This was even after the yellow star, even after the word *Jood* became something dirty, something foreign. The yellow star. The Star of David. The Star of Death.

Margie Franklin, she is a not a Jew. But every time I light a candle and say a silent prayer as darkness breaks on Friday night, it feels like a reminder of the person I once was, that somewhere, deep underneath my sweater, my second skin, my lies, she is still in there. Sometimes, in the wash of the cool yellow flame, I can even hear the sound of my mother's voice, so close, it is almost as if she is still with me. "Religion is breath," Mother told me. "And don't you ever forget it."

CHAPTER TWENTY-THREE

Sometimes I wonder if Pete Pelt fears discovery, the way I so often do. Does he keep his forearm covered, or does he not let it bother him now, the way a true American, or my sister, might?

In the annex, I asked him once, just before the end, how we would do it. If we could really hide ourselves forever, even after the war. "Two years has been so long," I said. "And every day, we are afraid."

He'd shaken his head, and leaned in and kissed me on the forehead. "Margot," he said. "Hiding who you are, it'll be so much easier than hiding where you are." He paused. "We will be out in the open then, living life. Just different names, that's all. No longer Jews."

"Can it really be that easy?" I asked him.

"Yes," he said. "It's like an annex in your mind. And no one can unlock your mind."

But what would Peter have said if I could've talked to him after that morning, when the Green Police ripped us out of the annex? Or after the war, after my father published my sister's diary for all the world to read, then see on the stage and now the silver screen? Perhaps he would look me in the eyes, and I would notice his eyes are darker than the sea, black as night. Perhaps he would look at me and say that now he understands, that you really cannot hide forever, even in your mind. A hiding space can only remain secret for so long. That always, eventually, you are discovered.

✻

Sunday morning, I am still thinking about what Shelby said, about how she and Peggy spied on Ron, and though I am holding on to my paralegal studies and readying myself to leave for Fairmount Park, I find myself walking in the other direction, toward the city bus stop. I tuck my studies into my satchel and board the bus toward Broad and Olney. I feel guilty about pushing my studies aside once more, and I promise myself again, double studying next week, or even triple, if I must. But today I cannot shake Shelby's plan from my mind.

I do not have to knock on the door, I think. *I do not have to be brave. I can just hide on the street and watch.* I will go, and just like Shelby, I will spy from a distance.

✻

On the bus, I close my eyes and lean my head against the dirty window. I think about what I might see when I get to Peter's house, what he might look like now, if I will even recognize him. I try to conjure up the fantasy image of him in my head, the man I have envisioned, over and over again, taking the train home from work, walking into our home in Levittown. But now, as hard as I try, I can only picture Joshua. *Joshua.* Joshua, I remind myself, is in Margate, with Penny.

Then I hear my sister's voice in my head, again, the way I so often do.

"I could fancy Peter," she is saying. She said this to me once. We sat together on her bed, in the room she, by then, shared with the dentist. We were both writing in our diaries, and I put my pen down to look at her. Her almond eyes were glossy, nearly feverish.

"But he loves me," I said. Or maybe I didn't say that. Maybe I said, "That's ridiculous."

She shook her head. "His eyes are dreamy."

"You should stay away from him," I said. "Father won't like it." But warnings, especially mine, bounced off my sister, as if her glowing skin made her immune to them.

"Oh, don't be such a paragon of virtue," my sister said, laughing a little.

※

I get off the bus and walk down Olney. The sun is warm today, my sweater too hot, and I feel my core temperature rising, my skin ready to burst, but I do not even push up my sleeves. I have lived through worse than feeling a little hot, haven't I?

I approach 2217 with care, whispering through the air, walking on my tiptoes so as not to be noticed, though the

146

early morning street is quiet, and I imagine most families in these houses are still sleeping. But I am a spy this morning, *not* a paragon of virtue. A genuine Ethel Rosenberg, I think. And I am trying to act the part, a thought which makes me smile a little. Then something catches my eye, and I stop, and my smile quickly fades away. Even from a few houses away, I can see exactly what rests in the small drive at 2217.

There are two cars there, parked side by side: a black Volkswagen Karmann Ghia convertible parked first, and then, right next to it, there is a Cadillac, its sharklike fins, its powdery pink color like silk, taunting me.

I have seen enough. I turn and run back toward the bus stop.

❄

My heart rises and then falls against the rhythm of the city bus that takes me back toward Market Street. A *pink* Cadillac. It is a woman's car, certainly. There can be no other explanation for that, can there? And it would not be a housekeeper there, this early on a Sunday morning, would it?

I hear my sister's voice in my head again, though this time it sounds like it did that very last morning, as she stood at the doorway to Peter's room. "Peter?" His name was a question.

I wanted to ask her then, *What, why?*

But then there was a man grabbing on to my arm, twisting it roughly, and pulling it against the coarse green flesh of his uniform. He didn't have to pull so hard. I would've walked. I would've just gone with him. Just seeing them there, I already knew we were defeated.

"No," my sister screamed. "I'm not leaving." She dug her

heels into the floor. She was holding it in her hands, the orange-checkered book.

The man picked her up and flung her over his shoulder, so hard that I gasped, afraid her neck might snap.

The book went flying across the room, landing somewhere close to where Peter and I had spent the night on the divan. My diary was hidden away, in between the layers of the cot where I was supposed to sleep in my parents' room.

❄

Back in my apartment, I cannot shake the picture of the driveway at 2217. But the farther away I am, the less certain I become about exactly what it was that I saw. Some spy I am. I can see now why Shelby convinced herself that Ron was not off with his hussy while she and Peg were waiting behind the oak tree. That was what she wanted to see, I suppose.

I lie on my blue couch with Katze and think about it. I cannot imagine that my father would ever own a pink car, but American men, who knows? And Pete Pelt, I am certain he is a very American man. Joshua drives a blue car, and so does Bertram, but I wonder if that is just by chance.

Just before dusk, I pick up the phone and dial Ilsa's number. "My dear," she says immediately, "is everything all right?"

"Yes," I say. "I'm sorry to bother you."

"You are never any bother," she tells me.

"I was just wondering," I say. "Would Bertram ever drive a pink Cadillac?"

"A pink Cadillac?" She laughs. "Oh, my dear, if you are

thinking of buying a car, take Bertram with you. Do not try to bargain with the salesman on your own."

"Okay," I say, letting her believe that is why I'm asking, because it's easier that way. "But a pink Cadillac," I press. "Is that a man's car or a woman's car?"

"Well . . ." She thinks about it for a moment. "It's more for a woman, I suppose. But certainly, Elvis is all man, and he drives one."

"Elvis Presley?" I ask.

"Yes, my dear. The one and only."

I cannot imagine the American Pete Pelt being anything like Elvis Presley, swaying his hips to rock-and-roll music, but it is possible that he might drive such a car, nonetheless. Maybe he got it at a very reasonable price and could not pass up the deal?

"My dear," Ilsa says, her voice catching for just a moment in her throat. "How is your secret case going?"

"Oh, that," I tell her, thinking of Gustav Grossman calling me early in the morning last week, sounding so lonely, making me feel so lonely, in return. In addition to him, I have received two women callers, both in the evenings, both offering me not much more than names and contact information. "It is really not such a big deal."

"Are you sure?" she says. I nod, forgetting that she cannot see me. "And there is nothing else?" she asks.

"Nothing else?"

"Nothing else that is bothering you?"

I sigh, sorry that I called. I should've asked Shelby about

the car in the morning. "No, Ilsa," I say. "Nothing else is bothering me."

"But you know if there is," she says, "you can tell me. I will help you."

"Of course," I tell her. "Of course I know that."

But I will not tell Ilsa anything else, no matter how much I love her. I will not tell her anything.

CHAPTER TWENTY-FOUR

THE NEXT MORNING, WHEN I WALK OUTSIDE TO GO TO WORK, I am surprised to find Joshua waiting for me outside my apartment. He is sitting on the bench out front, reading the *Inquirer*. All my worries about the pink Cadillac, Ilsa's questions, and even Joshua's weekend with Penny, they disappear for a moment. And I smile at how comfortable he looks sitting there.

"Good morning," I say, and he lowers the paper and smiles back. His gray-green eyes look bright in the early-morning sunlight and his face is a little red. I wonder how long he has been outside, waiting for me.

"Come," he says, standing. "Let's walk to work together. So we can talk."

I nod, and we quickly fall into step. I watch the shadow of our feet, moving together down Ludlow Street—his long strides, my short ones.

"Sorry about Friday," he says. "My father." He shrugs. "Do you get along with your father, Margie?"

"My father is dead," I say, the lie falling out so fast, so easy, that it doesn't even feel like a lie. What would Joshua say if he knew? If I were to tell him about all the letters in my head, never written? The great wide ocean separating us now, the great wide weight of lies.

"Oh." Joshua's face falls, and my body floods with guilt. But it is not a complete lie to say my father is dead, is it? After all, he is a different person now too. Husband to a new woman. Resident of a new country. Now-famous editor of my sister's book, carrier of her indelible legacy. "I'm so sorry, Margie," Joshua says. "I didn't know."

I nod, trying to think of a way to quickly change the topic, to steer the conversation away from my father. "I was always closer to my mother," I tell him.

"And your mother," Joshua asks. "She's still living?" The image of her comes to me, suddenly, like a heavy brick falling upon and crushing my chest. She is a sack of bones and loose flesh, whispering her plan to me with a feverish urgency. I shake my head and bite my lip to keep a sound from escaping: a confession, or a scream. I'm not exactly sure which one.

Joshua stops for a moment and puts his hand on my shoulder. "I didn't know," he says again, as if he should've, as if he might expect himself to know things about me, real things. "I'm so sorry," he says again. His voice is soft, and I feel his gray-green eyes on my face. The skin of my cheeks feels warm, flushed.

"Thank you," I say. "But they've been dead for many years now. I'm used to it."

"Any brothers or sisters?" he asks.

I shake my head, and my brain wants my lips to tell him about my sister, that she existed once, and not as some made-up character but as a real living, breathing, annoying, and lovable person. Three years younger than me, I would say. I loved her and I resented her. I failed her and I miss her. She died too young. She was murdered. I writhe in guilt. But my mouth says nothing.

Joshua opens his mouth, as if he is about to ask me more, as if he senses now there is so much more for me to say. His eyes hold on to me, with such intensity it is almost as if I can hear his thoughts: *How did they die? How is it you are all alone now?* I plead with him in my head not to ask these questions. And after a moment he nods, as if he understands, without me even having to say, that this is a subject about which I cannot speak. He moves his hand from my shoulder, and we start walking again, up Sixteenth Street. Matching strides. The space on my shoulder, where he touched, still feels warm, as if it's glowing, like candlelight.

"My father is all I have left, you know," he finally says. "My mother passed almost four years ago, this summer."

"I know. I'm so sorry," I murmur. He nods, and his eyes search the ground, as if he has lost something along the tops of his shiny black shoes. I think about how Shelby always says Ezra was much nicer to Joshua before Joshua's mother died. "You were closer to her?" I ask him.

He nods again. "She never thought I would be a lawyer. She'd tease me, say I was much too kind and honorable for that. She told me that one day I'd meet a nice girl and move out to the country and realize how silly the law was."

"But you didn't?" I say.

"No." He smiles. "I love the law. Not my father's law necessarily, but . . ." He shrugs and raises his palms in the air. We walk for a moment, not saying anything, and then he says, "She was incurable. Cancer. The hospital told us and then sent her home to die. My father has never been the same since."

I surprise myself now by reaching up and putting my hand on his shoulder, but I cannot stop it from moving there. He stops walking, turns, and looks at me, his eyes now filled with sorrow. "What about you?" I whisper. "Have you been the same?"

"Watching her die. It was . . . indescribable. She used to be this really vibrant woman. Heading up the Children's Hospital charity, always raising money for the less fortunate, and running the house and laughing. She had the most incredible laugh. It lit our house up." He pauses. "Then the cancer made her shrink. It took everything, even her laugh. Especially her laugh."

I close my eyes, and I can see my mother again and my sister now too, both their bodies, loose flesh and limbs, lying next to me in the darkness at night at the camp. Fleas were jumping off them like sparks, and yet they were too frail to slap them away. My sister moaned in her sleep; everything, every bit of life, had been taken from her.

"Ah," Joshua says as we turn onto Market Street. "Not the way I intended for us to start our Monday morning. I'm sorry."

"But it is impossible to forget, isn't it?" I say.

"Impossible," he echoes. We walk in step, past the glass front of Isaac's. "Anyway," he says, "the reason I was waiting for you is that I was wanting to hear all about your phone calls."

I blink and try to push the images of my sister and Mother away. Only, they stick there, in my head. They never go away, no matter how much I will them to.

"How many have you gotten?" Joshua asks, and then I remember, he is still walking here next to me, wanting to know about his case.

"Only three so far," I say.

"Three?" Joshua's voice turns in disbelief. "But I don't understand it. Is it that they're not reading the paper?"

"Maybe," I say softly, "it is that they're still hiding."

He raises his eyebrows, as if I've confused him, and then I know it: I've said too much. I'd opened myself for a moment, and then I'd forgotten to close back up again. I swallow back the taste of bile in my throat. "I mean, I—I am guessing," I stammer. "But perhaps these people, if they are immigrant Jews like Bryda Korzynski, they are used to living in fear. Used to hiding. Perhaps they are not ready to announce themselves, just like that."

"Hmm." Joshua strokes his beardless chin. "Maybe you're right and they are worried about losing their jobs." That was not exactly what I meant, but that could be the reason too.

We have stopped at the entrance to the office building, and Joshua holds the large glass door open for me to go inside.

We ride the elevator together, not saying anything else, and then Joshua leaves me at my desk with this: "Let me think on this some more, okay?" he says. "We'll talk later."

I nod. Charles Bakerfield, the wife killer, is already waiting for his nine A.M. appointment with Joshua. He sits in a chair by my desk, and once Joshua walks into his office, Charles looks at me and smiles a little.

"He'll be ready for you in just a moment," I say.

I sit down and start typing, but even after Charles goes into Joshua's office, I can't seem to shake the sensation of his wild eyes on my face.

CHAPTER TWENTY-FIVE

SHELBY BOUNCES OFF THE ELEVATOR AT FIVE MINUTES AFTER nine, and just by looking at her, I can tell something is different. Her cheeks are flushed, and her pink lips break into a wide toothy smile when she sees me. I don't even have time to ask her what is going on before she is standing there, next to my desk, shoving her left hand in front of my face.

There it is, a small but sparkling round diamond set in gold. Ron has actually, finally, asked her to marry him. Even before there was any mention of a hussy, Ron always struck me as the kind of man who would marry a calmer girl, like Peggy, though Shelby always insisted there would be a ring. And there it is, hanging in front of my face.

"Congratulations." I smile at her, and she laughs and bounces to her chair. I cannot help but wonder if the owner of the pink Cadillac is a woman and also Peter's wife now, and if she too is flashing a diamond much like Shelby's to her friends. The thought tightens in my chest. Is it possible that he has come here to Philadelphia, just as he said, and that he has married someone else?

I glance through the glass of Joshua's office, and I can see Joshua and Charles exchanging papers and words across Joshua's desk. *Guilty as sin,* Joshua had said. *I love the law. Not my father's law . . .*

Even with his head bent over his desk, speaking to a murderer, the sight of Joshua makes me smile. I think of him this morning, sitting on the bench outside my apartment building, reading the paper. The way his hand held gently on to my shoulder. And then I think, *Yes, it is possible*. In all this time, Peter could've fallen in love with someone else.

"Oh, Margie," Shelby is whispering across the desks now, and I turn my attention back to her. "The whole thing was so romantic. He took me to dinner at the Four Seasons on Saturday, and he had the ring hidden in a piece of chocolate cake. I nearly swallowed it!" She laughs, and the image of her choking on a ring does not seem at all romantic to me, but I suppose it is an American romance, one I cannot exactly understand.

I nod. "I'm so happy for you," I say. And I am. I wonder again about Ron's hussy, but I am not going to bring that up to Shelby now, when she shines in her happiness. After all, she seems to have satisfied herself, with her spying. I wish that I could've done the same.

"You'll be in the wedding, won't you?" Shelby is asking me now. "Peggy's going to be maid of honor, of course, but you'll have to be a bridesmaid."

I imagine that Shelby will most likely get married in the summer, outdoors, in a flower garden, because that is how I imagine American weddings. She will want to dress me in pink silk or taffeta, in a dress with no sleeves. She will not allow a sweater, even if I claim I am cold.

"Oh, please say yes," she says.

"Of course," I tell her, and I smile, though already I am wondering how I will possibly be able to be in her wedding without baring my arm, my soul. I wonder how Shelby would look at me if she knew the truth, and not just that, but how many people she would tell, about her friend, the Jew, damaged in the war, and surely some of those people would be anti-Semites, and then, what might happen? And even if no one nailed a flaming flare to my apartment door, still, it would not be long before Shelby would ask, before everyone would ask, about my family, about where I really came from. No. I cannot go back. I will never go back. I will invent another lie to get myself out of this, to keep my arm covered. I love Shelby, and I am happy for her. And that is one of the worst things about this life. As a liar, a pretend person, you cannot really truly ever be someone's friend. My American life, it is lonely. Often, it is very, very lonely.

❈

Just before noon, I watch Penny sashay off the elevator and walk toward her father's office. What good timing, I think. She is here for lunch. And within five minutes, she is making her way out of Saul Greenberg's office and over toward my desk. Today she is dressed in a powder-blue dress that accentuates both her trim waistline and her large pointy chest. She wears a snow-white hat, with her curls pulled back behind it in a twist.

"Has Josh gone to lunch yet?" she asks, barely glancing at me as she speaks. She is, instead, staring past me, arching her neck to see into the glass window.

"I believe he's eating at his desk today," I lie. "He mentioned he has a lot of work to do." He has not mentioned any of these things, and I remember why Joshua said he does not eat at his desk, because it is good for him to get out of this place, if only for a lunch break.

"Oh." She frowns. "I see. Well maybe I can persuade him otherwise."

"Shall I buzz him for you?" I ask before she has the gall to step inside his office, uninvited. She nods and takes the seat Charles Bakerfield was sitting in earlier this morning.

I pick up the phone, but do not actually depress the intercom button. I know it's wrong, but I do not want Penny and Joshua to have another lunch together. I do not want Penny walking in here, taking, taking, taking whatever she wants. Joshua and I, we had a moment on the street this morning, and I am not ready to let that go, yet. "Mr. Rosenstein," I say softly, "Miss Greenberg is here to see you about lunch." I pretend to listen for a moment, and then I say, "Yes, yes. I see. I will tell her." I hang up the phone, and my hands are trembling as I turn to look at Penny. "I'm sorry," I say, shrugging.

"Oh." She frowns and peers through the glass once again. Joshua is reading papers at his desk, and his brow is furrowed in concentration. He does not look up. "Well," she says, "I needed to see my father anyway." She walks back toward the elevator, and as soon as the doors shut behind her, I hear Shelby whistle softly under her breath.

"What was that, Margie?" she says.

"What?" I ask, innocently enough, as if I have no idea of the lies she has just witnessed me speaking.

"Oh, sweetie." She shakes her head. "If you think a little faking out the intercom is going to stop her, you've got another thing coming."

"I have no idea what you mean," I say. "Mr. Rosenstein has a very busy schedule today."

Shelby's lips twitch into a smile. "And I didn't even know you had it in you."

See, I am not a paragon of virtue. Really, I am not.

❖

After work, I watch the skies turn dark through the small square window behind my sofa. I should eat dinner, but I find myself sitting there, thinking about the way I deceived Penny, then about the pink Cadillac in Peter's driveway. Then, inevitably, as always, my thoughts turn to my sister. I wonder if it was possible that she deceived me the way I deceived Penny. Or maybe, not her who deceived me, but Peter?

In 1944, I became nocturnal, staying awake all night in Peter's room, sleeping in the afternoons on the foldout cot in my parents' room, letting the slow tick of Pim's clock lull me to sleep.

One afternoon I fell asleep, and I had a dream. Peter was there, and he was talking to me, whispering in my ear. Only then, Peter turned into my sister. *Don't be such a ninny, Margot,* my sister was saying. *He could never love you.*

I awoke, and Pim's clock said it was only 3 P.M., an hour when we were still supposed to be silent, to tiptoe in stockinged feet, to whisper. I found my diary beneath the sheets, and lay there and recorded my dream.

And then I hid it again, and tiptoed up the stairs to Peter's room. I would ask him, and he would remind me. In Peter's voice, the future sounded certain, always. It became a way to survive, a way of making it through fear and hunger. In Peter's voice, there was a future. What he said had to be the truth.

I stopped near the entryway to his room when I heard the sound of a giggle. A stifled giggle, because it was 3 P.M., and we were supposed to be quiet. If we weren't quiet, someone might hear us below, and then it would all be over.

But there it was, a giggle nonetheless, and unmistakably hers, my sister's. "Shhh . . ." I heard the sound of Peter's voice. "They'll hear us."

"So what?" my sister said. "So what if they do. Everyone already knows anyway," she said.

"Not everyone," Peter said.

Lying on my couch, in 1959, I'm not certain if this actually happened, or if it was all just part of my dream that afternoon. Since I've read my sister's book, my life in the annex has become blurry: what is real, and what was just a story?

When we leave here, we will be married, Peter whispered into my hair in the pitchest black of nights. *We will go together, to Philadelphia, Pennsylvania, United States of America. City of Brotherly Love.*

Even now I do not really believe that Peter's words to me were a lie, any more than I thought they were in 1944.

But sometimes I cannot tell what to believe. Sometimes, the only thing I'm sure is real is the thick dark ink on my arm, and that is only because it is permanent, inerasable, unchangeable.

❈

CHAPTER TWENTY-SIX

Tonight when I go to sleep, it is only me and her in the dream. Me and my sister.

We lie there in her room in the annex, writing in our diaries. We are on the bed, our hips and shoulders touching, our elbows moving against each other as we scribble words across our pages. My sister holds her fountain pen to the page, but then stops writing and chews on the end, contemplating, her almond eyes wide.

"What are you thinking?" I ask her.

"I'm not in love with him," she says. "It isn't love."

"What do you mean?" I ask her.

"I'm not in love with Joshua," she says, and then I look at her again, and she is Penny. Penny is sitting there, on the bed, next to me, chewing on the end of the pen, dressed in her frivolous tomato dress.

I awake and sit up startled, sweating. My sister and Penny. They are not the same. I loved my sister. I did.

Though it is only 4 A.M., I know I will not find sleep again tonight. I get out of bed and pull my dog-eared copy of my sister's book from the shelf. I have marked the page, the one where it is written, where my sister says it, that she doesn't love him, that she is not in love with him. This is proof, I've told myself many times, that anything that might have happened between her and Peter, even later on, that it didn't actually mean something.

Nothing can't mean something.

I'm not in love with him. In my head now I imagine her saying this to me. We lay together on the bed, hips touching, arms touching. I jumped a little when she said the words; then I took a deep breath and closed my eyes for a moment, remembering the feel of Peter's hand holding mine.

"Who?" I asked her nonchalantly, pretending as if I didn't know.

"Peter," she said, rolling her eyes at me, as if I were such a ninny that I could not even begin to understand the feelings of which she spoke.

"Of course you're not," I told her. "You're too young to be in love."

She chewed on the end of her fountain pen, thought about it for a moment, and then recorded something in her diary.

But there is so, so much Peter in my sister's diary. She knew so much about him, how he felt and how he talked, how he moved and how he breathed. What it was like to be there with him, in his room. This much, these details, they are not stories, and I have always told myself that she had to have taken them from me, from my diary, as if it were just a dress from my closet in the Merwedeplein that she was borrowing without even asking.

Because in my diary, I wrote of the way Peter's eyes looked as they gazed at me on the divan, washing past the moonlight, bluer than the sea. I wrote of the way he held on to me in the middle of the night when I forgot how to breathe, the way I remembered freedom when he spoke my name.

With every single part of my seventeen-year-old body and mind, I loved him. And I detailed all of it in my diary, so our story now, like my diary, it is lost.

CHAPTER TWENTY-SEVEN

❈

AT MY DESK, A FEW HOURS LATER, I AM STILL THINKING about my sister, then about Penny in her tomato dress, saying that she and Joshua, they are not in love. I wonder if Penny really and truly does love Joshua? Or more importantly, does he love her? As his secretary, I know that it is not my place to care, but as his *friend,* I do not think that Penny is right for him. I feel that sense of emptiness in my belly, the ache I feel every time I think of her and Joshua together, and I swallow hard to try to force it away. He doesn't love her, I tell myself. He is not in love with her. I cannot see it on his face, a gentle glow, the way I can see it on Shelby's face.

"Everything all right?" Shelby asks me, interrupting my thoughts. She is leaning across the desks, holding a paper in her hand in a particular way so the fluorescent light catches on her diamond and makes it sparkle. She looks awkward this way, and I think she is doing it just to display the diamond, if only to herself, a constant reminder that what she has wanted for so long, it is suddenly right there, in front of her. I hope that her marriage will be everything she thinks it will be, that Ron really and truly will be devoted to her.

"Yes, fine," I say. "What about you?" I ask her. "You are engaged to Ron, and you are happy that your spying has given you all the answers you need?"

She shrugs, and holds her hand out to look at the diamond again, and the way she casts her eyes downward, just a little bit, I wonder if there is some doubt still, that it's possible some of the excitement of the proposal has gently worn away and now there is the reality, which does not shine as bright. "He has asked me to marry him," she says. "And really, it is everything I've ever wanted."

"But if there is a . . . hussy," I whisper that last word across the desk. "It would be better to know now than later on." *I do not love him,* my sister said. But in my head, I hear the sound of my sister's giggle echoing from Peter's room. *Shhh. Not everyone knows,* he whispered to her.

Shelby shrugs and then says, "Don't look now, Margie." She gently yanks her head in the direction of the elevator. "But the queen bee is back."

I don't look, though I feel a weight that is a little too heavy in my chest. *I do not love him.* "Hello, Margie." The real sound of her voice startles me a little, clearer and higher than it sounded in my dream. I look up and force a smile.

Penny is pink today, the color of the Cadillac. Her dress is more casual than usual and it narrows, like an hourglass, around her small waist, hugging perfectly to her large pointy chest. She has forgone a hat, but her curls are still held back in a suspiciously perfect twist. "Josh is expecting me today," she says.

"I'll buzz him," I say, reaching for the phone.

"No need." She waves her hand and pushes past my desk, but then she stops and shoots me a look that tells me that she knows that yesterday I was lying to her, and also, it is saying, *Do what you will, I am smarter, prettier, more charming . . .*

I nod, and she walks past me, into his office.

A few minutes later, Joshua walks out, Penny draped on his arm. He stops for a moment by my desk and tips his hat. "I'm off to lunch, Margie."

"Okay," I say.

He smiles at me, and his gray-green eyes—they seem to be laughing, or dancing. They are alive with something, and the way they stare at me, it is like they are telling me a secret. He knows too what I did yesterday, and it amuses him.

"Come on, Josh." Penny tugs on his arm.

"Back in an hour," he says to me, tipping his hat again.

"Sometimes, I'd like to punch her smug little face," Shelby whispers, after the elevator doors have closed.

"Shelby!" I say. But I cannot hold back a small laugh.

"What?" She shrugs. "Don't tell me you're not thinking that exact same thing."

CHAPTER TWENTY-EIGHT

A FEW DAYS LATER, I AM STILL HAVING TROUBLE SLEEPING, and instead of pacing my apartment or continuing to stare at the ceiling above my bed, I decide to leave for work early. By 8 A.M., I am at my desk, before Shelby and Ezra or even Joshua have arrived for the day.

Just after I sit down in my secretary's chair, the elevator dings open, and Joshua steps off. Also early. I smile. He wears a navy suit today, with a red-and-navy-striped tie. He holds tight to his attaché, and when he notices me, he smiles his warm Joshua smile.

"Margie," he says. "Just the person I wanted to see." He puts his hat on the rack by my desk and waves for me to follow him into his office. "Come," he says. "Let's talk."

I nod, pleased that he has been wanting to see me, and that we are almost alone here. I stand up and walk into his office.

"Shut the door," he says, "and have a seat."

I do.

He sits down, folds his hands in front of him, his face serious. For a moment I worry that he might chastise me for lying to Penny the other day, but then he smiles again. "You're working early today," he says.

I nod, but I do not tell him the reason, that I have been unable to find sleep, my brain tumbling with thoughts of him and Penny together, the pink Cadillac, Peter. Pim in Switzerland with his new wife. And then, somewhere in the darkest clutches of night, there is my sister, frail and reaching for me at the very end.

Joshua clears his throat. "So I had another idea last night," he says. I nod again. "Maybe an ad in the paper is too public for some. Maybe we should also approach these people where they feel more comfortable."

"Okay," I say, but I am thinking that *these* people, they do not feel comfortable anywhere. That even your own skin, it is your enemy when it is marked, when you are nothing more, or perhaps nothing less, than a number. Or is that just how I feel? Bryda seems to have no qualms about it.

"Let's make up some flyers and take them to Beth Shalom," Joshua is saying.

"Beth Shalom?" I repeat, though I feel as if I am choking on the words, and they refuse to form in my throat into something real.

"Yeah, it's a synagogue, close to Miss Korzynski's part of town. A little bit of a poorer area with a lot of immigrants close by. And I'd be willing to bet a lot of the congregation there either work for Robertson or know people who do." He pauses and runs his hand through his curls. "I'll draw up the flyers, and then I'll just need you to take them down there, and speak to the rabbi, sometime before Saturday services. You can take an afternoon this week."

"Me?" I ask quietly. "You want me to go?"

"I would do it," he says. "But the rabbi there sometimes plays golf with my father, so I need you to keep this quiet. Don't even tell the rabbi which law firm you work for, all right?"

"You want me to talk to the rabbi?" I whisper. My throat is turning numb, and so are my fingertips. It is hard to breathe—sometimes this would happen to me in the dark, in the annex. It was so dark there at night that sometimes I imagined that's what it would be like if we were dead. Just a vast space of nothingness: no sound, no light, no air. The darkness frightened me so much that I would start choking on it, until Peter held on tighter and whispered in my ear, "Just breathe, Margot. Breathe. In and out. It is only air. Babies can do it. The Green Police can do it."

"Rabbis are just people," Joshua is saying, shrugging. "Just like the rest of us. No big deal, Margie." He pauses. "Why don't you do it tomorrow. Go down there, then take the rest of the afternoon off. You deserve it," he says. "You've been working hard."

❈

For a long while, after we talk, I stare at the keys on my type-writer, not moving, not typing anything. *A rabbi is only a person,* Joshua had said.

And a synagogue, it is only a building.

I shake my head. Joshua is wrong; it is not that simple; they are remarkably Jewish things, and thus that makes them different.

It has been almost fifteen years since I have been to a synagogue, and I promised myself I would never go to one again. Even though I sometimes long to go now as my lonely Shabbat candle flickers on my table, my fear, it will not let me.

But I cannot think of a good reason to tell Joshua no, and even in my head, this fear of Beth Shalom, a synagogue to which I have never been, begins to feels silly.

And besides, I remind myself, I am a Gentile now, a secretary. It is not the same. Not the same at all.

CHAPTER TWENTY-NINE

JUDISCHAUSEN WAS A LARGE TEMPLE IN THE CENTER OF Frankfurt, where I remembered going to Saturday services as a little girl with Mother sometimes. Even after the war, after I came to stay with Eduard in Frankfurt, I could still picture in my mind the way the glass windows rose in an arch, with a blue Star of David stained inside, giving off a particular glow in the light of the morning. In my head, I knew the rest of Frankfurt was not the same, that even some of the houses on Eduard's Street, Ulme Alle, had been annihilated, as if struck by a wayward tornado. But still, in my mind, Judischausen, it remained untouched.

One Saturday, not too long after Brigitta had left me off at his doorstep, Eduard asked me if there was anywhere I wanted to go, anywhere he could take me. I had already told him that my family, they were all dead. I'd watched his dapper green eyes fall against the light of his fireplace as he'd asked about my mother. "Even Edith?" he'd whispered, a faraway look on his face, so I'd wondered if he was picturing Mother, the way she was once, when she was a girl.

Before we left Frankfurt to move to Holland in 1933, Mother had taken my sister and me with her to say good-bye to Eduard. She'd told me then that he was just an old friend, from her girlhood days. But even as a young girl, I could tell it had been—or was—something more. He'd kissed her good-bye, once, gently on the mouth. "Oh, Edith," he'd said then, his voice filled with so much sorrow, I was surprised he wasn't crying. Eduard had loved my mother; this much I was sure of. But I also knew that Eduard was not a Jew, and my mother had been raised as a conservative one. Even before the Nazis, there were some lines that were not crossed.

"I want to go to Judischausen," I told Eduard that Saturday morning, when he asked.

"Judischausen?" Eduard shook his head. "You do not want to go there."

"Yes," I said. "I do."

"It will not be as you remember it," Eduard said.

"Nothing is," I told him.

So Eduard drove us slowly through the icy streets leading to the center of Frankfurt, where buildings had crumbled, destroyed by bombs. Frankfurt barely appeared to be a city at all by this point, much less a civilized one. But still, in my head, Judischausen would be the same.

Eduard pulled into a parking space and pointed across the street. "There," he said. I shook my head. We could not be there yet. I remembered the synagogue had risen high, and I saw nothing but disasters nearby.

I got out of the car and walked, as if inspecting the area more closely would change it. The blue Star of David glass had been blown away, and in its place was a gaping, empty hole, surrounded by the dust of bricks and mortar. One wall was still intact, but it had been painted with the ugliest of symbols, red swastikas. They rose and fell in parallel lines. One was not enough—the Nazis, they had felt the need to cover the wall with dozens of them, as if they were shouting.

I touched my heart, where my yellow star had once rested, sewn into my clothes, then my arm, where then, underneath, my number rested, sewn into my skin.

Judischausen had not just been destroyed by the war, but decimated by it: stripped, shaven, beaten down, tattooed.

I thought about Peter, about what he'd said as I'd lain there in his arms. *After the war I'll no longer be a Jew. I'm done with being a Jew.*

"I'm done with being a Jew." I spoke to Eduard softly, but with certainty.

"But . . . your mother?" he said, and his voice cracked on her name. It was religion that had kept them apart, I was certain of it. And religion that had taken her away.

"My mother is dead," I said.

Eduard shook his head. "You are who you are. This much you cannot change."

"What is religion," I asked him, "if it cannot protect you? If it kills you?"

"You are who you are," Eduard repeated.

I am thinking about that moment now, Thursday afternoon, just before 4 P.M., as I find myself clutching tightly to Joshua's flyers, standing at the doorway of Beth Shalom. This synagogue is a flat, square cement building and, I am relieved to see, almost unidentifiable as a Jewish place, except for the small green Star of David etched into the front of the wooden door. There are no large stained-glass windows, and maybe that is better. Nothing to shatter, I think as I take a deep breath and pull open the heavy door to walk inside. Every muscle in my body screams at me to turn and run. I do not want to go inside. I do not want to talk to the rabbi, a Jewish man of God. I feel he might look at me, maybe the way Bryda has looked, and call me a snake. It is so much easier to hide, to slip inside a second skin, so you can simply avoid anything that falls around the first skin.

But I cannot see a way around this, and I am already here. I will simply drop the flyers off, I tell myself, and then I will run. I will travel back on the bus that took me here, back to Market Street, back to my apartment and Katze. I will run, and then I will forget again. Forgetting is easy. It is almost as easy as hiding, or keeping secrets.

Inside the synagogue it is dark and smells faintly of rainwater and mildew. I follow the signs to the rabbi's office, which appears to be just off the main room, and I swallow hard to try to keep myself from gagging. I keep my eyes straight ahead, not allowing myself to look inside the main room.

I knock quietly on the office door, hoping that the rabbi won't be in, that I'll just be able to leave the flyers by the door, and run. *Run.*

But quickly I hear a response to my knock. "Come in," a man's voice says.

I take a deep breath, turn the handle, and walk inside his office.

The rabbi sits behind his desk, dressed in a gray suit. He is an older man with a thick graying beard, not so dissimilar looking to Ezra Rosenstein, only a bit thinner. Though the immediate, obvious difference between him and Ezra is the black yarmulke crushing the rabbi's silver-tinged curls. The nameplate on the front of his desk reads *Rabbi Epstein.*

"Can I help you?" he asks, looking up from his desk, raising his silvery eyebrows a little. I don't say anything for a moment. I want to speak, but I can't. I clutch tightly to the flyers, leaving sweaty fingerprints across the back of them. "Can I help you?" he repeats.

I clear my throat, but still no words will come. Suddenly I am a mute, my voice stolen, the way everything else has been. I hand the flyers to him across his desk. He picks up a pair of reading glasses, places them on the bridge of his nose, and holds the flyers out a bit in front of him. "'Join group litigation against Robertson's Finery . . .'" he reads out loud, and then mumbles the rest to himself.

He looks at the flyer, then back at me, then at the flyer again. "Do you want to have a seat?" he asks, pointing to the chair across from his desk. I shake my head.

"I won't stay long," I finally say, the words escaping me,

almost against my will. I force myself to breathe. *Breathe.*
Breath is harder than you think, when you are trying, when
you are thinking about the motion of your lungs, in and out
and in and out.

"You want me to distribute these?" he asks me, letting the
flyers drop to his desk.

I nod, and somehow I explain to him about Joshua, about
the lawsuit, about Bryda Korzynski. "She is missing a finger,"
I hear myself saying, as if that means something. It does,
though what I'm not sure. But I tell him this anyway, and he
listens carefully.

Rabbi Epstein listens the way a rabbi should. He nods his
head, and he lets me talk. When I finish speaking he looks at
the flyer again, creasing his brow in concentration so similar
to the way Joshua always does. He pulls on the bottom of his
beard a bit, just like Ezra. "And you are involved, in this case?"

I shake my head. "I am just a secretary, for the lawyer," I
say. "I am just a messenger." You cannot shoot the messenger,
can you? Especially one cloaked so deeply in her second skin
that her Jewishness has all but evaporated; this place is foreign to her.

He nods. Maybe he believes me. Maybe he doesn't. I don't
know if he cares. "I will hand these out on Saturday," he says.

"Thank you," I say, and I open my mouth as if to say something else, but then I don't.

"There is more?" he asks, looking at me. His eyes are
brown, like almonds, like my sister's eyes, though not quite,
because they are lacking the small green flecks hers had.
They do not look through me, like Bryda's did, but they look

at me with the kind of shrill intensity that makes me want to tell him more.

I had a sister, I suddenly want to say. *I love her. I miss her. I writhe with guilt. You might have heard of her. She was a Jew, and now she is famous for it. I was a Jew once too.*

But what I say is this:

"I have a question." I'm not even sure why or how these words escape my lips, except they do, and before I can stop myself, I am asking him, "What would happen to a Jew who pretends not to be a Jew?"

He raises his eyebrows. "What would happen?"

I nod.

"Well, this is America in 1959. Not Germany during the war. The Nazis are gone now."

Are they? Are they ever gone? I think about what Bryda said, that her boss, he is a Nazi. And I think about that gang of hoodlums beating up Jewish children, the swastikas still drawn on synagogues. The firebomb. At the thought, I feel myself sweating. I nod at the rabbi and move toward the door; my instinct to run is back.

"Miss," the rabbi calls after me, and I stop and turn and look at him again. "God knows," he says. "You can't hide from God."

CHAPTER THIRTY

I KNOW THAT I SHOULD EAT DINNER, LATER, WHEN I AM BACK at my apartment and the skies are dark. I know that I should. That I should be hungry and want and enjoy food as I must have once, as a girl on the Merwedeplein. I am certain I did. Mother's chicken soup. I feel I craved it once, before the war. The scent of dill and carrots and chicken fat stewing for hours on the stove. Only now I can barely remember what it is like to enjoy the taste of something. Most of the time I eat because I know I have to.

I am still thinking about the rabbi's words, that God knows who is a Jew and who is not. If that is true, then does He also know what happened with my sister, what I did? I shake my head, because I am not sure that I believe that God knows anything anymore.

But I think about Eduard's words as we'd stood together by the destroyed Judischausen: *You are who you are.*

Oh, Eduard. If only it were that simple now.

I don't think Eduard knew about the publication of my sister's book before he died, and he certainly never knew what my American life would become, how really, truly, deeply I would continue to hide myself.

You are who you are, Eduard said.

I was hiding that day when I showed up at his doorstep after the war. I was dressed in a nun's habit, Brigitta's idea— just in case.

"Yes, Sister?" he'd said, staring at me then. Eduard was tall and handsome, with thick black hair, and he seemed unchanged by the war, except for the streaks of silver dancing just around the edges of his ears. "Can I help you?"

I remembered the habit, and I shook my head. "I am not a sister," I whispered, the words catching in my throat. For a moment I could not breathe. "I am Edith's daughter," I finally managed to say, and I was surprised by how small my own voice sounded.

His green eyes curled in confusion, then, all at once, recognition. "Edith Hollander?" he said, referring to Mother by her maiden name. I nodded.

"Annelies?" he asked first. I shook my head and told him my name. He raised his eyebrows, and I thought, *My sister.* She always was the memorable one.

"You can stay here," Eduard told me, after I told him about the Red Cross lists, the rest of my family. Eduard placed a large hand on the protruding bone that had once been my shoulder. His green eyes, they were rivers. "Really," he said. "This can be your home. For as long as you like."

I stayed for nearly six years. While Eduard was at work during the day, I read my way through the volumes that filled his library: mostly literature, written in English. The only German books were the classics, which were the only German books we'd allowed ourselves in the annex too. And I understood, for Eduard, who was not a Jew, that maybe this was his small act of rebellion. I spent afternoons in the sunlight and privacy of his backyard rose garden, perfecting my English, sometimes reading the English words aloud, practicing them in my voice. In the evenings Eduard ate a hearty supper, prepared by his housekeeper, while I would take a few bites. Like Ilsa, he urged me to eat more, but I could not.

Sometimes I miss the simplicity of those days, the quietness of Eduard's house in Frankfurt, before I came to the United States, before the book, before the sweater. *You are who you are,* Eduard said. Yes, living there with him, for that time, I was.

❋

The phone rings, and I jump. I am on the couch, stroking Katze, and I think it cannot be a member of the Beth Shalom congregation. Already. But of course, it is not. It is Ilsa again.

"My dear," she says, when I pick up, "you're not in the middle of eating, are you?"

"No," I lie. "I've already finished."

She hesitates for a moment, and then she says, "You have been eating well, haven't you?"

"Of course," I lie again.

"Well, anyway, I just wanted to check up on you, see how things have been going this week."

"Fine," I say, forcing the word from my lips in my perfect imitation of cheeriness.

She hesitates for a moment. "Are you sure?" she says. "Because I have just had a feeling that something isn't right with you."

"Oh, Ilsa." I force myself to laugh and fight the image of Rabbi Epstein's face, staring, staring, staring at me. Eduard's strong voice, echoing in my head. *You are who you are.* "You really do worry too much." I imagine Mother or my sister, if they were here. They too would say: *I can hear it in your voice. Something isn't right. Stop being such a ninny. Stop lying to us, Margola.*

But Ilsa chuckles, and I picture her on the other end of the line, sitting in her country kitchen, tugging on her earlobe. "Bertie says I am a mother hen. And that I annoy you." She pauses. "But it's just, you know if you ever need anything. Anything at all, my dear."

"I know," I tell her, and this much I do know. "Thank you."

"Did you decide on your car yet?"

"My car?" I ask, not at all sure what she means at first.

"Your pink Cadillac?"

"Oh," I say, "that. No, not yet." I close my eyes, and I can see it again, in the drive at 2217. I have been too chicken to go back there again, too afraid of what and whom I might find. And besides, I have been consumed with Joshua and Penny, and this case. *This case.* The rabbi. *God knows.*

"Oh," Ilsa says, "my dear, we have been thinking more

about our trip, and we think we might like to do a whole tour of Europe."

"How nice," I murmur.

"Bertie is going to call an agent to book us a package. Germany, France, Switzerland—"

"Switzerland?" I ask, and it is a word that barely forms in my throat before it wants to choke me there.

"Yes, I have always wanted to see the Alps, my dear."

"The Alps," I say. "Yes, of course."

"You will come with us, won't you, my dear?"

"I don't think so," I say slowly, trying not to let on to Ilsa that it is very hard for me now to breathe.

"Well, at least give it some thought. I'm not going to let you off the hook that easily. I'd really love for you to come. Bertie and I both would."

�֍

Long after my phone call with Ilsa is finished, I find myself lying in bed, wide-awake, thinking again of the letter I have never written. *Switzerland,* I think. *My father.*

Not only is he editor of my sister's famous book, but also now he is husband to a woman named Fritzi Markovits. He is owner of a new life, lover of a new woman, holder of an indelible legacy.

Sometimes I imagine what might happen should I even find myself standing on *his* doorstep, ringing his bell.

I would not be disguised then in a nun's habit, my hair short and shorn, my flesh falling across my bones. Now I am still thinner than I was before the war, older, but all in all, I look very much the same girl who hid there on the Prinsen-gracht.

But even if I went to Switzerland now, found him now, even if he opened the door and his eyes shone with recognition, I know the first things he would ask me: how did I get away from the Nazis, and why did I stay hidden so long. And then, he would turn his brown eyes toward me, ripe with disappointment, or even disgust.

Where is your sister? How could you come back here without your sister?

If I made it past that, and I was still breathing, then I might say, *Where is my diary? Why is my sister's book, filled with stories, the one the world knows? Why have you always loved her more than me, even in death?* But, most likely, I would not say any of this. I would only stare at him, loving him and feeling angry with him. Wanting to hug him tightly to me and wanting to run.

Who is it? Fritzi might call from somewhere behind him, inside the house. *Who's at the door, Otto?*

No one, dear, he would answer her.

Then he would shake his head, and he would whisper to me, *You killed her. And I am the one keeping her alive.*

CHAPTER THIRTY-ONE

✤

EARLY FRIDAY MORNING BEFORE SHELBY HAS ARRIVED, Joshua buzzes me into his office. I wonder if he has come to work today just to talk to me, and the thought thrills me a little. "Well," he says, motioning me to have a seat. "How did it go with the rabbi?"

I hear Rabbi Epstein's words in my head again about God knowing who is a Jew and who is not, but Joshua, he does not. He has no idea. "Fine," I tell Joshua. "Rabbi Epstein will pass out the flyers tomorrow at the services."

"All right," Joshua says, smiling at me. "Very good, Margie. Let's see if you get some more calls next week, and we'll go from there." He pauses. "Mr. Bakerfield is coming in at ten, and then I'm off to Margate for the weekend. Hold all my calls, and leave the messages on my desk. Send Mr. Baker-field back when he arrives."

"Of course," I say, standing, walking to the door. "Anything else, Mr. Rosenstein?" I want him to say there is, that there is something. What, I'm not sure. But something.

But all he says is this: "That'll be all for now, Margie."

❈

At precisely 10 A.M., Charles Bakerfield steps off the elevator. He tips his hat, nods in my direction. "You can go ahead back," I tell him. "Mr. Rosenstein is expecting you."

He stares at me for another moment. Then he smiles and walks into Joshua's office and shuts the door behind him.

"Now, that one," Shelby whispers across the desks, "gives me the willies." I do not really know the details of Charles Bakerfield's case, except what I have gleaned from typing some of Joshua's notes and from what I recall from reading the stories in the *Inquirer* last year, after it happened. His wife was found strangled in her bed, but according to Joshua's notes, Charles claims it was an accident. "What a creeper," Shelby says.

"Shhh," I whisper to Shelby now. "He might hear you."

She shrugs. "What's he going to do?" she asks. "Kill me?"

It is such an American thing, to talk of death as if they are so far from its reach. Perhaps it is their inability to understand that murder, it is easy for some people. These people, they will kill, and they will kill again, and it will mean nothing.

❈

I was familiar with trials, even before I came to America and began working for Joshua. In Frankfurt, Eduard and I, we'd sit on the sofa in his parlor drinking tea and listening to the voices stretching out on his radio, recounting the events. In Nuremberg, in Luneberg, in Kraków, in Hamburg. The men, the Nazis, they were found guilty, and condemned to die by hanging. I wanted to watch them hang, watch them struggle to breathe, with the ropes tightening around their necks. But even if I could have, Eduard never would have let me.

After a while he would switch the radio off. "This isn't healthy, Margot," he would say to me. And my ears would yearn for more, for something. I'd have to bite back the urge to push Eduard away, to turn the radio back on. But Eduard was filled with kindness, and I never wanted to do anything that might cause him sorrow.

Sometimes when he was at work, though, I would come in from the garden and switch the radio on and listen without him. Sometimes, if I moved the antenna just right, I could get the American station and then I would listen to the smooth voice of Mr. Walter Cronkite recounting the events of the day. He was the one who told me that the men, the Nazis, in Nuremberg, they were to be hanged. Eduard told me too, later that same day. But Walter Cronkite, of course, said it better, with just the right amount of anger, defiance, and disgust. In Eduard's voice, I heard only sadness.

"There will be some justice," Eduard told me, but I did not think he really believed it, that any justice could actually be served.

I shook my head. "Hanging a few Nazis is nothing," I said.

"Margot," Eduard said again. "Turn the radio off. It's not healthy."

There was controversy after Nuremberg over whether

the ropes used to hang the Nazis were too long on purpose. If the ropes were too long, Walter Cronkite reported, it meant the men struggled and died slow and painful deaths, whereas if the ropes were shorter, their necks would've snapped immediately, quickly.

The executioner denied the claims, saying the ropes were just the right length. But I suspected he was lying, and that was something for which I was glad.

I know Charles Bakerfield, he is not a Nazi. But still, I agree with Shelby that he is, as she calls him, a creeper. Most likely, he is also a murderer, and it pains me that if he is set free, if he is not to be hanged for his crimes, that it will be Joshua's doing. That Joshua is the one who will help him get away with murder.

Charles Bakerfield walks out of Joshua's office just before lunchtime. He tips his hat at me and holds his wild green eyes on my face for maybe a moment too long. "Have a nice weekend," he says to me, smiling wide enough to reveal a golden tooth on the right side of his mouth.

Shelby is on the phone, but she shakes her head at me after the elevator doors shut. I shrug and continue with my typing, glancing out of the corner of my eye through the glass window as Joshua readies his desk and gathers his things for the weekend.

He walks out of his office and stops in front of my desk. I look up and he smiles at me, gray-green eyes dancing. "Well, I'm off to Margate," he says.

I nod, because he has already told me this earlier, and it feels like there is something else he wants to say but maybe not in front of Shelby.

"Have a nice time," I tell him. "Enjoy the sea."

He smiles again, and his face softens. "Have you ever been there, Margie?"

"To the sea?" I ask, and I am suddenly filled with sadness as I think of Peter's eyes, the way they held me, on the divan.

"No." He laughs. "To Margate."

"No," I say. "I have never been to the New Jersey sea."

"Well," he says, "it's really something. You'll have to go sometime."

He is just being nice, making conversation, I know that. But still, I can't help but think it sounds almost like an invitation. "Yes," I murmur. "Maybe sometime."

"See you Monday morning," he says, tapping on the side of my desk, and then I watch him walk lightly to the elevator.

"Don't you just love it?" Shelby shakes her head after the elevator doors shut behind him. "Our bosses out on the beach while we're stuck here." She wags her forefinger across the desk at me. "We're leaving early today, Margie, and I'm not taking no for an answer."

She switches on her radio, and I hear the soft strains of "Lonely Boy" drifting across the desks. Suddenly it is as if Mr. Paul Anka, he is singing directly to me. *"All I want is someone to love . . ."* I think about Joshua leaving for Margate, where he will probably spend the weekend with Penny, again. And then I think about the pink Cadillac. What if it was a mistake? A visiting friend? Or Peter's car? What if the American

Pete wants to emulate Elvis Presley? *Greatness is in bravery,* Joshua said.

"I'm actually going to leave right now," I tell Shelby, and I stand up and gather my things to put into my satchel.

She glances up from her typing and raises her eyebrows. "Well, Miss Franklin. Look who's breaking the rules now."

"It's only just a little early," I say, though I glance at the clock and see it is not yet 11 A.M. I swallow back the thought that I am doing something wrong. Joshua is already off to Margate. Most likely with Penny. Any work I have left, I can finish up early Monday morning, before everyone else arrives at the office. Joshua will never know the difference. And even if he does, I'm not sure he will care.

Shelby laughs, waves me toward the elevator, and goes back to her typing, so I know she's not going to tell anyone.

❋

I walk out of the office building and toward the bus stop at the corners of Market and Seventeenth streets.

I walk quickly, as I hear the sound of footsteps behind me. The gait of boots, heavy. I quicken my pace. The boots ache louder against the pavement. I am almost there, almost at the bus stop. And then there is a sound so loud it pierces my ears with its explosiveness. I jump. *Gunshots.* I close my eyes, and I picture Schmidt in his Nazi uniform, standing at the doorway to the train, his hand cocked on his gun. The shots echo in my ears, breaking them. "No," I say. "No. No."

"Miss Franklin?"

I turn to look behind me, and there is Charles Bakerfield.

He smiles at me in a way that makes my skin turn cold even underneath my sweater. "Don't be alarmed," he says. "It was only a car backfiring."

A car backfiring. I breathe. In and out. In and out. His green eyes fix on my face; his gold tooth catches the sunlight.

"Taking the bus somewhere?" He motions with his head toward the bus stop, just steps in front of me. I still cannot breathe. I try, but my lungs are too heavy to move. "I hate the city buses," Charles says, shaking his head. "So dirty." His green eyes wash across my face, as if he is examining me now, in a way that I have not felt in a long time, in a way that makes me feel an old horror. "Can I give you a ride some-where?" he asks.

My chest, it is so heavy, but I manage to shake my head.

"Are you sure?" Charles asks. "My car is right over here in the lot. It won't backfire. I promise you." He motions with his head toward the lot where I know Joshua parks, and I wonder if Joshua has left yet, if he is already in his car, driving toward Margate.

I see the bus pulling toward the stop, and I exhale. "No thank you," I say, and I stumble up the stairs of the bus, nearly falling with relief into the seat. Out the window, I can still see Charles standing there on the street, watching me, even as the bus begins to move away.

CHAPTER THIRTY-TWO

By the time the bus reaches Olney Avenue ten minutes later, I have forced the image of Charles from my mind. I have escaped him now, ridden the bus toward something else that also fills me with fear. Now I am thinking about the image of the pink Cadillac resting in the drive at 2217.

I get off the bus, but this time I do not walk like a spy. Instead I walk quickly, nearly breaking into a run to make my way to the 2000 block before I change my mind and run in the opposite direction toward home.

Though I have been on this part of Olney Avenue before, now at the lunchtime hour, on a Friday, it feels different somehow. Just before noon, Olney is awake with children walking to and from school on their lunch hour. Roses have bloomed since I have been here last. I do not see them, but their scent is intoxicating, nearly overwhelmingly so, until I feel I might vomit.

I reach my destination, and I stand there for a moment, in front of 2217, where the mailbox by the front door reads *Pelt*. There is only one car in the drive now, I notice, only the pink Cadillac. The black Volkswagen is gone. *He's at work,* I think. And then, before I can decide to walk to the steps or turn and run, the crumbling green door swings open and I hear the sound of a woman's voice.

"Don't worry, darling," she is saying. "You don't need to cry."

I listen carefully, and I believe it is the same voice I heard on the phone. My sister's voice, what it might have become now, all these years later. The voice of a woman who is strong and smart and confident, and who always gets what she wants.

But I look at her as she walks out of the door, and she is nothing at all like my sister. She is very tall and quite thin, dressed in fashionable plaid shorts and a bright pink top. She is red-haired and, I think, has freckles across the bridge of her nose. Certainly not in the least bit a Jew. *Of course.*

She yanks something hard across the doorway, and when I process what it is, I cannot help it, I let out a little gasp. It is a pram, and inside there is a baby, a girl I am guessing, judging by the pink she is draped in.

The woman turns and looks in my direction, perhaps having heard my conspicuous gasp, and I want to duck, or run, but my feet stay frozen. "Miss, do you mind?" she asks me. I turn to make sure it is me she is talking to, but I am the only woman standing there on the sidewalk. "This stroller is impossible to get down the steps."

I realize she is asking for my help, and I walk in her direction, toward the sound of her pure and self-assured voice. I climb up the steps slowly. One, two, three, four, five . . .

"Could you hold this end while I lock the door?" She pushes the handle of the pram in my direction, and then I have no choice but to take it or watch the baby plunge down the steps. I take the handle. "I don't know what I was thinking. A house with steps like this and a stroller." She shakes her head as she turns the key in the lock. The baby lets out another cry, and I grip tightly to the handle. It is metal and cold against my burning flesh. "Don't cry, darling," the woman says, making eyes at the baby. "Mommy will be there in a second." She locks the door, and she grabs the back end of the stroller. "Do you mind helping me carry this down the steps?"

I don't say anything. I cannot. But I am not going to let go of the handle either. Partly because I do not want the baby to fall, and partly because I am staring at her, this woman and the sharpness of her red hair, and yes, the cluster of freckles on the bridge of her nose. She is adorably and distinctly American.

We reach the bottom of the steps, and she smiles at me. "Thank you so much," she says. I nod as she turns the stroller, and then I can see the baby. She is a big baby, maybe closer to a one-year-old, or maybe just big. I do not know enough about these things to tell. She is swathed in pink, and for a moment I wonder if her name is Auguste, after Peter's mother, or Margot, or even Anne.

"What's her name?" I murmur, before I can stop myself.

"Eleanor," the woman says, smiling at me as she pushes the stroller toward the powdery-pink Cadillac. She waves as she helps the baby into the car and folds the pram into the trunk. "Thanks again," she calls as she slips easily into the driver's seat and backs out of the parking space.

Eleanor, I think. There was no Eleanor in Peter's family.

But then I remind myself, only Jewish people name their children to honor the dead. The Gentiles, they name their children to honor the living.

⸙

In my sister's published diary, there is a place where she talks about kissing Peter for the first time, and everything in that kiss, it changed her. She was no longer a girl, but a woman. Suddenly she was lovable.

Every time I read that passage, I feel as if I am reading a memory, the retelling of a dream, typed out right there inside a book probably millions of people have now read. That is me. Surely, these feelings, she found them in my diary first.

But there is something else. A line she wrote that catches me every time, a line that says my sister and Peter, they kissed by the window.

I did not write that. I did not do that. Peter and I, we always stayed on the divan when we were in his room. After a while the window frightened me, the idea that we could be spotted, or even become swathed in moonlight. When you are hiding for so very long, light becomes your enemy, a beacon of exposure. I never went to the window in Peter's room. We never kissed by the window.

"Who's Johann?" My sister asked, about my first diary.

"No one," I said. "I'm just telling stories."

My sister had a gift for telling stories. She told them sometimes to Mother when she wanted to get out of chores, or to Father just for fun, just to make him laugh. She told them to me as we lay there together, our pens dancing across the pages of our diaries. "Margola," she would say, "I have a fairy tale for you. With a happy ending. I adore happy endings, don't you?"

I often tell myself that in her diary, she was romanticizing what she thought love might have been, in hiding, and at her tender age. Perhaps she thought the window would make a nice symbol of the outside world, so close to freedom, and yet so far away.

But as I lie in bed, late into the night, thinking about the red-haired woman and baby Eleanor, I cannot stop imagining my sister and Peter standing by the window, holding on to each other tightly, kissing each other, as if it is not a story at all, but a memory I have now long since forgotten.

What if I have been wrong? I wonder. *What if I have been wrong about everything?*

CHAPTER THIRTY-THREE

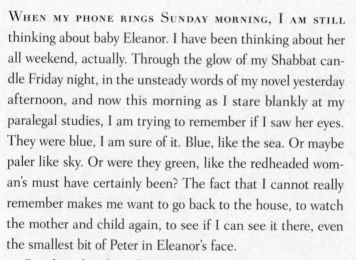

When my phone rings Sunday morning, I am still thinking about baby Eleanor. I have been thinking about her all weekend, actually. Through the glow of my Shabbat candle Friday night, in the unsteady words of my novel yesterday afternoon, and now this morning as I stare blankly at my paralegal studies, I am trying to remember if I saw her eyes. They were blue, I am sure of it. Blue, like the sea. Or maybe paler like sky. Or were they green, like the redheaded woman's must have certainly been? The fact that I cannot really remember makes me want to go back to the house, to watch the mother and child again, to see if I can see it there, even the smallest bit of Peter in Eleanor's face.

But then the phone begins ringing. Rabbi Epstein's Jews. Three women calling, all of them, one after another, as if they planned it this way, and I wonder if they are friends.

I picture them sitting inside Beth Shalom on hard pine

benches, their shoulders touching as they listen to Rabbi Epstein speak: Ada, Miriam, Reisel. I imagine them as older women and frail, their tattoos stretching over wrinkled flesh. But Ada tells me that she was born in Philadelphia, that her mother emigrated from Lithuania, and so I imagine she had the American version of wartime, that she is not even marked as a Jew, and that it's possible even that she is younger than I am.

"How much can you get for us?" the third woman, Reisel, asks me. She says it as if she is bargaining at the Reading Terminal Market, the way Ilsa always tries to. "Selling those peaches at such a price is highway robbery," she'll insist, and yet she'll buy them anyway, even if the vendor won't bring down the price. But most of the time, for Ilsa, they do. She has that effect on people.

"Right now," I tell Reisel, "my boss is just collecting names, and we will contact you when he has a plan."

"But how much can you get for us?" she repeats. "What is the price for being a Jew these days in Philly?"

I cannot tell if she is being serious or facetious, but I can feel her hatred, thick and overpowering, like the wool of a sweater, even through the telephone. "Should I give my boss your name?" I ask her.

She doesn't say anything for a moment, and then: "Why not? What else have I got to lose?"

❈

I think about Reisel, even after I hang up the phone. *What else have I got to lose?* she asked me. I wonder then, what she has lost. Or not what, but how much, who?

There were stories of guards—and not even the guards they hung after Nuremberg, but ones who slithered away into the world after the war—who came in at night after everyone was sleeping and took a woman out to rape her. Sometimes, if she was lucky, they brought her back. Mostly they beat her and then threw her away, like garbage. There was Josef Mengele, a doctor, who I heard Walter Cronkite talk about on the radio, afterward. "Angel of Death," Mr. Cronkite called him, for the medical experiments he performed on Jews, simply because he could. Josef Mengele was not at Nuremberg, though he should've been. What happened to him? I imagine he escaped like me and is hiding somewhere in America. That he has also found a second skin, working as a physician in an American hospital. America is a good hiding place, for Jews as well as Nazis—a faraway place where the war was something else, something entirely different.

I do not like to think about these things, about the camps, about what did happen, about what could've happened.

I do not like to think about them, but then Reisel's words, they do nothing but make me think about them.

❊

If we are counting up losses, really truly counting each and every thing, I would also include my diary from that time, those two years in the annex. Maybe it seems like nothing, not compared to the people, the places, the lives. But it was not nothing—it was something. Two entire years of my life. It was my story. If I had it now, that time would still be real. And so I often wonder about it.

For a long time I imagined that it was Miep who found my sister's diary on the floor in Peter's room after we were taken. I imagined that she picked it up. That she also found mine hidden under the mattress.

When the war was over, I imagined Pim returning to 263 Prinsengracht. He walked into the office and found Miep at her desk, and she pulled the books out of the drawer where she'd hidden them.

Pim had hope then that we were still alive, until he saw the Red Cross lists, the same ones that Brigitta brought to me, which said it, right there, my sister's name and mine, marked with crosses.

I do not imagine that Pim would've even opened the diaries until he thought we were dead. Pim would not ever have read our diaries without our permission. But then, once we were dead, I imagined that he opened them because he was grieving. Because it was all that was left of us.

If nothing else, Father is a good businessman, and when he realized he could get the diaries published, make money, profit from the books, I am sure he thought, *Why shouldn't I?* Perhaps he also thought at first that it was the only justice he could get for us, for all of us. Hanging a few Nazis, it was nothing. The world needed to understand more, to see more.

But this is where my imagination goes awry. What happened to my diary? Why did Pim publish my sister's and not mine?

For a long while I imagined it was the publisher who said to Father that he could not publish two daughters' diaries, that it would confuse his message, sully it, tarnish the face he might be able to give to the terrible suffering for the Jews, the face of a young, innocent girl who had so much life left to live when it was stolen away.

I imagined they said to Father, *This is the only way.* The only justice you can get for both your daughters.

And then I imagined they looked Father in the eyes and said, *Now, which one? Whose diary is it? Who is the face of the Holocaust, Mr. Frank?* And of course, who would he choose?

But now I do not know what to believe. Father is a good businessman. If he had my diary, I think of all the money he could make from telling the other sister's story, my story. So maybe it conflicts with my sister's; so maybe the world would be just as confused as I am now about who it was that Peter loved. But still, there is money to be made. Justice to be had.

Now I often wonder if the reason why my diary has not been published is that it was never recovered. I hope that is the truth. Because the other option is that Father has it, that he hangs on to it still, waiting, waiting, for just the right time to release it into the world.

CHAPTER THIRTY-FOUR

❈

I LIE IN BED AWAKE FOR A LONG WHILE, HEARING REISEL'S voice, imagining Eleanor's eyes, and thinking about my diary resting uneasily in Pim's hands. When I finally do fall asleep, I have the nightmare I have had so many times that sometimes now when I awake, I cannot remember if it is just a nightmare or a memory I've suppressed.

My sister and I, we are huddled together, in a pile of bodies in the camp. There are fleas jumping on us, and we watch them bounce in the air like sparks. We would be itching but we are too tired, too sick to move, and besides, we are no longer feeling anything.

Mother is next to us. "Hold on," she whispers. "Just a little while longer."

And then suddenly she is bleeding. Blood pours from her mouth, like a faucet turned up too high, red spilling everywhere, all over my sister and me, covering all of us.

I open my mouth to scream but no sound escapes me. My throat is too parched. I haven't had enough to drink in weeks.

✼

At 5:21 A.M., my phone starts ringing. I am lying in bed with my eyes closed, but nonetheless, I am not sleeping. My brain is heavy from my dream, and sleep has already felt like the furthest thing from my reach for a few hours. Still, I am good at pretending, lying there with my eyes closed, just because I know it is what I should be doing at this hour.

As I walk toward the phone, I find myself thinking about Peter again—*Peter van Pels, Pete Pelt, P. Pelt*—and I push my brain to remember the sound of Peter's voice, the pitch of it, how my name would sound as he spoke it. *Margot. You're really beautiful, even if you don't know it.* If he were to see the number in the paper, if he were to call it; if he were to find me listed in the phone book, Margie Franklin, as we always said—what would he even sound like now? What time would he call? Peter and I almost always spoke in Dutch. Would his voice sound different in American English?

"Hello." I pick up the phone.

"Margie, hello. It is me, Gustav, again." Gustav Grossman's broken version of English rings clearly in my ear, and any notion I have of remembering Peter vanishes. For a moment I am surprised, because I do not remember having told Gustav my name, but maybe I did. "I do not wake you, do I?" Gustav is asking.

"No, Mr. Grossman," I say. "You do not."

"I'm sorry I call back."

"That's okay," I tell him. "But I really don't have any news for you. I promise my boss will call you when he has some."

"I know that," he says. "But your voice, it has very beautiful sound, and I wonder maybe you have breakfast with me?"

Ilsa's warning echoes again in my head. Ilsa is wise and strong, and I do not know Gustav. He could be a wife killer, a creeper, a secret Jew hater, or even a Nazi.

"Margie." He says my name again. Gustav's voice sounds kind and broken all at once. Maybe Gustav and I, we have much in common, and suddenly, in Gustav's voice, I feel it again, that wayward sense of homesickness that I can never seem to squelch in America, no matter how hard I try.

"Yes, okay," I tell Gustav.

"How about today," Gustav says.

"Today?" I ask.

"Yes," Gustav says. "Why don't we meet today?"

❖

I agree to meet Gustav at 8 A.M. at Casteel's Diner. Though it is not far from the office, and in an area that is crowded in the mornings usually, I cannot shake Ilsa's warning after I hang up the phone. And I know what I am about to do, meeting Gustav this morning, is what the Americans would consider Mickey Mouse. That is to say, dumb. And I am not dumb. I was always the top pupil at the Jewish Lyceum, top self-learned in the annex. I know many languages. I survived the Nazis. I jumped from a train and somehow made it safely to America, Philadelphia, City of Brotherly Love. But still I have agreed to meet Gustav, this strange man from the other end of my phone who really could be anyone, because I think we are both lonely, lost souls in a great big American city.

Yet, I am no Mickey Mouse, no matter what Shelby might have you think. So I quickly dial the number to Joshua's house before I am about to leave.

"Hello," a woman's voice answers, and it throws me because I was expecting Joshua's voice. I think of the woman, baby Eleanor, and the pink Cadillac, but then I shake the thought away. No. *Penny.* "Hello," she says again, and my heart tumbles.

"Hello," I finally say. "This is Margie Franklin, is Mr. Rosenstein there?"

"Oh," she says. "Hi, Margie, it's Penny."

"Hello," I say. There is the space of silence, and though it is the sound of nothing, it feels excruciating to me.

"Josh can't come to the phone right now," she finally says. "Can I take a message?"

I hesitate, remembering that moment at my desk when I pretended to intercom Joshua as she stood by, eagerly craning her neck to see into his office. I suspect that what I tell her now will never reach Joshua, but I say it anyway. "Can you tell him I am meeting with someone, for our new case, at Casteel's before work today?"

"Hang on," she says, "let me grab a pen." She waits, what is probably the appropriate amount of time for pretending, and then she says, "All right. Casteel's before work today." She pauses. "Anything else?"

"That is all," I say.

After I hang up, I cradle the receiver in my hand for a moment, imagining the weight of Penny's smirk on the other side of the line.

CHAPTER THIRTY-FIVE

I WALK DOWN MARKET STREET PAST THE LAW OFFICE TO GET
to Casteel's. It is early and the air is still cool, the street
uncrowded. My breath rasps in my chest, then my throat, and
I remind myself. Breathe. Just breathe. It is not so hard.

I feel my heart pounding in my chest, my throat closing a
little bit. What am I doing? I wonder. Why am I meeting this
man who I do not know, just because he is a Jew and lonely
like me? He could be anyone, I remind myself.

I close my eyes for a moment, and I see Penny's face, then
the redhead's, and then baby Eleanor. *What color were her
eyes?* Why did I not think to notice them?

Suddenly I hear the heavy footsteps behind me again. I
quicken my pace. They quicken too. Pounding, faster, faster.
I think of Charles Bakerfield, offering me a ride on Friday.
Was he following me? Or was he just being nice?

He's a creeper, Shelby said.

I am trying to breathe. But I cannot. My chest hurts from the effort of breathing and running—it is too much. The boots, they get louder and louder, and louder, breaking my ears, and then I am back on the Prinsengracht again. May 1942, just before the call-up notice came. Mother had asked me to stop by there after school, to bring Pim a letter at the office that had come for him that morning. I'd held it in my satchel all day, and on the way home, I took a different turn from my sister. She was skipping, anyway, with her friend Hanna, as if the yellow star across her heart, it meant nothing.

I walked quickly, though my legs were already tired. I was scared to walk alone, or even leave the house since I'd overheard Father talking, telling Mother that now Jews could be arrested, just for being Jews. "They do not even need a reason," he'd said to Mother, when he thought my sister and I weren't listening. "They see a yellow star and that's enough."

I turned the corner, just before the Prinsengracht, and I heard the sound of footsteps behind me. The heavy gait of boots.

I sped up to a run, and the boots, they sped up, too.

"Stop, *Jood*." A man's voice called out to me, and I couldn't breathe; the words fell on me, like the hardest of rains, flooding me, sweeping me down toward the Prinsengracht, drowning me. Yet my feet stood still on the pavement as if they were stuck there. I wanted to run, harder, faster. I didn't. The sound of the man's boots got heavier in my ear.

I turned, and he was behind me, dressed in his Green Police uniform: thick black boots, long green coat, hat like a bell, obscuring all but his black and penetrating eyes. "What

are you doing, a young girl on a business street at this time?"
He spoke to me in Dutch. I had trouble understanding the
words at first, though by then I was already quite fluent in
Dutch. With fear, my brain still turned back to its first language, German. I tried to answer, but my voice, it trembled
in my throat and refused to make a sound. "*Jood,*" he yelled in
my face, his breath hot and smelling of cigarettes. "Answer
me, *Jood.*" He grabbed my arm roughly, twisting it a little.

"I am going to see my father." The words fell out of me,
somehow. "He works on this street."

He twisted my arm a little more, a smile twitching against
the white hairs of his mustache, a smile that said he was
deriving pleasure out of frightening me.

"What's your name, *Jood*?"

That was the time to lie, the time to find a second skin;
only I was too young then, too innocent to understand
how important lying was. I told him my name. If I had lied,
maybe the call-up notice never would've come a few weeks
later, and we wouldn't have had to go into hiding so quickly,
just to save me.

He let go of my arm. "Hurry up," he told me. "Run. Your
yellow star, it's making me sick."

Uw gele ster, het maakt me ziek.

There is the Dutch. It comes back to me sometimes, even
still, in 1959.

❁

Just as I reach Casteel's, I feel a large hand grasp my shoulder, tugging at the corner of my sweater.

Stop, Jood.

I hear the sound of a scream, somewhere, in the distance. It rises, like a siren, getting louder and louder, hurting my ears.

It takes a moment for me to recognize that that sound, it is my own.

"Margie," a voice is saying, whirring in my ear. *Margie, Margie, Margie.*

The name falls and breaks like a clap of thunder followed by a torrent of rain. "Margie, are you all right?"

The voice is familiar, and the screaming stops. I look around, and I realize I must've fallen down as I was screaming, because now I am sitting there, on the dirty morning sidewalk on South Seventeenth Street, staring at the tops of black, dressy, familiar shoes. *Joshua.*

"Margie." Joshua's voice echoes in my head. "I'm sorry. I didn't mean to frighten you. I was just trying to catch up with you." His large gentle hand reaches down for mine, and I hold on to it, allowing it to pull me up, back to my feet. "Are you all right?" he asks again.

"Yes," I finally say, but he does not let go of my hand. He laces his fingers through mine, and he shoots me a worried smile.

Suddenly I am embarrassed that Joshua heard me screaming, that he saw me slink to the ground. It has happened to me before, these fits, as Ilsa would call them. Where something will startle me, and I will crumble. "It must be some kind of residual stress," Bertram guessed, "from the war." And Ilsa had encouraged me to see a doctor, but always I refused.

"It's nothing," I told her, and then, for so long, I've been able to contain myself.

"It's nothing," I tell Joshua now.

"Are you sure?" he asks. "Because you seemed pretty upset. Did something happen?"

His eyes look at me in a way I have not seen before. It is neither seriousness nor sadness, but something else. Concern? Have I worried him? Does he think I was getting mugged here on the street? That would certainly be a better explanation for my screaming than the truth, but some lies make me feel too terrible, so I will not tell him that.

"No," I say softly. "Nothing happened. I just . . ." *Twisted my ankle. Saw a ghost. Heard a ghost. Am a ghost.* "I just startle easily, is all."

"Are you sure?" he says again, his gray-green eyes holding on to me.

I nod, and he slowly steps back and lets go of my hand.

"Shall we go in?" he asks. It is not until Joshua says this that I think about how he got here. Penny must have actually given him my message. I flush with embarrassment. Of course. She does not look at me the way I look at her. Why should she? I am Margie Franklin, the Gentile secretary wrapped oh-so-tightly in her sweater. And she, she is Penny Greenberg, the wealthy Jewess who weekends in Margate.

I shake the thought away and take a few tentative steps to the front window of Casteel's. Is he inside? Gustav Grossman? I put my hand up to the glass and press my face close, peering inside, but all I see are two elderly women drinking cups of coffee.

"Margie." I hear Joshua saying my name again. His hand touches my shoulder gently, and I close my eyes for a moment before I walk toward the door to Casteel's. Joshua opens it for me, and I walk inside, where I am greeted, at this hour, by the smells of stale coffee and greasy bacon. The air is fog and silt, and it covers me, as if in a dream. So many empty tables, no men inside to speak of. "I'll grab us a table," Joshua says. "We can get some breakfast, talk."

I nod and walk in the other direction, up to the counter. "I was meeting a man here," I say to the pink-striped waitress, who is standing behind the counter, holding a pot of coffee.

"A man?" she asks. Something about her tone reminds me of Shelby when she teases me about finding me a man.

"Have you seen him?"

"What does he look like?" she asks. I shrug, and she says, "So you were meeting a Joe Doe for breakfast, hon, and he didn't show?" She laughs a little, as if I am an amusement to her.

"Tall," I hear myself saying, though I know as I speak, the words make no sense. "Brown curly hair. Blue eyes, like the sea."

"Nope." She shakes her head. "Haven't seen him."

CHAPTER THIRTY-SIX

JOSHUA HAS CHOSEN US A TABLE BY THE WINDOW JUST IN case, he says, Gustav still decides to show. But I wonder if he'd already arrived, heard me screaming, saw the commotion on the street, and he ran. That's what I would've done had it been the other way around. I would've run far and fast, holding on tightly to my sweater.

Joshua asks the pink-striped woman for two cups of coffee and two plates of eggs, though I do not think I can stomach eggs at this hour, but I do not tell him that.

"Now, Margie," Joshua says. "I want you to tell me exactly what was going on and why you agreed to meet a client on your own." It's only now that I realize he sounds annoyed, that I have overstepped my bounds as his Gentile secretary.

"I'm sorry," I say. But I don't tell him the truth, about Gustav telling me about the loneliness of America, about how Gustav and I have something to discuss, something in common, about the wayward sort of homesickness that burns a hollow space in my chest. What I tell Joshua is this: "He was very persistent about meeting in person today. I called to let you know . . ."

"Okay." Joshua sighs. "But don't do it again, all right? If someone wants to meet, put them on my schedule."

"At the office?" I say, raising my eyebrows.

"Good point," he says. "This is becoming more complicated than I thought." He sighs again and runs his hands through his curls. "I hate this secrecy, this . . . sneaking around. As if we're doing something wrong." He shakes his head. "It's ridiculous, isn't it? I'm a grown man. A lawyer. And still, I'm under my father's thumb."

I nod, but I am thinking about my own secrecy. My own father. All the lies I have told because of him.

"I know I shouldn't complain so much about my father," Joshua is saying now. "He's given me a good life, an easy life, especially when you look around and see how Jews my age in other parts of the world have had it. Or, hell, even right here, in Philly."

I nod, but I press my lips together, not saying anything. What if Ezra had practiced law in Germany, and passionate, contemplative Joshua had been marched to his death at Mauthausen? He would not have survived very long, in that world. There is a softness about Joshua, but maybe that is only an American softness. In another world, Joshua too, it's possible he would've found a kind of strength that he did not even know existed.

The waitress plunks our plates down in front of us. Each

is full with eggs over easy, hash browns, two pieces of buttered toast, and three large slices of bacon. Joshua pushes the bacon aside with his fork, and I am surprised. I would've expected him to eat it, such a liberal Jew. Or is it just that he does not like the taste of bacon? Joshua takes a bite of his eggs, and I push mine around on my plate with my fork.

"He's given me a good life, an easy life," Joshua repeats, as if he is trying to convince himself. "But sometimes I wonder what it would be like to feel truly happy."

"And what would make you feel that?" I ask him. I catch his gray-green eyes with my own, and hold on to them for just a second, until he breaks my gaze and he smiles.

He shrugs. "Sometimes I think about starting my own firm, where I could work on the kinds of cases that would help people. Like this suit against Robertson." He shrugs again. "So maybe it's not going to make me rich, but it means something. There just has to be more out there than defending murderers, you know?"

I nod. I imagine some people, Shelby, for instance, might feel annoyed by Joshua's complaints—*poor little rich boy*. But I am not. Though neither do I feel sorry for him. Joshua is a wealthy American Jew, in the year 1959, which also means he has choices. Freedom. "Why don't you start your own firm?" I ask him. I think about what I told Shelby once about a sense of duty to one's father. But how far does one's sense of duty go? When does loyalty to one's father end, and a child's self begin?

Joshua shrugs again. "I can't leave my father," he says. He pauses as he sops up egg yolk with his toast and eats a little.

"My mother left him, both of us. It wasn't her fault. She didn't want to leave, of course. But . . . it destroyed him," he says.

"And you cannot work on your own and still be his son?" I ask gently.

He shakes his head. "If I left the firm, my father would see it as a betrayal. He'd never forgive me. It's all he's ever wanted, his only son following in his footsteps. And now. . . since my mother passed, well, I'm the only thing in the world he has left."

"What about what you want?" I ask.

"Me?" He laughs a little and finishes off his meal, save the bacon. "Aren't you going to eat anything, Margie?" he asks.

"I'm not very hungry this morning." He frowns, so I add, "And I ate a little before I left my apartment." Then I take a bite of the toast, just so he will stop staring so hard at my plate. Only, he diverts his eyes, instead, to my face, and he stares even harder, as if he is searching my eyes for the secrets that he may have begun to suspect are there.

"What about you?" he finally asks. "Your paralegal studies still going well?"

"Yes," I say. Then I think guiltily about the number of Sundays I have ignored them lately.

He nods. "And that is what will make you happy, Margie? Is that what you want out of life?"

I hesitate for a moment, and then I nod again, chewing the toast carefully, making an effort to chew, chew, chew each bite.

"But you are afraid of something," he says.

"Why do you say that?" I put the toast down and hold tightly to my sweater.

"The way you screamed, out there, on the sidewalk," he says. He reaches his hand across the table and lays it gently on my wrist. The gesture is meant to comfort me; I know that. And for a moment it does. I can breathe, and the air in front of us feels serene like the delicate blowing of bubbles under water.

I wonder what Joshua would say if I told him. If he knew it all, everything. *I am not Margie Franklin,* I might tell him. *I am not Polish. I am not a Gentile. I'm a Jew. I was marked as a Jew, the thick dark ink on my arm. It is not a badge of honor, it is a battle scar, a wound so deep I will never find a way to heal it. My name is Margot.*

But before I can tell him anything, Joshua moves his hand, and his head is turning. "Can I help you?" I hear him saying, and that is when I look up, when I see him for the first time sitting at the table across the aisle from us, staring at me, with a glassy sheen to his dark brown eyes. He is older than me, my father's age, I might guess, with graying hair that sticks out in wiry curls around his temples, and bushy gray eyebrows to match.

"You are Margie?" he says to me. I nod. *Gustav Grossman.* Not at all what I imagined, which was what? Peter? A Peter replacement? "You are even very more beautiful in person than on the telephone."

"This is who you're meeting?" Joshua whispers across the table.

"Gustav?" I say to him just to be sure, though I already feel certain it is him. He nods, and he smiles at me, revealing yellow crooked teeth. He stares hard at my sweater, my heart, and nods.

"Yes, very beautiful, indeed."

My cheeks burn, and Joshua frowns and folds his arms across his chest. "You are interested in our group litigation against Robert Robertson?" he asks Gustav sternly, in what I imagine is his courtroom voice.

Gustav shrugs, and he smiles at me. "You very young too, Margie, yes? A sweet, sweet flower."

I pull my sweater tighter around my chest, and Joshua looks from Gustav to me to him, then back to me. He reaches across the table for my hand again and holds it between his own. "Look," he says pointedly to Gustav. "I think you've got the wrong idea here, pal. Miss Franklin is taken."

"She is?" he asks. *I am?* Joshua looks at me and winks across the table, and now there is a smile twitching on his lips. He is lying. Of course. Being kind. Trying to scare Gustav off. This is some kind of sweet or misguided urge to protect me. I cannot decide whether this thrills me or annoys me. Gustav is odd, yes. But also, I believe he is most likely harmless. And Joshua, he is the one who is taken, isn't he?

"I'm very sorry," Gustav says. He looks at me. "On telephone you did not say." He shakes his head. "America is very lonely place. In Berlin, before war, I very handsome boy. I have very many friend."

I close my eyes and think about my sister and me, walking home from the Lyceum, before the yellow star, when we still skipped on the streets, flanked by the laughter of our school-mates and the gentle flow of the canals. "But you have made it to America," Joshua says to Gustav, and his eyes soften a little.

"Yes," Gustav says. "But many time, I would give all my life, to be boy in Berlin again." He pauses. "Not Berlin now. But Berlin that was."

In the annex, Peter and I had talked of America as if it were a cloud: rich and full, beautiful and soft. And America, it is harder than I dreamed it would be, though beautiful too. But sometimes I too would give anything to be back on the Merwedeplein with Mother, Father, my sister. Before the yellow star and the restrictions on Jews. When my sister and I could chase each other on the grassy knoll, the sounds of our laughter resonating against the nearby cobblestones like raindrops.

"In America," Gustav is saying now, "I have no one."

"But you must have someone," I hear myself saying. "Someone here who reminds you of home." Joshua clings tightly to my hand, and I look across the table at him, his chestnut curls, his gray-green eyes, his uniquely Joshua smile. Gustav doesn't answer.

Joshua moves his hand to pull his gold pocket watch from the confines of his black suit jacket. "We should probably be getting to work," he says pointedly.

Gustav looks at Joshua then back at me. He hesitates for a moment, and then he says, "I'm sorry I waste your morning."

"It's okay," I say.

Joshua pulls a card from the cardholder in his pocket and

hands it to Gustav. "If you want more information about join-ing the suit, you give me a call. But call me and only me."

Gustav nods, and Joshua and I stand and walk out of Casteel's together, holding hands. I know it is only pretend, that when we hit the sidewalk, Joshua will drop my hand and shoot me a smile.

But still.

I am right, of course, and one block up, he drops my hand. "Maybe it wasn't such a good idea to put your number in the paper," Joshua says, sounding just a little bit like Ilsa.

"He seemed harmless enough," I say. "Just lonely, that is all."

He frowns. "Margie, that's how every single criminal I've come across seems, at first."

I think about Charles Bakerfield offering me a ride, and I cringe. I wonder what Joshua would think about that, but I know I will not tell him, because then I will also have to tell him about leaving work so early.

"No." Joshua shakes his head. "I didn't like the way he was looking at you. I'm sorry, Margie. This is all my fault." He pauses. "I'm taking the ad out of the paper."

"Okay," I say, and as we walk together in the office build-ing, I cannot seem to erase the smile from my face.

CHAPTER THIRTY-SEVEN

A WEEK PASSES, THEN TWO. THOUGH JOSHUA HAS TAKEN the ad out of the paper, I still receive a few more calls from Rabbi Epstein's Jews, bringing our number of interested people up to twelve. "That is still not enough," Joshua tells me early one morning, sighing the heaviest of sighs, and I nod. "There has to be a better way."

Joshua has taken a new case, handed down to him by his father: Herbert Bittlesby, who killed a man by accident when he was driving after a night of drinking. Herbert is a thin, nervous-looking man, who twitches his brown eyes in an annoying fashion. Shelby does not find him creepy, and she tells me she feels sorry for him. I assume this is because he is an accidental murderer, and a nervous one at that, but still, he is a murderer all the same.

Each time Herbert arrives at the office, which has been three times so far, and also the one time that Charles

Bakerfield has come back since offering me a ride, I can't help but think about what Joshua said, that he would like to leave this place, to start his own firm, to do good in the world. *There has to be something else,* he told me. I want Joshua to leave, but I also don't. If he leaves, what will happen to my job, to me, if I cannot see him every day? And he might ask me to come with him, but then, would my days be filled helping him find mistreated Jews? Finding a better way to do what he is doing with this group litigation, out in the open?

"Margie." Shelby interrupts my thoughts one afternoon, about two weeks after Joshua and I have shared breakfast. "Peggy and I are going to John Wanamaker's to shop for dresses on Saturday. Do you want to come?"

"Dresses?" I ask her.

"Wedding dresses."

"For you?" I ask.

She shakes her head. "I want to see what styles look good on both you and Peg. She's taller than you, so it might be tricky, but we'll find something. I promise I won't be one of *those* brides who makes you wear something truly awful."

"Saturday I can't," I say.

She frowns. "You're studying?"

I shake my head, and I commit myself to the only lie that I think Shelby will find acceptable. "I have a date," I say. Then I add for good measure, "With a nice American man."

"Not Joshua." She frowns.

"Of course not," I whisper.

"Who is it?" she asks, her voice lilting with excitement, and then I feel a little bad for creating this imaginary man.

"You don't know him. He lives in my building." I pause. "And whatever dress Peggy likes, that'll be fine by me."

❁

Saturday. Even if it were not for the fact that I would not try on dresses in front of Shelby and Peggy, I would not go to Wanamaker's with her on a Saturday. Saturday is the Shabbat day, the day of rest.

God created the universe in six days, and on the seventh day He rested. The seventh day, it is holy.

I am across an ocean, a lifetime, housed within a second skin, no longer a Jew. No longer a believer in God. My candle, my whispered Hebrew prayer, my day of rest, they are a comfort in their steadiness, their ability to stay unchanged. Every single week.

It is not religion; it's ritual.

Religion is breath, Margot, Mother said.

But what I have come to understand as I watch the lonely flicker of my candle and listen for the faintest echo of Mother's voice is this: sometimes we breathe because we have to, not because we want to.

CHAPTER THIRTY-EIGHT

"All right," Shelby says, waltzing off the elevator a few minutes before nine on Monday morning. "Peggy and I found the perfect dresses. You like pink, don't you?"

"Of course." I nod obligingly, thinking about the pink Cadillac in the Pelt driveway. Actually, I hate pink right now. But still, I am about to ask Shelby about the sleeve length, when the elevator doors open again, and Ezra storms out, his face the color of Penny's tomato dress.

Shelby quickly has a seat and picks up her phone, raising her eyebrows at me, so I pick up my phone too. Ezra does not stop by my desk or even glance at me to inquire if Joshua is with someone. Instead, he storms right past and swings open Joshua's door, a rolling, raging thundercloud about to explode.

I crane my neck to see through the glass window, and Joshua is speaking on the phone, though he quickly hangs up when he notices his father standing there in front of him.

Ezra slams Joshua's door shut, and his anger is momentarily muffled, the sounds of yelling muted through the paper walls. Until suddenly his anger becomes clear, and I hear the words, "Robertson . . . What kind of an idiot do you take me for?"

My heart thuds rapidly in my chest as Shelby shoots me a nervous look. We have been discovered, Joshua and I. I begin to sweat, to shake a little. I might vomit. I close my eyes, and I feel the roughness of hands against my neck. *There are no hands.* Not here. Not now. But still, I feel them, dragging me down the steps, bruising every single bone along the way, yet I could not cry out.

I will not cry out, not here. Not at my desk.

"Margie," Shelby whispers. "Margie, what's wrong?"

It is an effort to breathe. In and out. In and out. In and out.

"No," Joshua's voice booms back, unexpected. "I'm not going to drop it." There is more yelling, more words I can't make out. I inhale, exhale. The hand grabs my neck. *No, it doesn't.*

"Yes, you are," Ezra yells. "I'm your boss, and you'll do as I say."

"Is that all you are," Joshua yells, "my boss?" There is quiet for a moment, and I feel even through the walls that I can hear the heavy sounds of Joshua and his father breathing. Then, more muffled words I cannot understand.

Joshua's door flies open, and he is standing there, at the entryway, breathing hard. He looks to me, then Shelby, then back to me. "Margie," he says loud enough for a few of the other lawyers to walk to the edge of their offices to stare at him. "I'm leaving."

Shelby stares at me hard and shakes her head a little. I can feel her panic gripping me across the desk.

"Will you come with me?" Joshua asks. His gray-green eyes break on my face, and he says my name, his voice softening: "Margie?"

Shelby shakes her head again, and her eyes, they remind me of Ilsa's now, ripe with worry.

I clutch my satchel from underneath my desk, and somehow, I'm not sure how, I stand up. I look at Joshua. His eyes catch mine, and they are filled with something, or a combination of somethings: sadness or anger, mixed with excitement.

"Margie, sit down," Shelby whispers just as Ezra walks out of Joshua's office and looks to me, then Joshua. Ezra doesn't say anything, but his face is even redder than before. He clenches his fists tightly at his sides, and he stares hard at Joshua. His eyes are green, I see now, greener than Joshua's. Joshua breaks his gaze and looks at me again.

"Come on," he says to me gently, and he nods in the direction of the elevator.

I walk behind him, feeling the weight of Ezra's green eyes and Shelby's brown ones, as if both of them, they are burning holes through the back of my sweater.

❈

Once the elevator doors shut Joshua exhales. And then so do I, letting out breath I did not even realize I'd been holding.

"Thank you," Joshua whispers to me. But I do not answer him because I am thinking that we have been discovered, and we have escaped, and yet I can feel my fingers trembling. I tighten their grip on the strap of my satchel.

I realize now that I do not know where it is we are going, that I may have just quit my job, and that if I am not getting a steady paycheck, I will not be able to continue to pay my rent. But I still cannot speak.

"I'm sorry it happened like that," Joshua is saying, "but I would've asked you to come anyway, you know, when I left this place. I don't think I can work without you anymore, Margie."

I don't think I can be without you anymore. No, that is not what he said. Work. Work without me. This is all about work. "Okay," I finally say, and the word sounds hollow, far away, in my voice.

The elevator pulls us down, down, down, slowly, gently. We have been discovered, and we are escaping, in such an American way. No rough hands on the back of my neck, no bruised shins bumping against the staircase. We float down in an elevator, unscathed.

"I guess you're wondering what happened in there?" I realize Joshua is still talking, and maybe I have missed some of what he's been saying. I nod, though I think it is fairly clear what happened. "My father played golf with Robert Robertson, and Robertson mentioned seeing the ad in the *Inquirer* a few weeks ago. My father is a smart guy. He put two and two together." Joshua laughs drily. "I guess my father figured there could not be two Mickey Mouse lawyers in this city wanting to form a group litigation against Robertson."

The elevator falls slowly and comes to a stop. "You're not a Mickey Mouse lawyer," I say.

"I know," he says. "But my father sure thinks I am."

The elevator doors open, and Joshua and I step out into the lobby. I stop by the sandwich cart, mainly because I am unsure exactly where we are going, and Joshua seems to be walking slowly, as if in a dream. He stares at me and shakes his head. "I finally did it, didn't I? I told my father the truth about what I want to do with my life."

"The truth?" I say, and my voice escapes in a whisper, as if that word, it is so foreign to me now, I can barely comprehend its meaning.

"That I don't want to defend murderers, that I don't want to work for him. It felt good. It felt really, really damn good." He pauses. "You know what? I think my mother would be proud."

The truth.

Joshua is still talking, his voice bubbling with excitement. He is saying something about finding an office, or maybe starting out of his home, about how he will build something from the ground up, how we both will, together.

Together.

"Joshua." I say his name, and he stops talking and smiles at me. His gray-green eyes catch in the sallow light of the lobby. They are so full of life and American entitlement. His truth, it is so easy. I put my hand to my mouth, realizing I have just called him by his first name out loud, the way I do so often in my head. But he doesn't seem to notice.

"Don't worry, Margie," he says, grabbing my hand. "I'll make sure you still get paid. And once things get off the ground, and you get certified as a paralegal, we'll really make a run of it, you and I."

"Okay," I say. He drops my hand, and then he raises his own hand, as if he is about to touch my cheek, to trace it with his finger, the way Peter once did, only he stops just short and then instead reaches and slowly tucks a brown curl behind my ear.

"Thank you," he repeats, letting his hand linger by my cheek. "For coming with me. For believing in me. It means so much, Margie. I can't even tell you how much. Really."

I nod. "Joshua." I say his name again. And it is right there, on the tip of my tongue. The skin has peeled itself back, and so easily, I could say it. *Joshua, I am not Margie Franklin. I am not a Gentile. I want to come with you, but I do not know if I can help you with your case, you see, because I too, I am a victim of Jew haters. Only, I do not even like thinking this word—"victim"—much less saying it, out loud.*

Joshua is so close to me, I can feel his breath on my face, and his fingertip, it traces the outline of my cheek now, gently. "Margie," he whispers, and I have the strangest feeling that he is about to kiss me.

"Mr. Rosenstein!" A familiar voice shouts Joshua's name, from the bottom of the stairwell, just on the other side of the elevator. I look up, and Shelby is standing there, gasping for breath, so I know she has just run down the seven flights of steps. Her pale freckled forehead is shining with sweat.

Joshua moves his hand away from my face, turns toward her, and frowns.

"Mr. Rosenstein," she shouts again.

"What is it, Miss McKinney?" It is hard to tell whether he is confused or annoyed, or a little of both.

"It's your father," she says, gasping for breath. "I've called for an ambulance."

❖

It takes Joshua a moment to process what Shelby is saying, and when he does, he turns and runs, without hesitation. He presses the elevator button hard, over and over again, and then gives up and runs for the stairs.

Shelby walks toward me. Her face is beaming red, her hands shaking. I reach out for one of her hands, and we walk toward the elevator holding on to each other.

"What happened?" I whisper.

"I don't know," she says, and her voice trembles. "He just collapsed. He was standing there, and then he was on the floor, and I couldn't even tell if he was breathing." She gets the words out, as if she is choking on them, in between tears. "Oh my God," she is saying. "Oh my God."

I think about the look on Joshua's face as he ran, as he pushed the elevator button, over and over again. And I know that Joshua loves his father. Even with everything else. Ezra is his father, and he loves him. Of course he does.

"It'll be okay," I tell Shelby as we step into the elevator, and it rises again. "Everything will be fine." But inside, I feel the same as when I held on so tightly to my sister's hand, standing in line at the camp.

It's just a little ink. It's nothing, I told her. *Don't scream, don't cry, don't be afraid. Keep your head down and your voice low. Keep moving forward, do as they say. Everything will be fine.*

CHAPTER THIRTY-NINE

❖

AFTER THE AMBULANCE HAS TAKEN EZRA AND JOSHUA AWAY, Shelby and I sit across from each other at our desks, staring at each other but not saying anything for what feels like a long while. I wonder if it is okay for me to be sitting here after I have quit, though I realize all I have done is taken the elevator down with Joshua and then back up with Shelby, and besides, with Ezra now riding in the ambulance, I do not think there will be anyone else here who would ask me to leave.

Shelby's fingers twitch in the air, until finally she fumbles through her bag for a cigarette. She tosses the pack of Kents to me, and I hesitate for a moment before taking a cigarette out. Shelby always says smoking relaxes her, so maybe I should try it.

Normally, the girls don't smoke inside the office, just some of the lawyers. But with Ezra being pulled out on a stretcher, and Joshua leaving with him, it seems as if all decorum has been suddenly thrown away.

I clutch tightly to the cigarette and notice that my hands too, they are shaking. I put it loosely in my mouth and lean forward to catch on Shelby's lighter, and then I feel smoke burning in my lungs, as if I am running too hard, too far, too fast. I have had enough, and I crush the cigarette out in the empty coffee cup on Shelby's desk, which she is using as an ashtray.

Shelby takes another drag on her cigarette, leans back in her chair, and closes her eyes. "I've never seen it before," she whispers, after a little while.

"What?" I ask her.

"Death. So close, right in front of me. Just like that." I nod. "Have you?"

Now I close my eyes, and I can feel the weight of my sister's small hand, holding on to me, on the train. Mrs. van Pels, naked and small and without her rabbit fur. Mother, whispering to me at night in the camp, her breath rattling in her chest. "No," I lie. "I haven't."

"Oh, Margie, it was awful. I don't know how Peg does it all the time. I could never be a nurse like her." She shakes her head and blows a funnel of smoke in my direction. "And Mr. Rosenstein, he's such a big, powerful man. You just don't imagine him falling like that, you know?"

I nod, though in my head, I am revising slightly my image of Pim, coming straight from the camp after it was liberated to the Prinsengracht. Why have I always imagined him as the Pim I knew in the annex, still strong, with broad shoulders and girth much like Ezra Rosenstein? The Pim straight from the camp must've been a smaller man, broken, skeletal. I try to make the image come that way, but I cannot, no matter how hard I try to force it.

The clock by the elevator strikes noon, and Shelby squashes her cigarette in the coffee cup and stands up. "I'm going to the hospital to see what's going on," she says to me. "You coming?"

I think about Joshua's face, as he stood there, in the lobby. *I cannot be without you anymore, Margie. No, work. Work without you.* But I imagine Joshua, like Shelby, has never stood so close to death before. And then he rode there, all the way to the hospital in the ambulance, with his father.

"Yes," I tell her, standing up, grabbing my satchel. "Of course."

❖

Shelby and I ride the bus together up Market Street, toward the University of Pennsylvania Hospital, where I wonder if Peggy is on duty. I hope she is, because she is caring and assured and the kind of nurse who brings real comfort.

Shelby is quiet, which is so un-Shelby-like that I turn to look at her several times, just to check if she has fallen asleep. But she is still there, her shoulder bouncing next to mine on the city bus, her gaze straight ahead, serious, trancelike. I keep expecting her to ask me what happened, just before, when I followed Joshua down in the elevator, but she does not.

I turn and look out the window at the city blurring by me. Then I shut my eyes for a second, and all I can see is Pim, Pim, Pim. And not the way he is now, an old man about to turn seventy, living in Switzerland with a new wife, a lot of money, and, I imagine, a mountain-high pile of correspondence about the book he published. No. I picture him the way he was then, in the annex, when sometimes he would look at me, seeming defeated, and I would want to hug him, just to inflate him again. I would want to hug him and tell him he had done so much to keep us safe. He had done so much. For me.

I was the one the Germans wanted, I might have told him. *You could've given me away. But you didn't.*

I never told him this, though.

One time in the annex—it was night—and everyone was sleeping, even Peter. I got up from the divan in his room to tiptoe back downstairs, but then I saw Pim, awake, just sitting there in the front room staring at the wall.

"Margot," he whispered, not noticing me until I stood there, right in front of him. "You're not sleeping."

"Neither are you," I pointed out.

"But you are still a growing girl. You need your sleep, Bubbeleh." He hadn't used his pet name for me in so long that I'd almost forgotten it had existed. And then there he was, saying it again—"Bubbeleh"—the word hanging in the stillness of night in the annex. His voice was warmth, and it captured me. He patted the space next to him, and I sat down there.

I laid my head against his shoulder. He had strong, broad shoulders, even then. "I could sleep here, maybe," I whispered, because suddenly I was so very tired. I remembered what it felt like to want to find sleep, in the darkness. I remembered what it felt like when night had once been my friend, not my enemy.

"Go ahead," Pim whispered into my hair. "Close your eyes. I will keep you safe."

"Pim," I whispered, my voice tracing a circle in the darkness. "I love you."

"I love you too, Bubbeleh," he whispered back.

This memory is so distant, so hard to keep clear in my brain. Every so often I find it, and I try to keep it close to me. But as quickly as it comes to me, it fades away again. Too much has happened since then, to both of us.

Mostly now I can imagine Pim there, after the war, standing at the door to the office at 263 Prinsengracht, his heart full with the hardest and roundest of emotions: hope. I imagine Miep handed him the diaries once, and at first he refused them. "No," he would've told her, handing them back to her. "My girls will be back."

And then he waited, and he waited, and he waited.

"Otto," Miep's kind, small voice would've said to him as she placed her tiny hand on his shoulder. "Take the diaries. Read them. They are something."

"I tried to save them, and I failed," Pim might have said, tears perched in his brown eyes.

"There was nothing you could do," Miep would've told him. "You did everything you could. You kept them safe for years."

"But it wasn't enough," Pim might have said. "Both of my girls, gone."

"Take the books."

He took them.

Nothing can't mean something, Mother had said, of the ink.

But Pim, his eyes saw the world so much differently than Mother's, everything in opposite. Pim would've said it like this: *Something can't mean nothing.* Or: *Someone can't mean nothing. Two someones can't mean nothing.*

Oh, Pim.

"What did you say?" Shelby asks me, finally speaking as the bus has stopped a block from the hospital, and she stands to get off.

"Hmm?" I murmur.

"You were just saying something?"

"No." I shake my head. "I wasn't saying anything."

"Yes," she said. "You were talking about a pin."

"Oh, that," I say, and I can't believe I have thought about him so much that I have spoken his name, out loud, accidentally. "Don't worry about it," I tell Shelby. "It was nothing."

CHAPTER FORTY

SHELBY AND I WALK THROUGH THE WIDE EMERGENCY entrance of the University of Pennsylvania Hospital, with our arms linked, but not the way they are when Shelby, skipping, pulls me toward the bar. Now it is as if we are holding each other up. We are tied together, pulling each other's weight, like sisters. *No,* I remind myself, *friends.*

Shelby has been here before to visit Peg, and she leads me straight to the emergency area nurses' station, where Peg works. The waiting area surrounding the station is crowded, and I briefly look around and see a young woman bleeding from her arm and a small child crying at her feet. My stomach turns, and I look back, to focus on Peg, who is tall and serious and confident in her starched white nurse's uniform and pointed hat, and who walks quickly in circles behind the station, grabbing charts from a large white filing cabinet.

Shelby lets go of my arm and runs to her sister, and Peg

turns, reaches across the desk, and wraps Shelby in a hug. I struggle to breathe for a moment as I am standing there by myself, watching them.

Peg points to the elevator, Shelby nods, and then she is back at my side. "Come on," she says.

"What did Peggy say?" I ask.

"He's up in critical care. They think it was a massive heart attack."

I think of Joshua, and I am overcome by sadness. *Is that all you are,* he'd yelled at his father this morning, *my boss?* Of course, that wasn't all he was. Joshua knew it then, and even more, I am sure, he knows it now.

"But he's still alive," Shelby is saying now as the elevator rises, her voice hopeful.

The elevator doors open and I see, right away, a small crowd of them, huddled together in the blue waiting area. My eyes fall immediately on Mrs. Greenberg, Penny's mother, whom I have seen from time to time around the office. She is a large woman, tall and big-boned, and has never struck me as the least bit graceful, as her daughter is, though now her spine is hunched, her expression pale blank. She wears a green hat and clutches a pile of tissues in her hands, and she holds on to her husband with one arm, Joshua with the other.

My heart bursts to look at Joshua, and I hold tightly to Shelby's hand, holding myself back. After a moment he looks up, and he catches my eyes. His gray-green eyes are red-rimmed with sorrow, and they are lacking their usual light. I let go of Shelby's hand to wave, and he waves back and shoots me a meager smile.

Joshua turns, whispers something to Penny's mother, stands up, and then he is walking toward me. His smile is even and somber and strong, and his eyes they are speaking to me, as if suddenly I am the only one. I am the only one who can understand him. And I can. I can.

"Josh, honey." I hear her voice from somewhere not too far behind me, and I startle. It is shrill and wily and I have the urge to cover my ears, to keep it from hurting me. "I brought back coffee for everyone."

I turn, and Penny stands there, pure as snow in a white tapered dress cinched at the waist with a snakelike navy-blue belt. Our eyes meet for a second, and then Penny looks away quickly. "How sweet," she murmurs, walking past me and handing the coffee tray to Joshua. "The girls from the office came down." She leans up and kisses him purposefully on the cheek, her pink lips, as if she is marking him, right there, like that.

"Thanks for the coffee, Pen," I hear Joshua say, and I cannot look anymore. I cannot stand there and watch while he kisses her back.

"I have to go," I whisper to Shelby.

"Margie," she says. "Wait, don't leave me here all alone."

But she is not all alone. Her sister is just downstairs.

I let go of Shelby's hand, and I do not wait for the elevator. I pull open the door to the stairwell and run, quickly, down the three flights.

CHAPTER FORTY-ONE

THE EARLY MAY SUNSHINE HITS MY FACE, WARM, NEARLY too warm for springtime. It is almost summer now, my favorite season once, when I was not afraid to bare my skin and jump into the Baltic Sea or the IJsselmeer, where the water was crisp and blue. We missed experiencing one full summer while stuck in the annex and two halves. Also, two springs gone, just like that. As a girl, I used to love all the things spring and summer: the feel of water and sunshine against my skin. But I do not like the summertime in Philadelphia, the way the heat makes lying even more oppressive, makes my secret an even bigger burden to bear.

May used to be a month of promise: the end of school was so near, the sweetness of summer and all the freedom that came with it. May is also Pim's birthday month, and even now, every year as the date approaches, May 12, I still think of him, getting one year older. This year, he will be turning seventy.

In May of 1944, Pim was turning fifty-five. He was still young enough to be our Pim, but almost old enough to be something else. He was graying then, but just around the temples. Now I wonder if he is completely gray, looking more like a grandfather than a father, though he cannot be a grand-father without me and my sister, a thought which makes me desperately sad.

"I know!" my sister said in 1944, the week before his birth-day, one midafternoon as we lay in her room. Her voice was just a little too loud. I shushed her, and she rolled her eyes at me. She was next to me on the bed, her hip folded easily against my own. "We should write Pim a poem for his birth-day this year." She spoke a bit softer.

I looked up from my diary and nodded in agreement. Yes, that was just the kind of thing Pim would love. Maybe it would even cheer him up, make his birthday something spe-cial despite our being trapped. We were rats, and we were Jews. But we still celebrated things. Miep brought flowers and cake and we lit the menorah for Hanukkah. "We should write it in English," I told her. "Show him how far we've come in our studies."

"How far you've come, you mean," she said.

"You know some English now too," I told her, and she rolled her eyes again. "And Pim will be so happy to see we have learned something while we've been here. Like two pres-ents in one."

"Fine," she agreed. "An English poem, for Pim's birthday."

To Pim on His 55th Birthday

Pim, Pim, you do not dim
Even sometimes when things look grim
Your smile is wide and your hair is trim
And we think we are not on a whim
Or even out there on a limb
To say we love you, our darling Pim!

We chanted it to him, like a song, on the night of his birthday. May of 1944, and so many Allied bombings in Europe that, surely, the war was almost over. Pim would not spend another birthday in the annex. None of us would.

Mother smiled wide that night, and Pim laughed and hugged us both close to his chest. "My girls." He shook his head. "What good English." He kissed each of us on the top of our heads, twice. "I will cherish this," he said. "Forever."

Even now, the words, they play in my head from time to time. A silly, stupid child's rhyme. The paper we wrote them on, I'm sure it was destroyed so very long ago. But I wonder if sometimes the words, they still play themselves in my father's mind too.

❦

After I leave the hospital, I take the bus back to Market Street, and then I find myself wandering, almost aimlessly, on the street, hearing the words from Pim's birthday song in my head. I am not lost, but I am without direction, and even though they sound the same, they are not. It's just that now I'm not sure exactly where I'm headed. Not back to work. Not now, because what is there, waiting for me? Not home, not in the middle of the day, when all I have there is Katze.

I cross the street, and then I see it there, the way I have before. I wonder if my feet took me here on purpose, overtaken by homesickness that I can never get through no matter how much I think I can, or might want to. It is always lurking there, just beyond the surface. Even in the Jewish law firm. Especially in the Jewish law firm.

The letters up in front of me, they gleam a putrid red on the marquee, the color once, of the swastikas defiling the broken wall of Judischausen. They assault me, but still I stop there, and I stare at them. Bright red letters: *The Diary of Anne Frank. Introducing: Millie Perkins. Starring: Shelley Winters.*

I buy a ticket, and I walk inside the theater.

CHAPTER FORTY-TWO

IT IS COLD INSIDE THE THEATER, AND SUDDENLY I AM hungry. So hungry that my stomach hurts and rumbles, and I cannot remember exactly the last time I have eaten something whole. I buy some popcorn at the concession stand in the lobby and find myself a seat inside the wide empty theater. It is empty, of course, because it is the middle of the day, and people are working, and so many people have already seen this movie. And I imagine it is not the kind of movie you would come back to see twice.

I take a seat in the last row, quite close to the exit, and where I can see everyone else who might come into the theater.

It is cold, and I pull my black sweater tight across my chest, hanging on to my arms to warm up before digging my hand into the carton of popcorn. The corn is warm and salty and buttery, and I chew it, and I chew it. My chewing is loud, though, of course, there is no one else here to complain.

The lights dim, and the curtain rises. The screen is black at first, and there is an overture, the heavy sound of trumpets, then strings, which I imagine the director felt was both serious and emotional all at once. Oh, the drama—the overture seems to go on forever. I wish the movie would just start already.

Finally, there is a picture. A sea of clouds, awash with seagulls as the actors' names play across the screen, the *i* in Millie's name dotted with an upside-down teardrop. I roll my eyes, just the way my sister always did. There is a note that scenes were filmed in the annex thanks to the city of Amsterdam, and something clenches in my chest so hard I cannot breathe. I am not prepared for this part, to see it again. I did not know they filmed there, at the actual spot where we once lived.

The movie begins: a man is standing there on the Prinsengracht. Oh, the Prinsengracht. Just the way it was, just the way I remember. The canal, then the street right beside it with the beautiful, old, linked, brick, multistoried buildings. I reach my hand out, as if the Prinsengracht is close enough for me to touch it. *Home.*

Up on the big screen, the man turns, and I realize he is supposed to be Pim, returned from the war. He bears a likeness to Pim, but only distantly, some long-lost cousin we never even knew. The man enters the office, then climbs the steps to the annex, and he wraps himself in a scarf he finds—whose it is supposed to be I am not sure. Mother's, maybe? Though she had nothing of the sort. Then the woman who is supposed to be Miep enters, reaches for a book on some sort of shelf—the diary, I assume, and says it has been there the whole time, where my sister left it.

I shake my head, and bite my lip, to suppress the urge to yell out, *No, no, that is not where she left it. It was on the floor. In Peter's room. It fell from her hands as they carried her out. She never kept it on a bookshelf! She hid it away, in her mattress, just like I did with mine.*

But then I see her—Millie Perkins—and I forget about the book for the moment. She bounces into a room, into the annex. The place is familiar, but the people, they are all wrong. Millie, she is nearly laughable. She is a woman, not a girl. She is a model, slim and graceful and filled with infallible beauty. She is way too old to be my sister, way too polished. But wait, where is Margot? Oh, there I am, somewhere off in the background, like a second-class citizen. At least I am attractive, more so than in real life.

I chew my popcorn, throwing it in handfuls in my mouth. It tastes so good, buttery and salty and warm. I eat, and I watch the screen as if in a trance. My eyes cannot let go of these people and their story. I do not know them. This story, it is filled with so much danger and romance and hope. Why is there so much ridiculous hope?

You're all going to die, I want to shout at the screen, *all of you.*

You will be stripped and shaven and broken and tattooed. Fleas will dance off your body like sparks, and the air will become a film that suffocates you until you can no longer breathe. Stop smiling, Millie. Honestly. The annex is not that beautiful. The world is not that beautiful. My sister, she understood that.

And then there is Peter. Oh, Peter. He is not at all as handsome as I remember him being in real life. He is the one to which the silver screen does no justice. The movie is in black and white, and so there are no eyes blue enough to be the sea. He is strangely goofy, making eyes at Millie Perkins like a dummy as she chases after Mouschi.

When I see them together, I laugh a little, and I dig into the popcorn. My hand scrapes the bottom of the cardboard carton. I chew louder, and I need a napkin, but I am not about to stand up to walk back to the concession stand to get one.

Margot is quiet. So quiet. She barely says a word the entire time, as if she spent two years of her life a mute in the background, not at all the kind of girl who would kiss Peter, in his room, in the darkness. No, in the movie she is the kind of girl who, one night, after she has been ill, blurts out at the dinner table that she wishes everything would end already. I hear these words come out of her mouth, and I start laughing. I am laughing and laughing so hard, that then I am crying. The screen is blurry; it is hard to see, to focus. The strangers on the screen swim in front of my eyes.

Then Millie and Peter stand in front of the window, where the sky tumbles, large and beautiful. They hold on to each other, just the way the book said they did. There are sirens so loud and so obvious—movie sirens—from the street below. Then the screech of brakes, and Millie and Peter, they cling to each other so hard, so fast, their lips meeting. And Margot, she is nowhere to be found.

I close my eyes, and then I am holding on to him on the divan.

Peter? My sister stands there, saying his name.

There were no sirens. Just quiet one moment, my sister's voice, then banging on the annex door.

On the big screen, the music swirls. The lovers embrace and are still kissing with deep movie-star passion, just as Shelby said.

I stand up quickly, forgetting about the popcorn, and the carton tumbles, spilling kernels to the sticky floor.

I know what happens next. And I cannot watch anymore.

I run through the front of the theater, and I hit the street, where the sunlight is too bright and burns my eyes. I squint as I run back toward Ludlow Street, the stupid poem we wrote for Pim playing itself in my head. Only suddenly I cannot remember the order of it at all.

Pim, Pim, you are so dim. You like to do things on a whim. Your hair is gray; your world is grim. You are dead to me now, my dear sweet Pim.

CHAPTER FORTY-THREE

PIM AND I, WE NEVER FOUGHT THE WAY MY SISTER AND MY mother did. We never yelled or screamed harsh words at each other. I did not write angry things about him in my diary the way my sister did about my mother.

It was just that we all knew, all of us. My sister belonged to our father, and I belonged to my mother. We were split that way, two and two, and we always had been. Sometimes I wondered if it was by default, if Father would've paid more attention to me if given the chance. Was Mother only mine because she and my sister could not get along? But now, afterward, I have come to understand that could not have been it entirely.

Peter did not love his parents, not the way I loved mine. Sometimes he fought with them, but not like Joshua and Ezra do, or even like my mother and my sister did, when fire exploded between them, sparks of love and hate and passion falling into one. Mostly, they ignored each other. And Peter seethed, quietly.

"What about our parents?" I asked Peter once, in his room in the annex, in the middle of the night. "What will happen to them when we go to America." I thought about Mother and Pim, about the way she had begun to cling to him in the annex, holding on to his arm with her thin fingers in a way she had never done on the Merwedeplein.

We were together all the time, every second, every day. For two years. I didn't even have the capacity to imagine it then, this person I have now become without them. But Peter simply shrugged, as if he could imagine life without them. I remembered his story about bringing Mouschi into the annex, how he felt his parents didn't care about him. "They gave you life," I reminded him.

He frowned at me, and reached across the bed for his cat. "Not everyone is a good parent like yours." He paused. "Not every father is smart and kind the way yours is, Margot." He stroked Mouschi's fur roughly with his fingertips. "You know why I never talked to you at school, really?" he asked.

"Why?" I murmured. But I was thinking that the Lyceum felt so far away, like something in a dream. School. Books. Teachers. Walking through the halls with shoes and a light step, and an easy sense of contentment. Had I ever really done those things? Had I ever existed in a life, really and truly of my own, outside the confines of this annex on the Prinsengracht?

"You had so much," he was saying. "And you took it all for granted. You thought everyone had what you did."

"And you could tell that, without ever having talked to me?" I could not keep the annoyance from my voice.

"Yes," he said. "You did well in school. Everybody loved you there. All the teachers. Your home on the Merwedeplein was so large and nice. And your father always lit up when he talked about you and your sister."

"How do you know all this?" I asked him. I had no idea where Peter lived before the annex, or how his father had talked about him. I'd seen him before at school. I'd noticed him and his blue, blue eyes. But we'd never spoken. I'd never thought much about him before the annex.

"I just do," he said. "You and your sister, you never understood how lucky you are."

"You don't know everything," I told him, standing up. It was the middle of the night, and the moonlight cast an eerie slant on Mouschi's face, lighting his eyes yellow until they were glowing. I felt as if my own face was glowing hot, under Peter's words, the idea that somehow I was spoiled, like my sister. That I did not appreciate the things I had, or that I just assumed that everyone's parents loved them the way Pim and Mother loved us.

"Come on. Sit back down," Peter whispered.

"I don't think so," I huffed. "I think I'll go back to my room tonight."

"Margot," he called after me, gently. But I was already tiptoeing out, down the stairs, to my cot in my parents' room, where Pim's gentle snore rattled in his chest and Mother gasped quietly in her sleep.

I lay on the cot for a long while, with my eyes open, wondering if Peter was right, if I never understood it, everything I had. Everything I would eventually lose.

CHAPTER FORTY-FOUR

IN THE TWO AND A HALF WEEKS SINCE EZRA'S COLLAPSE, Joshua has been to the office only twice. I have been in every day, since Joshua called me at home the morning after and asked me to please come in to work, at least until he knew where things stood with his father. And so I understood, I had not quit my job at all, but only ridden down in an elevator and then back up. Still, for some reason I have felt different sitting at my desk. But maybe that is just because Joshua's office has remained mostly empty, only darkness clouding his glass window.

Each morning when he has not come in, Joshua has been phoning in, presumably from the hospital, with instructions. And Shelby and I have been rescheduling appointments, pushing back courthouse meetings, and, at Joshua's request, handing Ezra's most pressing cases over to other lawyers in the firm.

His voice on the phone is solid and cool, all business, nothing else. And the two times I have seen him, when he has come in, Joshua has not looked at me, in the eyes, not even for a second. He has walked off the elevator, in casual brown spring pants and a short-sleeved plaid button-down shirt. He is a different man without the suit and the tie. Younger and larger all at once. He seems to take up more space somehow, now that his father is not around. His voice booms a little louder. And he has run into his office, past my desk, without so much as a look.

Without Joshua in the office, I find myself daydreaming at my desk and thinking again about Mrs. Pelt and Eleanor. What if I was wrong? I wonder. What if she was not Mrs. Pelt at all, but just a friend with a pink Cadillac who liked to visit? She hadn't told me her name. But she had implied that she'd chosen the house somehow. Maybe she owns it and Peter rents it from her? Maybe she is just the landlady? But no matter how many what-ifs fall in my brain, none of them feel true or right, and yet even though Joshua is not here, I cannot bring myself to leave early, to go back there again. Every time I think of it, I am stopped by that image from the movie, the two of them kissing by the window as sirens blare in the background. It is a fake image, but still, when I reimagine it, over and over again in my head, my mind does not picture their movie faces, but their real ones.

"Margie," Shelby whispers across the desk one afternoon, interrupting my thoughts. I look up, and she is pulling her pack of Kents from her satchel. She holds them toward me. I shake my head. In Ezra's absence, now, all the girls have begun taking their smokes at their desks. I wonder if it is the changing times, the brink of a new decade, as Shelby says, or if it is just that Joshua was not the only one in the office who was afraid of Ezra's wrath. The air feels more still in here, calmer somehow, without Ezra, even though it is now tinged with a steady haze of smoke.

Now Shelby lights her smoke and then smiles at me. "We've set a date for the wedding," she says.

"Oh?" I say, because in the midst of everything else, I have nearly forgotten about Shelby's wedding, about the pink bridesmaids' dresses she and Peg found.

"Saturday November twenty-first," she tells me, inhaling her smoke, then exhaling.

November. It will be cold, and thus we will most probably wear long-sleeved dresses. But Saturday, my day of rest. I hope it will be after sunset. Before I have a chance to ask her anything, she divulges all the details: the Rittenhouse. At 7 P.M. "It's a little ritzy, but Ron wants only the best for me, and so does my father—"

"Shelby," I say, interrupting her, and she taps her smoke in the empty coffee cup and looks up. "Are you sure?"

"Am I sure?" She laughs. "Wouldn't you want a wedding at the Rittenhouse, Margie?"

"I would want a marriage," I tell her.

"A marriage?"

"A partnership with someone who loves me and respects me." *We will go to America,* Peter said. *We will be married. We will no longer be Jews. We will change our names. Become the*

Pelts. And all the while was he really kissing my sister by the window? Did he make it to America only to marry a redhead?

"Ron does love and respect me," she says, an edge of annoyance to her voice.

"I'm sorry," I say, because I did not mean to offend her. "I just want you to be happy."

She smiles at me. "I *am* happy. Have you ever seen me happier?"

The truth of it is, sitting there, tapping her smoke into her coffee cup, she looks a bit more nervous than I am used to seeing her, as if she too is hiding. But I wonder in Shelby's case if she is hiding from herself. "Just ask him about the hussy," I whisper across the desks. "It will be better to know the truth now than later."

"Oh, for goodness' sakes, Margie. You're a fine one to talk. Look at you, you're such a prude, sitting there in the heat, in your sweater."

I avert my eyes back to my typewriter, and Shelby and I don't say a word to each other for the rest of the day.

❈

It is the end of May by the time Ezra is released from the hospital, but even then, he does not come back to work.

"He's recuperating in Margate," Shelby tells me one morning, on a day when the temperature is predicted to hit ninety degrees, and I am dressed in my gray dress with the thinnest black cotton sweater I own, which is already, even in the morning, suffocating. Shelby and I have barely spoken since the other day when I pressed her to talk to Ron, so at first I am surprised she is talking to me.

"So Ezra is getting better, then?" I ask her.

She shrugs. "Joshua said recuperating, so yes, I think he is."

"Joshua told you?" I ask.

She nods. "He called me at home this morning to let me know he was moving his father down to Margate. And that he would be in for a full day of work tomorrow."

"He called *you* at home?" I ask, wondering why her and not me. And also, how silly I have been, to believe that his calling me, at home, meant something. Something other than work.

"Oh, Margie," Shelby says.

"What?" I ask her.

She looks at me for a moment, as if there is something more she wants to say, but then she seems to think better of it because she shakes her head. "Nothing," she finally says. "Just forget it."

"You're still angry with me?" I ask her.

"No, Margie. It's just . . . You're worried about me, that's why you want me to talk to Ron, right?" I nod. "Well, I worry about you too. Joshua will never see you the way you see him. He's your boss, and besides that, he's with Penny. And besides that, he's Jewish, and he's a lawyer. And you're . . . you."

I feel my cheeks turning hot, and my brow is already sweating from the heat, but I feel it turning hotter. *I cannot work without you, Margie.*

You're you, Shelby said. And yet she has no idea, none in the slightest, what that even means.

The elevator dings open, and just then Joshua steps off. He is dressed in his most handsome tailored black suit with a green-and-white-striped tie. He clutches tightly to his black leather attaché and walks, with a purpose, in my direction. It was not so long ago, I think, that we were walking off together, in the other direction. But, also, it feels like it has been forever. *You're you,* Shelby said.

"Margie." Joshua taps his hand on the side of my desk, then removes his hat and places it atop the rack. "Can I see you in my office?"

Shelby is most likely raising her eyebrows at me, but I do not turn to see. I stand and follow behind Joshua inside his office without even giving her a second glance.

※

The air is cooler inside Joshua's office, the room dark from lack of use. Joshua turns on the light now and puts his attaché down on his desk. "Shut the door, would you?" he asks me. I do, and then he tells me to have a seat.

He sits in his chair, so we are across the desk from one another. It is not a far distance, and yet, as his gray-green eyes turn to meet mine for the first time in weeks, it feels like an interminable space.

"Margie," he says, his voice and his expression softening. "I feel I owe you an explanation."

"You don't," I say, though that is a lie. I ache for it, to get that moment back, when Joshua and I stood in the lobby, by the sandwich cart. When his hand tucked a stray hair behind my ear and traced the outline of my cheek. When Joshua looked at me, for a moment, as if I were more than just his secretary, as if he was about to kiss me. When I almost told him, *This is the truth. This is who I really am.* Shelby has no idea.

"My father is very sick," Joshua is saying now. "And I need to do everything I can to make him happy." He pauses, and I think about everything he told me about his mother, about how hard it was to watch her disappear.

"I'm so sorry," I tell Joshua. "This must be very hard for you."

"Thank you," he says, and he casts his eyes downward, as if searching for something on his desk, in the papers that I have piled up there in his absence. "Anyway," he says, "all that stuff I said about leaving . . ." His voice trails off, and he shakes his head. His chestnut curls are still rumpled from his hat, and I have the urge to reach across the desk and fix them. "I was saying it in anger, and I shouldn't have. And I certainly shouldn't have involved you." He pauses. "While my father recovers, I'm going to make sure I do what needs to get done here on my cases and some of his too."

"And your dream of starting your own firm?" I say.

"That was silly," he says. "Stupid."

I nod, but I am thinking that Joshua is lying again. Maybe just to me, or maybe, also, to himself.

"As I said on the phone a few weeks ago, I want you to stay on here, as my secretary, of course. We'll be ceasing our group litigation, but you can keep your raise. For your continued loyalty," he adds.

I am not sure how I feel, about Joshua saying we will cease

working on our secret case. On one hand, I'm relieved, but I'm also, surprisingly, a bit annoyed. How can Joshua let Bryda and the others go, just like that? What about that night, when his eyes lit up, when he confessed to me his fear, that if Jews are not seen as equals, something terrible could happen again?

"You will stay on, won't you, Margie?"

I cannot work without you, Margie. I nod.

"Good." He sighs, leans back in his chair, and runs his fingers through his curls. I notice now his green tie looks too tight, and his neck is red, as if he is being suffocated by it, or it could be that he has already gotten too much sun in Margate. "For now, we'll be doing everything we can to make sure Mr. Bakerfield does not get convicted of murder. His trial is coming up in three weeks."

"But you said he was guilty," I say softly.

He leans forward in his chair, but he does not look at me now. He looks past me, toward the door, the glass window, as if there is something out there, just beyond his reach. "It is not our job to judge a client's guilt or innocence," he says, his voice devoid of emotion, as if this is a rote phrase he has practiced in his head, wanting it to take on meaning.

"I see," I say, standing, not sure whether I am annoyed or disappointed, but wanting suddenly to be back at my desk, even if that will mean Shelby's eyes staring at me just a little too hard.

"Oh, and Margie," Joshua says as I am about to open the door.

"Yes?" I turn back, and for a second our eyes do meet.

Joshua's eyes are melting, full of hurt and pain and tiredness, and I feel the weight of all of that on my own sagging, sweating shoulders. I want him to say something profound, something that will make me feel the way I did that morning, not so long ago, when he looked me in my eyes and spoke of the truth as if it were something glimmering and full of light, like Shelby's diamond.

"Miss Greenberg will be stopping by for lunch. See to it that you send her right back."

"Of course," I say again, and I drop my eyes before he does, before I can see it there, what it is exactly Joshua is thinking when he talks about Penny.

Five minutes before noon, Penny steps off the elevator, dressed for summer in a sleeveless floral print that is tied at her tiny waist with a pink ribbon. She clutches a wicker handbag—or no, it is too big; it is not a handbag but a picnic basket, and food overflows from its top.

"I have come to rescue Josh," she announces, not to anyone in particular. Shelby rolls her eyes in my direction. And then Penny stops in front of our desks and shoots me a tiny, irascible smirk as she pulls her Marilyn sunglasses atop her head. "Hello, Margie," she says. "Josh is expecting me." I nod, and she leans in closer. "How's he doing?" she whispers, as if we are friends, confidantes. Only, it is not a real question, as she does not wait for me to answer her. "This has been so tough on him." She sighs. "I expect we'll even move the wedding up, so his father can see it. It will help in his recovery, I'm sure. He'll be so happy."

"The wedding?" I ask, my voice trembling as my eyes search Penny's left hand for a diamond like Shelby's, or I would guess, twice the size of Shelby's. But I see nothing. Her thin pale fingers are bare.

She leans in closer and lowers her voice. "Of course, it's not official yet, but everyone has always known Josh and I would be married. Since we were little kids and our mothers pushed us into the sandbox together." She laughs and pulls back. "Anyway, he's expecting me for lunch."

I nod, and I don't even offer to buzz him as she stands up straight and parades herself into his office. She shuts the door behind her, so I don't even hear it, the sound of their laughter breaking against the sticky afternoon air.

CHAPTER FORTY-FIVE

A WEEK LATER, I AM SITTING AT MY DESK, STILL AVOIDING Shelby's eyes. It is nearly lunchtime, and each day I have watched the clock with trepidation, wondering if this will be the day that Penny will step off the elevator flashing a giant diamond in my face.

But today, just before noon, the elevator opens, and instead of Penny, Bryda Korzynski steps off, dressed in her blue Robertson's Finery uniform. My heart falls immediately into my stomach.

"I speak to Mr. Rosenstein," she says sharply as she approaches my desk, her brown eyes hard like stones, breaking me in two.

"Miss Korzynski," I manage to say, though my throat is parched and my voice barely escapes my throat. She narrows her eyes at me, and then walks purposefully toward Joshua's office door. "You can't go in there," I hear myself saying. "He's with another client." Charles Bakerfield has been inside Joshua's office all morning, his trial now two weeks away.

Bryda stops and turns, her brown eyes searing. "Then I wait," she says, sitting in the chair by my desk.

"Is there something I can help you with?" I ask, swallowing hard as I speak, trying not to choke on the words. *Just breathe. Breathe.* "Or can I schedule you an appointment for later in the week? He might be a while in there."

"You?" She shakes her head. "You come to my apartment. You say Mr. Rosenstein help me. Then he ignore me. He do not take my phone calls."

Her phone calls? They have not come through me, so Joshua must have given her his direct number.

Bryda glares at me now, and I pick up the phone to buzz Joshua, which is something I would normally never do when he is in a meeting with a client. But it is as if her eyes, they force me to do it. My fingers tremble as I press the button.

"What is it, Margie?" Joshua asks. "Is it my father?"

"No, no," I say quickly, feeling bad that I have frightened him in such a way. "I'm sorry to interrupt. But . . . Miss Korzynski is here, and she wants to see you. And she's refusing to come back later."

"Oh." He sighs. I cannot see him through the glass because Charles's tall frame, he is blocking my view, but I imagine Joshua putting his hand to his forehead, then running his fingers through his curls. "I didn't get a chance to call her back," he says. "Can you tell her?"

"Tell her?" I ask, surprised, though maybe I should not be, as Joshua has already asked me for so much with this case.

"That we're dropping the case. Let her off easy. You can say we just weren't able to get the support we needed, all right?"

"I . . ." I turn and lower my voice so she hopefully cannot hear me. "I don't think I can," I say.

He sighs again. "All right, then stall her for a while, until I'm finished here, and then I'll talk to her."

"Joshua." His name escapes me again, but this time I correct myself. "Mr. Rosenstein, I—"

"I'm hanging up now, Margie. I'm in a meeting, remember?"

His end goes to static, and then there I am, adrift in a flood, without even Joshua's large hand to pull me to safety.

❀

"Well?" Bryda's thickly accented voice hangs in the air. I turn and look at her, and though her brown eyes break me, suddenly I do not hate her anymore. To be a Jew, and to be treated badly for it. Even here, even in America. *We will no longer be Jews,* Peter said. But it strikes me how unfair it is, that you cannot be who you are, that you will be continually punished for the way you were born. Bryda, like me, lived through Auschwitz. She is mean and bitter and tired, but perhaps she has a right to be all those things. Suddenly I feel like a coward. Running, running. Still running, all these years later.

"What happened to your finger?" I hear myself asking, and then the moment the words escape my lips, I hold my hand to my mouth, realizing I have misspoken. That I have asked for too much.

She frowns, but something softens a little in her eyes. "There was accident," she says. "In camp."

"But you said it wasn't what I thought," I murmur.

"I say accident." She frowns. "My mother, she so sick, so tired. One day, she slip and drop brick on my finger and crush it." She pauses. "That not what you thought, was it?"

I shake my head because I suppose she is right. I did not think of an accident in the camp. "I'm sorry," I say.

Then I realize I do not hear the sound of Shelby's fingers on the keys or even feel the haze of her smoke washing across the desks. I glance in her direction, and she is staring at this interaction between Bryda and me with all the intensity with which she inhales a movie at the cinema. I swallow hard, and turn my eyes back toward Bryda, who has now fixed my face in a steady glare.

She narrows her brown eyes; she is full of hate and anger again, and now all of it, it is aimed directly at me. As if I were the one who carried her away in the middle of the night. Who accidentally took her finger. Who purposely took her family. *You know what worse than Gestapo? Snake.* "You not going to help me, are you?" she asks.

I don't respond, and she seems to take this as a no. Joshua said to stall her. How am I supposed to do that, when she is standing here, prodding me? "You," she yells. "You did this, didn't you. You told Mr. Rosenstein not to help me."

"I'm only his secretary," I hear myself saying, the words

seeming to float in somewhere from far away, disconnected from me. "The truth is, he just hasn't been able to get the support he needs for the case."

She narrows her eyes, so they are slits, barely even alive. "I see way he look at you," she says. "You more than secretary."

I can practically feel Shelby's eyebrows arching across the desk, wondering who this woman is and what she knows that Shelby doesn't.

"You don't know," I say, and I am angry now too. What right does she have to come here, to think she knows every-thing about me? This is America, and if I want to wear a sweater, to be someone that I'm not, well, then that is my right, isn't it?

"You," she mutters again. "You in your sweater. Thinking you better than me." She shakes her head. "I hear there doctor who take tattoo away. Just right for you. Then you be liar and out in open, yes?"

She stops talking, and everything in the office feels very still, as if everyone, they are listening to Bryda and her accu-sations. Shelby's eyes are wide brown saucers. I am sweating, and I can feel hands on the back of my neck, the rough green skin of a uniform. *Walk,* Jood. *You cannot hide from us,* Jood. *We will always find you,* Jood.

"You not even worth my breath," Bryda mutters, and then she turns and walks purposefully toward the elevator, getting on, and not even looking back as the doors shut behind her.

"Margie?" Joshua says my name. Now he is standing at his doorway, Charles behind him. How long has he been standing there? What has he heard Bryda say to me? "I heard yell-ing. Is everything all right?"

"I . . ."

"Let me finish up here," he says to me. "And then we need to talk." He walks back inside his office and shuts the door, and then Shelby whistles softly under her breath. "What was that all about?" she whispers.

But I do not answer her. I cannot speak now. I can barely breathe. Bryda's words ripped off my sweater, and I am raw and aching, as if my forearm, it is bleeding. *What did Joshua hear? What is he thinking now?*

I look up, and I expect Shelby to be staring at it, my arm, my sweater. But she is not. Her gaze meets mine, evenly.

"Margie?" Shelby's voice floats across the desk. *Hiding who you are, it'll be so much easier than hiding where you are,* Peter said. *Like an annex in your mind.* "Why was she telling you about a doctor who could remove a tattoo and calling you a liar?" Shelby's curiosity has gotten the best of her, and so she is questioning me now as if she is no longer mad. Or perhaps she isn't. Now it might all be water under the bridge, as she would say. "What tattoo?" she is asking.

I close my eyes, and I am standing there at the camp, the numbers being singed into my arm. *It is just a number. Noth-ing can't mean something. A badge of honor,* my sister says.

I open my eyes, and Shelby is still there, her eyebrows raised, waiting for an answer. "She's crazy," I finally whisper. "I have no idea what she was talking about," I lie. I lie and I lie and I lie. It is all I know now; all I have. Everything I am.

Shelby nods and teases a Kent out of her pack. "She sounded pretty crazy. That accent and that creepy missing finger." She holds the pack of Kents in my direction, just the way she always does. Nothing is different. Nothing has changed. I shake my head and then watch her light her smoke on fire. She takes a drag and blows smoke in my direction. "And what was she saying about you and Joshua? You being more than his secretary?"

Her brown eyes pierce me as if they are expectant or even nervous. I realize she is much more interested in this than in the tattoo. Margie Franklin, of course, she would not be the kind of girl to have gotten a tattoo, or to have had one forced upon her. Gentile skin remained untouched, unblemished, during the war, unless a soldier got a tattoo by choice, and it would not even occur to Shelby that I might be anything other than a Gentile.

"I don't know," I say. "Like I said, she's crazy." Of course, Shelby will believe this. *You are you*, she'd said to me. *Joshua could never look at you the way you look at him.*

"Is she the one Joshua and Ezra were fighting about?" Shelby asks. I nod, slowly, still finding it hard to breathe. "Well . . ." She waves her cigarette in the air, her diamond glinting off the fluorescent light. "Good riddance, then."

I hold my breath for a moment more, waiting for Shelby to understand that I am a liar, and I am a Jew. That I am marked and ruined. That my sweater covers only so much, and my lies, they cover the rest. But Shelby finishes her smoke and goes back to her typing, and doesn't say another word about Bryda Korzynski. Shelby is so gullible; she believes every word I say to her, as if it is so easy just to believe the best in people. Ron could have a thousand hussies, I realize now, and she would not even believe it.

�֍

Charles Bakerfield walks out of Joshua's office just before noon, and Joshua follows close behind him. Charles steps onto the elevator, and then Joshua taps his finger on my desk and grabs his brown hat from the rack. "Lunch," he says, rather sternly.

I am still having trouble breathing in the wake of Bryda's accusations. Shelby may have bought my lies, ignored Bryda's comment about the tattoo. But Joshua . . . what did he hear her say? What is he thinking now? We have barely spoken since Ezra's heart attack except for that one time in his office last week, and I cannot read the expression on his face now. Is it sadness, or is it anger? Or is it something else entirely?

"Come on," Joshua says gently now, his features softening, his gray-green eyes dancing across my face gently. "Let me buy you lunch, Margie. And we'll talk."

I glance at Shelby, who has slowed her typing to watch my reaction. I can practically hear Bryda's words reverberating in her brain: *more than a secretary.* I think Shelby has even forgotten already about any talk of a tattoo, and instead she is wondering exactly what it is Joshua and I have been doing at these lunches. I feel my cheeks turning red, but I shrug in her direction and then grab my satchel and follow Joshua toward the elevator.

The air is sticky on Market Street; my sweater, stifling. I can hear the sound of my sister's voice, though now it feels much like Bryda's voice: *Why are you still punishing yourself for being a Jew? Here, in America?* And maybe that is exactly what I'm doing, punishing myself. Because I still deserve to be punished, don't I, after what I have done?

Hiding who you are, it will be so much easier than hiding where you are, Peter said.

Is that what he's been doing, married to a redhead, with a baby whose name is devoid of meaning? Is it possible Peter is a father, a husband? That Peter stopped loving me? Or that he never even loved me at all?

"Margie." Joshua says my name as he holds open the heavy glass door to Isaac's. "Please order more than an apple. Let me buy you a sandwich, at least?"

"I'm not very hungry," I say, and that is even more true today than usual because my stomach still feels the twists and turns of Bryda's words. I am afraid any food I eat might come right back up.

"Half a ham?" he pleads.

"I don't like ham," I say, the way I always say it to Shelby. What is it with these Americans and their pork?

"No ham," he says, hesitating for a moment, as if the words mean something to him. And I wonder if he is connecting the pieces, Bryda's words, in his head. "Turkey, then?"

"I'm really not very hungry," I say, but Joshua orders a half turkey and an apple for me, chopped liver for him, and then we make our way to the table by the window. *Our usual table,* I think. Though that almost feels silly. Joshua and I do not have a usual anything, do we?

We sit down, and Joshua hands me the plate with the turkey. I take a bite, just to appease him. But I do not taste it. I chew and I chew and I chew, and it seems to take forever.

"So what was Miss Korzynski yelling about?" Joshua asks, in between voracious bites of his chopped liver. Joshua eats like such a boy, the way Peter used to, as if every bite of food might be his last.

"You didn't hear?" I whisper, still hopeful, but knowing with the paper of the walls in the office, that is most likely impossible. Joshua heard.

"I heard her say something about you overstepping your bounds as a secretary, and then her yelling at you about her tattoo. So I figured you told her, about our case, and she didn't take it well."

I almost want to laugh at the way he has interpreted things, or cry. And now I wonder, how many times have I mistaken his conversation with Ezra through the paper-thin walls for something else? Angry words float across, but not the entire context? But now I do not even care; my body floods with relief. Joshua heard "tattoo" and assumed Bryda was talking of her own. Of course! That is the perfect lie, the perfect story. Why did I not think to tell Shelby that when she asked? It seems I should be better at lying, when I have been doing it for so very long now. But still, it is such an effort for me.

"I'm sorry," Joshua is saying now. "I should've been the one to tell her. I should've returned her calls. I've just been swamped." He doesn't say anything for a moment. "Maybe I can think of another lawyer to take her case . . ."

"Maybe," I say, but I wonder how many lawyers can there be in the city of Philadelphia who will be willing to fight a Jewish fight for no money?

"It was going to be an impossible road," he says. "Look, we barely had anyone signed on to the case." I nod as I think he is trying to convince himself more than me. "Oh, and just so you know, I've called Rabbi Epstein to let him know we're dropping the case. So if you get any more calls, you can tell them what you told Miss Korzynski, or you can just have them call me directly, and I'll tell them."

I nod again, but I am thinking that he does not sound at all like the Joshua who once sat across this table from me, his voice thick with excitement as he spoke about bravery, or the Joshua who confessed his fear: *Until Jews are seen as equals, I worry it could happen again.* "Anyway," he is saying now, "you did such a great job with this that I'd like you to take a bigger role in Mr. Bakerfield's case. I need someone to go and talk to a few character witnesses, Bakerfield's friends, before the trial."

"And you want me to do it?" I ask. He nods. And I close my eyes. I picture the way Charles looked at me that day, near the bus stop, when he offered me a ride. What would he have done to me had I gotten in the car with him? Was he just being friendly, or was there something much more sinister going on? Either way, I cannot imagine taking the bus to these surely wealthy homes on the Main Line, Charles's friends, asking these men to extol his virtues.

I look at Joshua. He stares at his food, so I cannot tell what it is he is thinking at this moment. Can this really be it, the reason why Joshua has asked me to lunch this morning—not because Bryda has revealed me, but because he wants to assign me more duties outside the secretarial realm? Certainly, he could've asked me this at the office, where Mr. Bakerfield's case is no secret.

Joshua looks up, and his gray-green eyes meet mine for a moment, but then they break, and he looks away, and he shakes his head a little bit.

"Joshua," I say. He looks back at me. His expression softens as he hears me say his first name, and I don't correct myself this time.

"What is it, Margie?" His voice is imbued with tenderness and hope and maybe a sense of loss, the sense that something is now missing from him that he is never sure he can get back. I know that feeling, so, so well. Joshua reaches across the table for my hand, and his touch, it makes my fingers tingle.

"Are you really going to marry Penny?" I ask.

"Penny?" He says her name like it is typing paper, flat and pale and blank. He pulls his hand away from mine and runs his fingers through his curls. "I suppose I will, yes." He pauses. "It's what my father's always wanted for me, anyway. And he would love nothing more now than to see us married."

"But do you love her?" I ask.

He hesitates for a moment, and his eyes catch mine. "I could never be with someone who wasn't a Jew, you know," he says. "I just couldn't."

I am confused for a moment, because he has not answered the question, because his words, they don't make sense, and then it occurs to me, what it is he is saying. *You are you,* Shelby said. I am the one who is not a Jew. Margie Franklin, she is not a Jew but the Gentile girl Peter was to find in the city of Philadelphia. *We will go to America,* Peter said. *We will be married. We will no longer be Jews.*

But it is not Peter talking to me about being Jews now, it is Joshua. And why, I wonder, is he telling me this? Does this mean he has thought about me the way I have thought about him, watched me through the glass, wondered what it might be like to run his fingers through my hair? That he has noticed me? That he has not been able to resist the impulse to reach his large hand toward my face, at least once? *I cannot work without you, Margie.* That our lunches and our talks, they have been about something more than a secret case? "Joshua," I say softly, "I am not who you think I am."

He shakes his head and turns his eyes away again. "My father always said, Penny and I, we would make beautiful babies. He's right about that, isn't he?" Joshua has missed it, the first truthful thing I have said to him in three years. But maybe it does not even matter. Even if he knew the truth, Margie Franklin, the Jew, she still would not be wealthy and beautiful and charming the way Penny is. She still would not be the one Joshua's father would want him to be with. *But what about what he wants?* I wonder.

"But do you love her?" I ask. I want him to admit that he doesn't. That he does not love her. *I do not love him,* my sister said. But I did. I do.

278

"It's not always about love," Joshua is saying now, again letting his fingers thread through his hair. "Life is more complicated than that, Margie. You get to a point in your life where it's time to stop playing around. And then you just need to bite the bullet and do the things you're supposed to do."

I think of it, questioning character witnesses for murderers, then sitting at my secretary's desk, watching Penny Greenberg—no, Penny Rosenstein—saunter in for lunch with her Josh. In no time she will sport a round belly, filled with life, with Joshua's life.

"I don't think I can," I whisper. And I stand and push my chair back.

"Margie." Joshua says my name. At first it rings with surprise. Then he says it again. "Margie, where are you going? Margie, come on . . ."

I hit Market Street, already sweating, and I turn the corner onto Sixteenth, then Ludlow, but I keep walking, past my apartment, past the bus stop even. Though I am warm, sweating, and tears build in my eyes, I keep on walking.

I do not stop for a long while, until I hit Olney Avenue.

CHAPTER FORTY-SIX

❖

MY WALK, IT IS A FAR ONE, ESPECIALLY NOW, IN THE HEAT and under the weight of my sweater. But I have walked through much worse, and after I am far enough away to put the sound of Joshua's voice out of my head, I am not in a hurry. I want to arrive by the five o'clock hour so I can stand there, watch him pull up into the drive after work.

His car—the black Volkswagen, the kind of car one would never imagine a Jew to drive. A nice and masculine comple-ment to his wife's powder-pink Cadillac. *His wife.* Is it possi-ble still she is his nanny, his landlady, his friend, his housekeeper even? But her words from last time about the steps and the stroller—words that implied that she lived there and she had chosen that—swim carelessly in my brain.

I approach 2217 cautiously. There are no cars out front. Not even the pink Cadillac, but I resign myself to sitting on the bottom step to wait.

I think about Peter's eyes, blue as the sea. The way they lingered on my face even after the man in green pulled me up from my neck and started dragging my limp body out of his room.

"Margot," he called desperately after me, before one of the men clamped a large hand across his mouth, muffling the sound. I hear it now, my name in his voice, not the way it was that morning but the way he said it as we lay together on the divan. He whispered my name, into my hair, like the sound of wind chimes, blowing back and forth, their sound pleasant and high and sweet. *"Margot."*

Margie, Joshua said. *I could never be with someone who wasn't a Jew.* His gray-green eyes flickered in the light shining in past the window of the delicatessen. How could he marry Penny? I wonder. How could he marry someone he doesn't even love? Maybe Joshua isn't even the man I thought he was. I am pretending, pretending, always pretending. But so, it seems, is he.

"Hello there." I hear a woman's voice, the redhead's voice, and I look up and she is standing before me on the sidewalk. I have been lost in thought, not even noticing the pink Cadillac, which now I see is parked in the drive. She holds Eleanor tight to her hip, and the baby makes a fist in the air, then examines it, and decides it looks ripe for chewing.

I hold my eyes tightly to the baby's face, her eyes. Her cheeks are round and fleshy, her tufts of hair the color of sunlight striking snow, and her eyes, they are a remarkably deep sea blue.

"Do you live around here?" the woman asks, and I startle

and look back to her face. Her eyes are green, darker than Joshua's, lighter than Ilsa's. And now they seem wary of me.

I stand. "No," I say. I clear my throat. "But when I was here a few weeks ago, I couldn't help but notice your box." I point to the mailbox by the crumbling green door. "I knew a Pelt once," I say.

"Oh," she says, her eyes softening. "Well, maybe I could be related, then." She smiles. "Would you like to come in? Eleanor needs a nap, and I need to get dinner ready," she says. "But we could have a glass of lemonade, talk. You look like you could use a cool drink dressed the way you are."

I want to walk inside the duplex. I want to see them, the pictures she might hang above the mantel of the three of them: her, Eleanor, and Peter. I want to know that he is here, in the city of Brotherly Love, just the way he once promised. I want to watch his eyes light up, one more time, even if it is only in a photograph. "Okay," I say. "Yes. Thank you."

And I follow her up the steps into the duplex.

CHAPTER FORTY-SEVEN

THE INSIDE OF THE DUPLEX IS DARK AT FIRST, UNTIL THE redhead switches on the light. "Excuse me for a moment," she says. "Let me just run Eleanor back to her crib." I nod, and in the new fresh light, I have a look around.

The living area is spacious, deep rich hardwoods like Ilsa's covered with an Oriental-style bright red rug and flanked with unmatching green chairs. I approach the mantel, and just as I imagined, it is covered in pictures. A few of baby Eleanor. One when she is very, very young, a newborn. One with the redhead, Eleanor, and an older gray-haired woman who I guess to be the redhead's mother. Another one with the gray-haired woman and an older mustached gentleman who holds a protective arm around her shoulder.

"Ignore the dust," the redhead says, walking back in and running her finger across the glass of the picture of her and her daughter, leaving the impression of her fingertip. "I'm not a very good housekeeper, I'm afraid. And now that I've gone back to work, I've gotten even worse."

"What do you do?" I ask. I imagine Peter would've married someone like me or my sister, or the working women we might have become, anyway, had it not been for the war, or had we not been Jewish, or had we been born in America.

"Oh." She laughs. "My friend owns a restaurant, and I've been waitressing there. It's only temporary," she says, "until I find something better." She walks into the kitchen and motions for me to follow her. There is a small square oak table that barely feels big enough to seat three, and I try to imagine Peter, his long legs spread out in front of him, cramped in a space like this. How tall was Peter? Now I am only seeing the movie Peter in my mind, and it is ruining everything.

She pours the lemonade and hands me a glass. "I'm Petra, by the way," she says. It is a nice name, Petra. I guess it to be Russian or Slovakian in origin, though Petra looks so clearly Irish with her thick red hair.

"That's pretty," I tell her. "I'm Margie."

She smiles. And for a moment I think she might tell me that her name is short for Petronella. "Petronella van Daan," the pen name my sister used for Peter's mother in her diary. The name the entire world knows as that of Peter's mother. Oh, the irony. For Peter to have found his fake-named mother, here in America. But Petra does not say her name is short for anything.

"So who is this Pelt you know?" she asks me. "There aren't too many of our family in Philadelphia, I'm afraid."

Of course not.

I take a sip of my lemonade. It is tart and sweet and curls against my tongue, which is parched from my walk in the early summer afternoon. "Peter," I say, and my voice comes out in barely a whisper. "Peter Pelt."

I expect her face to turn, for her to smile, then laugh, and say, *Well, Margie, you have come to the right place*. I sit at the edge of my chair, half expecting him to walk in, home from work, any moment. *I'm home, darling*, he might call. And then, how will he react as he walks in, attaché tucked under his arm, pulling his hat from his curls, and seeing me, sitting there, in his kitchen?

"Payter," she says. "I don't think I know of a Payter?"

At first her words don't register, because I am still imagining him, standing there at the cusp of the doorway. Tall and strong and handsome. His American-ness, his Gentile-ness, they will have aged him gracefully and perfectly. He will smile at me. He will forget all about his wife. He will turn and his eyes, blue as the sea, they will capture mine. *Margot*. He will whisper my name, and it will become a summer breeze that dances so gently against my neck that my brain begins to tilt and whirl the way it once did in his room in the annex.

"Pete?" I ask, clinging to the smallest iota of hope.

"Nope," she says. "It must be another Pelt clan entirely."

"P. Pelt," I whisper.

"Oh." She looks at me funny, as if I have given away too much, because I remember my lie, that I noticed the word "Pelt" on the mailbox. "I'm P. Pelt," she says. "Petra Pelt."

"And your husband?" I ask.

She frowns. "We're getting a divorce," she says. "Pelt is my maiden name. I've gone back to it now. My husband is a Bellwether, nosebleed that he is." She pauses and shakes her head. "Anyway, I've just moved in a few months ago, and I've listed the house and the phone with just my first initial because I don't want the whole world to know I'm a woman living here, all alone with her baby." She laughs nervously. "You won't go and advertise this now, will you, Margie? My mother is convinced I'm practically inviting Jack the Ripper to come on in." Petra's green eyes are sad and tired, and I understand now that she is hiding too.

"I just thought Peter would be here," I whisper.

She shakes her head. "I'm sorry," she says. "What you see is what you get. It's only me and Eleanor."

CHAPTER FORTY-EIGHT

BACK IN MY APARTMENT, I TAKE MY SWEATER OFF. IT IS TOO hot for a sweater, and anyway, there is no one to see me now other than Katze.

I lie on my blue couch, and Katze tumbles himself in my lap, kneading and kneading, unable to settle himself in one place. I think about Petra and Eleanor, about their lonely secret life on Olney Avenue. I promised Petra I would stop by soon, as she said she was in need of some girlfriends who did not know her in her life as Mrs. Bellwether. And though I can entirely understand the sentiment, I also know that I will not be finding myself at 2217 Olney Avenue anytime soon.

Peter is dead. Like my sister is dead. I know it so solidly in my heart that it aches and falls and burns in my chest. Perhaps I have always known it. But I hate to think that hope, which has for so long been the only thing I have had left, that it is also nothing but my enemy.

Peter is dead, and I wonder even if he isn't, if he is somewhere else, unlisted, or living under a different name, or still somewhere in Europe, or even if he had been there, Petra's husband, would it be too late now? Whatever we had, we were teenagers then. Maybe we had nothing. Maybe we had everything, but we were only teenagers. Before the war, I never even considered love, marriage. I was too busy with my studies. I was a child, and I felt I had so much time for all that other stuff.

I sigh and lean back against the couch, and run my hands across Katze's warm orange fur. I want to know everything. I want to be able to understand everything, to decipher what is real and what is not. That is what I hate most about the aftermath of Hitler's terrible regime, that everything that I have done and that has been done to me, I cannot recall it with the clarity in which I used to be able to recall school lessons. I had a photographic memory for trigonometry and Latin words, and yet there is a whole two-year period of my teenage life—maybe more—in which I find myself at a loss.

The bare flesh of my arm burns into my blue velour couch, and I find myself turning my head to look at it now: my forearm. *This is real,* I think, the way I so often have. This is the only thing I have left from that time that is completely real. It is undisputable evidence of what was done to me, how much was taken, who and what I used to be, where I came from.

I think about what Bryda said earlier, that she knew of a doctor who could remove my tattoo. But even if it would mean no more sweaters, no more hiding, I know I would never have it erased. It is really the only thing that remains of Margot. The only thing I know to be true.

I stare at the numbers now, and it surprises me the way they are still so bold, the way they are still right there, thick dark ink. *Nothing can't mean something,* Mother said.

I think about that morning in the camp. September 1944. A month from the annex, from Peter, from the way my sister said his name as the men in green carried us out. What had she been saying then, really? Had it been an accusation or a fantasy? Had seeing us there ruined her story or her reality?

Peter. Peter van Pels. Peter Pelt.

I do not love him, my sister said. *It is not love.*

She was angry with me that morning, when the Green Police came. She did not talk to me in the truck. Our parents thought her silence was born from fear. I knew better. *Peter?* The way she'd said his name, it was as if he'd betrayed her. We both had.

But by the time we were dropped off the train in Auschwitz, nearly a month later, her anger had passed. We clung to each other that morning, waiting, waiting, waiting in line, as the Polish woman screamed over and over again, so loud I thought her voice might break me. *Jestes diablem. Jestes diablem.*

"No," I whispered to my sister then. "No, no, no."

"Shhh." She clung to my hand. "Don't listen to her, Margot. Sing something happy in your head. Imagine a beautiful place, the sea. Swimming in the North Sea with Mother and Father and you and me." She did not mention Peter, not ever again, after the annex. At the camp, she was my sister, my protector, my savior, and I was hers. Everything else fell away.

My hands trembled against hers as we watched the Polish woman, as they held her down, tattooed her. "She's so brave," my sister said.

And now I can envision this moment a different way than I so often have envisioned it. In my head, this way feels just as true.

Is it possible I did not push my sister behind me, to protect her, to have her watch that it was not so bad? Is it possible I trembled, like the coward I always was and most certainly always have been?

"I cannot be brave," I whispered to her. "I am not brave."

"Yes," she told me. "You are."

She stepped in front of me in line, and held out her arm to the officer, and she did not scream or even flinch as the tattoo singed her flesh.

❁

I see it there now, on my forearm: thick dark ink. And I squeeze my eyes shut tightly, trying to picture it there on my sister's arm. She was one number higher than me. She stood right behind me.

Or was she one number lower than me? Had she stood right in front of me?

I push my brain to remember, the way the ink looked on her forearm as she lay there on the dirty ground in the camp, as she clung to my arm on the train. What was her number?

It has been so long, I cannot see it. All I can see are her

almond eyes, the way they held me at the end on the train, begging me.

Nothing can't mean something, Mother said.

But if she is right, then what I am left with now, it is nothing. It means nothing. It is almost as if Margot, she never even existed at all.

❊

Suddenly I notice the brewing darkness, and I push Katze from my lap and pull the Shabbat candle from beneath my kitchen sink. I set it on the counter, force the flame to rise and fall, and say my silent prayer.

It's not religion. It's ritual.

I could never be with someone who wasn't Jewish, Joshua said.

I stare at my candle, watch it burn and flicker brightly, as if it is taunting the gloaming.

"But it *is* religion," I say to myself, out loud, my words hanging there in the air.

CHAPTER FORTY-NINE

MONDAY MORNING I SLEEP LATE, AND IT IS A SURPRISE TO awake to a gentle summer breeze coming in through the slightly open window, blowing past the pale blue curtains Ilsa sewed for me just after I moved in here. The numbers on the clock read 9:17, but I have not slept well, my body, my brain, restless and tumbling. In my dreams, baby Eleanor was crying for her father. Though not Peter, I thought as I awoke. *Bellwether.*

I wonder what has transpired during Joshua's weekend in Margate. Perhaps he has even asked Penny to marry him, and she will parade into the office this morning wanting to shove her diamond in my face. She and Shelby, they may even share a laugh and some bride's notes, should Penny deem it acceptable to behave in such a way with the girls in the office. Though I venture to say she will. That nothing will dampen the good mood that a diamond from Joshua will put her in.

I groan and pull the pillow over my head, willing sleep to find me again. But I know it will not. And though I have not decided, consciously, not to go to work today, I do not move to dress and get ready, and I know that I cannot go in. That I cannot face even the possibility of Penny and her diamond.

Instead I get out of bed, pick up the phone, and dial Ilsa's number.

"My dear," she says, upon hearing my voice. "What is it? What's the matter?"

It's possible she can hear the way I'm breaking, just from my tone as I have said her name. Or it could be because she always seems to be so worried about me.

"I think I quit my job," I say. *And Peter's dead,* I add to myself, in my head. *And I have nothing, no hope, left anymore. Not even Joshua.*

"Oh," she says, and the word is weighted, as if she understands there is more there than just a job. I wonder if she was able to intuit this much from our recent dinner, or if it is just a guess on her part, right now. "Well," she says, "I'm coming into the city, then. We'll have a girls' day today."

"I don't know if I'm up for it," I say.

"I'll be there in an hour, my dear. Bertie is off today, and I'll have him drop me at your place."

Then she hangs up, before I have any time to convince her otherwise.

❖

I sit there for a few moments, still holding the phone in my hand, wondering if Joshua might call to ask me when I will be in and why I am not at my desk. But then I suspect he won't. *I could never be with someone who wasn't a Jew,* he said. And didn't that change everything? That he said it, what everyone else had already seen, that there was something else between us, more than just boss and secretary, but that whatever that something was, it was never going to turn into more.

I think about Mother and Eduard, and I wonder what their life might have been like together once. If they shared a passion or if they held themselves back. But that was different, anyway. Eduard really truly was not a Jew. Margie Franklin, though, she is just a lie.

I look at the number on my arm again, trace the digits with my finger. And then I go and dress in my green dress and pink sweater.

Bertram honks the horn once as he pulls his Fairlane up by the sidewalk on Ludlow Street, and I watch out the window as Ilsa climbs out of the car. Her petite frame is wrapped in a deep green sundress, which I know will bring out the color of her eyes, when I am standing closer.

I lock my apartment and walk outside to meet her, and as Bertram honks again, waves in my direction, and drives away, Ilsa wraps her tiny arms around me. "Oh, my dear," she says. "Let's walk to Wanamaker's and look for some nice summer dresses, shall we?"

I nod, and let her cling to my arm, the way Shelby always does. But in a way, I feel safer holding on to Ilsa. I am suddenly sad for her, that she could never have a baby, because she would've been the best kind of mother, fierce and smart and beautiful and protective, and always, always with a plan. Not so dissimilar from my own mother.

"So are you going to tell me what happened?" Ilsa asks as our heels click in step against the sidewalk.

"I don't know," I say.

"Margie." Her voice is kind and stern all at once.

"My boss," I finally say, because there is no way I can tell her about P. Pelt. And now I am beginning to understand, that maybe this is really what it has been about these past few months. Not Peter, but Joshua. Who have I really been thinking about as Shelby's love songs have played on her Friday afternoon radio? Who have I been watching through the glass, waiting for the moments when he says my name?

"Yes," Ilsa says. "What about him?"

"He wants me to do things I cannot," I tell her.

She stops walking, turns to me and frowns. "What kind of things?" she asks.

"Help him defend murderers," I say, but what I am really thinking is, *Watch him marry a woman he doesn't love.* Watch her walk in every afternoon gloating that she is his wife.

She tsks and shakes her head, and we start walking again. "I am surprised he cannot be more sensitive, after all you have been through."

"He doesn't know," I say softly. "He doesn't even know I'm Jewish."

"Oh, my dear," she says, shaking her head again.

We turn the corner, and we are up the street now from the cinema. The red letters are still there, blinding me, on the marquee, and I wonder how long they will remain. Is this the longest-playing movie ever in the city of Philadelphia? Surely, it only feels that way to me. I look away, not wanting to see them again. My sister's name against the bright white light of late morning, the way the letters appear in red, in the movie's title, they are nothing at all like my sister, the way she was as a person, not some silly, nearly invented icon.

"Have you seen it?" Ilsa asks as we pass by.

"What?" I ask, playing dumb. Only this never works with Ilsa. She nods her head in the direction of the marquee. "Oh, that," I say. "Yes, of course. Hasn't everybody?" I cannot keep the bitterness from my voice. It is so sharp, so biting that it almost surprises me. *Oh, the lies.*

"I wasn't sure if you would have," she says slowly, as if she is treading water with her voice. "Did you like it?"

I remember what Joshua said, sitting there, so very close to me on the stool in O'Malley's bar. *It's not something you can like, is it?* Like school. Or the doctor's. I sigh. "I don't know, Ilsa," I say. "Let's not talk about this now."

Ilsa shrugs, but in true Ilsa fashion, continues to talk about it. "I saw it," she says. I nod. Of course she did. Everyone has. The entire world. "It was beautiful, in a way. Only very sad. I kept thinking of you."

She stops walking, and she turns and takes my hands in her own. She rubs my fingers between hers, as if she is warming them. "That was you, wasn't it, my dear?" she asks me. I am so surprised by her words, by the easy way she says them, that all I can do is shake my head, back and forth and back and forth. My brain feels numb, and yet my head aches. How could Ilsa say this? Just like that. How could she know?

My heart pounds in my chest, and I am sweating, pools of water building down my arms, swallowing my ink. "No," I whisper. "No."

"Eduard told me, when he first wrote me about you, that your name was Margot Frank."

"No," I whisper again, but it is so strange to hear it, someone say it aloud. *Margot Frank.* Someone whom I know and whom I even love saying those words. I have not heard them spoken out loud in so long that they cannot be real. It feels like a stranger's name, or the name of someone I once knew, long ago, but whom I can barely remember.

"But then you arrived and said your name was Margie Franklin," she is saying now. "And I thought you were Americanizing yourself, the way we all have when we have come to this country. I thought nothing more of it. I never got a chance to read the book. But recently, after Bertie and I saw the movie . . . And then lately, the way you have seemed so on edge, the way you just reacted when you saw the marquee. My dear . . ." She puts her hand to my cheek and turns my face toward her. Her green eyes are filled with kindness and sadness.

"Ilsa," I whisper. "I am not the person you think I am."

"I understand that," she says. She reaches for my cheek again and strokes my hair back gently, the way a mother might do to a very small child.

"No," I say. "You don't. I am not her." Because this is the

truth, I am nothing like the girl she saw in the movie. She is only a character, the boring fictional sister of an icon. Nothing about it seems real to me, except that we were Jews, and we were hiding.

"Okay, my dear." She pauses for a moment. "I do not know what happened to you then. But I love you now. In my heart you are the child that I never had. I worry about you." She pauses again. "I want to help you," she says. "And if you are her, well, then your father is still alive, isn't he? He is living in Switzerland, yes?" It occurs to me that this was maybe the real reason for the invitation to join her and Bertram on their trip. *You can go home again,* she'd said. *I've always wanted to see the Alps.*

No. No. No.

"You don't understand," I whisper.

"You are afraid," Ilsa says.

"I'm the reason she's not here," I whisper.

Ilsa frowns, confused. "Who?" she asks.

"My sister," I say. "I killed her."

And now that I have said it out loud, finally, at last, the truth, I feel my hands shaking against the weight of Ilsa's, and then I am not sure I can stand any longer.

Ilsa leads me to a bench, on the sidewalk by South Seventeenth Street. We are not too far from Casteel's, and I cannot help but think of that other morning, when Joshua found me and led me gently inside. Where we shared a meal together. And where Joshua pretended that he was mine and I was his.

"Tell me everything," Ilsa says now, when we are both

sitting. Her voice is calm but stern, and her green eyes, they pierce me, until the whole story comes out of me, all of it. I tell her about Peter, and about the way my sister said his name, just before the Green Police stormed the annex. I tell her about the line at the camp, how I cannot remember now my sister's number. And then I tell her about my mother's plan, the train taking us from Auschwitz to Bergen-Belsen, when I escaped the Nazis.

"We were lumped in a cattle car," I tell Ilsa, and the words tumble from me now as if I am in a trance, describing a nightmare I have relived over and over and over again, and yet have never spoken of before this moment. "With so many women. Every one of us was just a heap of bone and loose flesh. It was hard to tell whether anyone was dead or alive, unless they happened to move a limb or twitch an eyelid."

Ilsa shudders, but then motions for me to keep on talking.

"The train started moving slowly, and we were by the door. I was holding on tightly to my sister's hand, and I saw our old neighbor, Schmidt, guarding our car. My mother had promised he wouldn't shoot me. And then I knew I had to jump, or the train would be moving too fast, and then it would be too late. I couldn't stay on the train any longer."

"And then what happened?" Ilsa asks, her eyes the size of silver dollars.

"I jumped," I say. "I let go of my sister's hand, and I jumped. There were gunshots. And screaming . . . And that is all I remember until the next morning, when I woke up on the ground not too far from the train tracks."

I close my eyes, and I am imagining that morning again, the feel of Brigitta's hand on my shoulder, her German whisper in my ear. I could not hear her at first because the sound of gunshots and my sister's screams, they were ringing so loudly in my ears. But I had not been shot. And I had not taken her with me. I'd let go of her hand; I'd left her there to die, to take Schmidt's bullets for me.

"Oh, my dear." Ilsa wipes at the tears on my face with her thumbs, then wipes at tears on her own face. "It is so heavy to be you, to carry all of this around, for so long." She pauses. "I do not believe you killed your sister," she says. "I do not believe that even for a moment."

"That's because you are you," I tell her. "And you believe the best in people." In this way Ilsa, she is not so dissimilar from my sister. But Ilsa was not there. During the war. Then, anyone was capable of anything.

She is shaking her head now. "You are telling me that maybe your sister was telling stories about her and Peter. But what of herself? Was she strong and full of life and courageous as the movie suggests?"

I nod. "Yes," I say. *You are such a paragon of virtue,* I hear her saying in my head, laughing, chewing on the end of her fountain pen.

"And you say you cannot actually remember those last few moments on the train?" Ilsa asks.

I shake my head.

She thinks about it for a moment, and then she takes her hand in mine. "My dear," she says, "I want to tell you a story . . ."

In 1944, the train started.

It was taking them from one camp to another, from Auschwitz to Bergen-Belsen. Margot and Anne were lumped in a cattle car, with so many other women, heaps of bones and loose flesh. It was hard to tell whether they were dead or alive, unless they happened to move a limb or twitch an eyelid.

The train moved slowly, at first, and Margot was by the door. *He won't shoot you,* Mother had promised, and Margot saw him there, Schmidt, guarding their car.

I will run, and he will shoot me, Margot thought. Oh, the idea of running, out in the fresh air, though. It felt glorious and unbearable, after so very long.

Margot held on tightly to her sister's hand. They had to jump, or the train would be moving too fast, and maybe they would die as they hit the ground, from the impact alone. A heap of bones and flesh: they might snap. But it was then, or it was never. And Margot promised Mother.

"Run," Margot said to her sister, pulling as hard as she could on Anne's arm. But Anne was too sick, too weak. She couldn't run. Her almond eyes were saucers.

"No," she whispered back. "I can't make it. Run. Without me."

"I won't leave you," Margot cried. "You're my sister. I won't leave you."

"Yes," Anne said. "You must."

Schmidt turned his head, and he stared directly at them.

His hand moved to his belt to grasp the handle of his gun, and that's when Anne pulled all the strength she had to reach her hand up, put it tightly on Margot's shoulder, and push her hard enough so that her body found the door and it fell, crumbling into one with the parched earth.

Ilsa's story, it is a nice one. It is a story of bravery and selflessness and redemption. It is a story that makes Margot nothing more than one of the millions of other Jews who suffered, the ones now whose dead sisters are not icons. It is a story that makes me nothing more than a victim of the Nazis and then, somehow, like Bryda Korzynski, a survivor of them too.

It could be the truth. It might not be. When I close my eyes and envision the scene, I can see it happening that way, just as Ilsa described. My sister insisting that I go, pushing me from the train. I imagine it the same way I can imagine my sister stepping in front of me in line, getting tattooed first. I cannot tell you if this is the way it happened. I wish I could. But I cannot.

"You have suffered so much," Ilsa is saying now. She reaches up and strokes my hair with her hand, and I lay my head down on her fragile bony shoulder. "Oh, my dear," she whispers into my hair. "It is time for you to become whole again."

CHAPTER FIFTY

Eventually, Ilsa and I stand up from the bench and continue walking down the street. It feels strange, that nothing around us looks different, that not even the air has changed after I have told Ilsa so much, and Ilsa has given me a story that I may be able to cling to.

As we walk, I think about her words, that it is time for me to become whole again. What does that even mean? I wonder, until we hit the front entrance to John Wanamaker's, and then her words begin to make sense.

Ilsa pulls open the heavy door, but I stop, let go of her hand, and give her a hug. "I have to go," I tell her.

"Where?" Ilsa asks me.

"There is someone I need to see," I tell her. I think about that last moment in the annex with Peter, my sister, and me. What might have happened, had the Green Police not stormed in? I would've asked my sister what she meant, why she was saying his name that way. And Peter would've stood. He would've looked me in the eyes with confusion or he would've gone to my sister. Either way, I would've fought for him. I would not have run away—I did not run away; I was ripped away. And that is entirely different. I wouldn't have let Peter go, just like that. I would've at least tried. The way we were together the night before, that last night in the annex. That meant something. I know it did. The way Joshua had looked at me, put his hand on my face. *I cannot work without you, Margie.* He was saying more than that. He was.

"Someone?" Ilsa is saying now, arching her eyebrows.

"My boss," I say. Ilsa said it was time for me to become whole. And now I cannot imagine myself as someone whole, someone real, without Joshua.

"Your boss?" Ilsa raises her tiny eyebrows, and her voice now reveals that she has also long suspected there is more between me and Joshua than my inability to work with murderers. But I do not clarify any further.

"I'll call you later," I promise her again.

"Margie," she says.

"I will call you. I promise." I hesitate for a moment. And then I add, "And please, don't tell anyone the things I have told you."

"Of course," she says. If it were anyone but Ilsa, I might worry, but I trust Ilsa more than I have trusted anyone since my blood family, and I know she will keep my secret.

"Margie," she says my name again. "Wait—I could come with you."

"Thank you," I tell her. "But this is something I need to do alone."

She hesitates for a moment before leaning in to give me another quick hug. And then she stands back and watches me go.

❊

It is nearly lunchtime by the time I arrive at the lobby of the office building, and as a result I have to wait a while for the elevator. I pace the marble-tiled floor in front of it, Ilsa's words echoing in my brain. *You have suffered so much. It is time for you to be whole again.*

I have been hiding for so long that it has become all I am. And I realize I am not even truly certain why I am still hiding, except now it is all I know. A promise I made so long ago that has no meaning anymore. *Ilsa knew. She has known for a while.* And yet she has said nothing until now. She has cooked me dinner and worried about my weight, and called me "my dear" as if I were her flesh and blood. Is it possible that no matter who you once were, what your past is, how terrible that past is, that you can somehow transcend it? I thought I could, that I would, when I first moved to America. I thought my life would be free and open, and I would find Peter and we would marry. I did not imagine the way my father would put my sister's book into the world filled with such a different version of life in the annex than the one I remember, the way that would change everything. The way everyone would know my story but me. But I hope that Ilsa is right, that it is not too late. Even now.

Finally the elevator doors ding and slide open. A group of men in suits, not lawyers from the firm, but men or clients from one of the other companies in the building, step out, past me. Henry holds on to the button to keep the doors open for me, and I am the only one going in, the only one going up, at this hour of the day.

"Miss Franklin," Henry says, shooting me a kind smile. His warm brown eyes melt against my face. "I thought maybe you was sick today when you didn't ride up first thing this morning."

"No," I say. "Just a little sidetracked, that's all, Henry." Maybe I have been sidetracked for years now, I think. But I don't share this thought with Henry.

The doors open onto the seventh floor and Henry tells me to have a good afternoon. I smile at him and walk quickly toward my desk. It is empty, I see, which means Joshua hasn't replaced me yet, even temporarily. Not that I would've expected him to, this fast, but still I also cannot imagine Joshua working efficiently without a secretary.

Shelby is at her desk, but she does not appear to be working. She is staring at something—maybe the window by Joshua's office?—and she lets her cigarette dangle loosely in her right hand.

"Shelby." I say her name, and she jumps a little.

Her chocolate eyes turn, then fall. I wonder if something has happened with her and Ron, but before I have a chance to ask, she is saying, "Oh, Margie, where have you been?" I look past her to Joshua's glass window, trying to get the tiniest of glimpses of him. But I quickly see the light in his office is off, the office dark, and that Joshua is not inside. *He's at lunch, with Penny. Of course.*

Still I ask Shelby now, "Where's Joshua?"

"Oh," she says. "You don't know, do you?"

I expect her to say it, that over the weekend, Penny and Joshua got engaged, that of course he could not be expected to work on the cusp of such a happy and exciting occasion. Her eyes, when she saw me, it had nothing at all to do with Ron. "Know what?" I ask, my voice breaking.

"Ezra," she says, her voice thick with a sadness that I am not used to from her. I turn and look at her, and there are tears in her eyes. One escapes and runs down her cheek. She quickly wipes it away.

"No," I whisper, not wanting to believe what she is telling me. If this is true, then why has no one called to tell me? But then I think guiltily of the way I walked out of Isaac's on Friday as Joshua called after me.

Shelby nods. "He passed away on Saturday."

My fingers feel numb, the air suddenly too thick. "Where is he?" I whisper.

"Ezra?"

"Joshua?"

"Oh." She grabs a tissue from inside her satchel and blows her nose. "Margate," she says. "He called in this morning." She pauses. "He asked for you."

"He did?"

She nods. "I tried to cover for you, Margie. I lied and told him you were in the bathroom, but he said he knew I was lying, that you weren't in. Where in God's name were you, anyway?"

"I have to go," I tell her. And I turn and walk back toward the elevator.

"Margie," she calls after me. "Margie."

I press the button for the elevator, but it is still lunchtime, still slow. Shelby stands up from her desk and runs over to where I'm standing. She puts her hand on my shoulder, and I turn to look at her face. Her brown eyes well up with confusion and sadness. "What is going on with you?" she asks. I don't answer, and the elevator doors open. Henry raises his eyebrows at me in surprise, but he does not say a word.

"Joshua really asked for me?" I say. She nods, and I step inside the elevator.

"Margie," Shelby calls after me. "Where are you going?"

"Margate," I say, and there is just enough time before the elevator doors shut for me to watch Shelby's lips fall open in surprise.

CHAPTER FIFTY-ONE

WHEN I REACH MY APARTMENT BUILDING, I FIND ILSA sitting outside on the bench where Joshua once waited for me. She is holding a tiny John Wanamaker's bag and glancing nervously at her slender gold watch. "Margie." Her eyes break into a smile when she sees me.

"You didn't have to wait," I say.

"Bertie is picking me up here, remember?" She pauses. "I thought you would still be talking to your boss, for a while."

I had been thinking I would go to my apartment, take some money from my stash underneath the mattress, and then make my way toward the Greyhound station, where surely there must be a bus that could take me to Margate. But now I have a different idea.

"Have you ever been to Margate?" I ask Ilsa.

"Margate, New Jersey?" I nod. "I've been to Cape May," she says. "Bertie's cousin Alice has a house there. I think

Margate is nearby." She pauses and looks me up and down. "My dear," she says. "What's in Margate?"

"Joshua," I say.

"Joshua?" She pats the space on the bench next to her, and I sit down. "This Joshua, he is your boss?" I nod. "And you are in love with him?" I meet her green eyes, wondering how they are so wise, how she knows so much. And really, that I am not as good at hiding things as I think. At least, not from Ilsa. I nod again, and then she reaches for my hand and clasps it tightly. "Bertie should be here in ten minutes. And then he will drive you to Margate," she says. "We both will."

CHAPTER FIFTY-TWO

IN THE BACK OF BERTRAM'S FAIRLANE, I CLING TO THE
brown leather seat and look out the window, waiting anx-
iously for a glimpse of the sea. I can smell it faintly as we grow
closer, the salt air curling in my nose, a smell so foreign now
yet also so familiar. Once you have smelled the sea, I don't
believe you ever forget its particular scent.

Bertram hasn't talked much, but in true Bertram fashion,
he did not argue or even seem upset that his afternoon off
was being detoured by an hour-long drive to New Jersey.

"Margate?" he'd said, raising his copper eyebrows at Ilsa as
we both got into the car and Ilsa instructed him to drive
there. Ilsa nodded, and Bertram said only, "Illie, pull the map
out of the glove box, will you?"

"Are you sure you don't mind?" I said to Bertram. "I could
find the bus."

"Nonsense." Ilsa's green eyes lit up as she found the atlas, and I could feel her excitement bursting through her skin. "We don't mind at all."

And then all Bertram said was, "Check the map, Illie. The White Horse or the Black Horse Pike looks better for Margate?"

Bertram held one hand on the steering wheel and slid the other across the seat to rest gently on Ilsa's knee as Ilsa studied the map and then declared the Black Horse Pike to be our route.

"Black Horse it is, then," Bertram said, pulling away from the sidewalk, but keeping his hand on Ilsa's knee.

I watch her as she still holds the atlas on her lap now, and I cannot help but think of Peter. Of the way his finger traced the name of the city of Philadelphia. *City of Brotherly Love. Certainly Jews cannot be in hiding there.* And yet what have I been doing, all this time? Peter had brought me here. But no, I think now. I have brought myself. Peter and I were supposed to be together. Or maybe we weren't. Maybe nothing in the annex was meant to be any more than a story, a fantasy, a way to survive the horribleness of having our childhoods ripped away, our lives ripped away. *We will go to Philadelphia,* Peter said. *Be married.*

I do not love him, my sister said.

Was she the only one of the three of us who was really, truly being honest? Understanding that the life in the annex, it was a pretend life. It was no life at all.

"Where in Margate are we going?" Bertram asks as we are getting closer and closer to the sea. The smell of salt grows stronger, and I close my eyes and inhale, letting the salt tingle in my nose as I try to remember the address of the house. I sent things there on behalf of Ezra and Joshua in the past few weeks. "Knight," I whisper, recalling it. The house is on Knight.

Ilsa finds the street on the map and gives Bertram directions. Their voices rise and fall in the background as I look out the window, at the houses. As we get closer to the sea, it seems they get bigger, grander, more beautiful. They are delicate and regal all at once, on stilts and swathed in windows. Any one of these could be the Rosensteins'.

But the one that actually is the Rosensteins' soon becomes obvious. It is at the end of the drive, the house closest to the sea. Their name is splashed across the black mailbox in white letters. It is not the biggest house on the street, but it seems fashioned of glass, and close enough to the sea that you might almost be able to taste the salt on your tongue from the back deck, which hangs close to the sand.

"This is it," I say.

Bertram stops the car. Ilsa turns around and smiles at me. "Shall I come in with you, my dear?" I shake my head. "Bertie and I will go get a late lunch, then, and come back in an hour. Should that be enough time?"

"I don't know," I say, because I have no idea how Joshua will react when he sees me. Maybe five minutes will be enough, or maybe, hopefully, it will not. "I can take the bus back," I tell her. "You don't have to wait."

"Nonsense," Ilsa says. "Of course we'll wait." She leans in to the backseat to hug me. "Good luck, my dear," she whispers in my ear.

✿

As Bertram's Fairlane drives away, I stand in Knight Street for a moment, across from the Rosensteins' house. In a way, it is not so dissimilar to our home on the Merwedeplein, in that it is grand and tall and lofty, and the place where a well-off family very obviously lives. We had nice things, before the war, before we were hiding. I should not be so intimidated by the big, big house by the ocean. And yet, still I am.

After a few minutes a powder-blue Chevelle pulls up, and nearly immediately, I realize it is driven by Penny. She rides with the top down, a white scarf wrapped around her petite head. She is dressed in a slender black dress and wears big Marilyn sunglasses. My heart falls as she parks the car in the street next to the house, then turns my way and immediately locks her eyes on me.

She pulls her scarf off her head, gets out of the car, and runs across the street. "Margie, is that you?" she says. She pulls her sunglasses down the bridge of her nose and gives me a once-over. "If you're here for the funeral, you're too late. It was this morning." She frowns, and I realize I am completely inappropriately dressed for a funeral, should that have been my reason for coming here. I am wearing my pale green dress with my pink sweater.

I try to glance at Penny's left hand, nonchalantly, but she clings tightly to her black leather clutch, and I cannot tell whether there is a diamond there or not.

"No," I finally say. "I'm looking for Joshua."

"You came all the way here for Josh?" She raises her eyebrows, and looks at me in a way that says, *Silly, silly girl. Josh would never want to see you.* I think about what Shelby said once about wanting to punch Penny in her smug little face, and I clench my hands uneasily at my sides. "Well," she says, pulling her sunglasses back up over her eyes. "This really isn't the best time. We're preparing the house for the first night of shiva tonight. That's when—"

"I know what shiva is," I say. Though there were many shivas I did not get to sit, for my mother, for my sister, we sat one on the Merwedeplein after Gram Hollander died in January 1942. It was only a pretend shiva, though, as my sister said, since we did not want to attract attention then from the Green Police for having a large gathering of Jews. That was the first time I'd seen Mother upset, really truly upset, by the war.

"You cannot even die with dignity anymore," Mother had complained to Father.

Penny stares at me hard, and then she says, "Josh is really in no state to be discussing work right now."

"This is not about work," I tell her.

"Well, whatever it is you came for, it's going to have to wait. This is just the worst possible time." She puts her hand, her right hand, on my shoulder. "You go back to work, and I'll tell Josh you've sent your condolences, all right?"

No, it is not all right. I am not okay with allowing Penny to be my gatekeeper, telling me where I can and cannot be, what I can and cannot say, and most especially how and when and why I am allowed to talk to Joshua.

"I am going to walk down to the beach," I tell her. "Can you ask Joshua to come down there to talk to me?"

"Oh, Margie." She sighs. "I am sure you are a lovely secretary. But that is all you are. All you'll ever be."

Penny's words rush in my ears, making me suddenly dizzy, because it is possible, more than possible, that there is truth in them. *You're you.* Shelby's voice echoes in my head.

I am me, I think. And not the Gentile, Polish American secretary. I have spent so many years hiding, and as Ilsa said, it is time for me to become whole again.

"I will be waiting on the beach," I tell Penny. "And then, in a little while, if Joshua does not come down, I will knock on the door, and come inside the house."

I can feel the weight of her frown on my back as I turn and walk down the staircase that leads me to the sand and the sea below.

CHAPTER FIFTY-THREE

I TAKE OFF MY PUMPS BEFORE I STEP INTO THE SAND, AND then I dig my toes in. The beach is warm, and the grains of sand cling between my toes. The sea swells before me, giant and unyielding, even to the snow-white gulls who swoop down and then back up against the pale blue sky.

The New Jersey sea, it is not at all like Peter's eyes. It is greener and blacker, murkier. It reminds me more of the color of the canal running alongside the Prinsengracht, the water we could stare at for so long, but could not touch.

The sea I always imagine in my head is the North Sea, which truly was as blue as Peter's eyes. We vacationed there, the four of us, before the war got so bad that we could not. I can still picture my sister and me, digging our small hands into the sand while Mother and Father sunned themselves on long chairs. My sister and I dug a moat in a circle around them, pulling at the sand until it coated our arms and dusted under our fingernails. And then we filled the moat with buckets of water, so anyone who would try to get to our parents, as they lay there with their eyes closed, could not.

"Let's do a castle," I said to my sister, after the moat was finished.

She shook her head. "Let's keep digging," she said. "I've heard if you dig deep enough you can dig straight through to the other end of the earth."

We did not need to dig that far then, though still we tried, until our arms grew tired, our fingers parched and ready to bleed. "Girls," Mother said when she awoke. "Fill that hole back in. Someone might fall inside and kill themselves."

My sister smiled at me and whispered, "We were so close, I think. Maybe next time we'll get there."

There never was a next time, of course. By the next summer, there were no vacations left for Jews. There were not even movies or bus rides or bicycles.

❋

"Margie?" I hear Joshua's voice, and I turn away from the sea. He runs down from the house, in his black suit, a yarmulke crushing his curls. He has taken off his shoes and cuffed up the bottom of his pants, and he has removed his tie and unbuttoned the top two buttons of his white collared shirt.

"Penny told you," I say, nearly in disbelief. Even though she had told him my message once before, this time it had felt different.

"Penny?" He shakes his head. "I saw you out the window.

I thought it looked like you and then I saw the sweater, so I figured . . ."

He stops running now, and his breath is hard and heavy in his chest. He is close enough to me that I could reach out and touch his arm or run my finger around one of his chestnut curls, but I do not.

"What are you doing here?" he asks, still breathing hard. He does not sound angry or annoyed, as Penny would've had me believe, but confused.

"I went into the office to talk to you, and Shelby told me about your father," I say. "I'm so sorry."

He nods, and he gently takes my arm and leads me to the edge of the sea. "Do you want to sit?" he asks. I nod, and he pulls his suit jacket off and lays it on the ground for us. I sit down first, and then he sits next to me, close enough so our shoulders touch as we both hang our feet out and dangle them in the edge of the water. It is warmer than I expected it would be.

"I wanted to talk to you this morning," Joshua says. "You know, before all this happened." He waves his arms around in the air, pointing back toward the house. "I wanted to apologize for Friday, at lunch. I felt I offended you somehow, and that wasn't my intention."

"I know," I say. "And I'm sorry too. I shouldn't have said those things about Penny and then just run out."

"You're right, though," he says. "I don't love her." My heart swells when he says it, not because I hate Penny so, but because I know it is the truth, and he is admitting it to me, and also to himself. "I love her as a friend, of course. I always have, and I always will, but . . ."

He sighs and props himself back against his elbows, extending his face up toward the sun. And I do the same. Our shoulders are still touching, our faces beaming in the sun, our toes dancing against the water. If there has ever been a perfect moment since that last one, in the annex, lying in Peter's arms before my sister walked in, this is the one: sunlight, the sea, the warmth of Joshua's body next to me.

"How did you do it?" Joshua asks, after a little while. "When your father died?"

"Do what?" I ask.

"I am not even sure what to feel. My father is gone. And I'm numb. Completely and totally numb." He sighs. "You said you didn't get along with your father. How did you mourn him and hate him all at once?"

I think about Pim: Pim standing there, as surely he did, at the doorway to 263 Prinsengracht, just after the war. Pim holding on tightly to our diaries, thinking to himself that something, it couldn't mean nothing. Pim now, in Switzerland, seventy years old. Seventy! I try to imagine him with snow-white hair, a slightly shrunken spine, but that same look of brightness in his eyes. *Lay your head here, Bubbeleh. I will protect you.*

"My father isn't dead," I say softly. It is the first time I have said the words out loud, to anyone. And now they sound so real that they startle me all over again, the way my father's name shocked me when I first saw it written there as editor on my sister's book. Otto, Father, Pim—for certain alive and breathing in Switzerland.

Joshua shakes his head, confused. "I thought you said both your parents were dead."

"My mother is dead," I say. "And my sister."

"You had a sister?" he asks, sitting back up.

"Yes," I tell him. I sit up too, and I look at him. His gray-green eyes are purely green in the sunlight, and they hold my face in a certain way that tells me he is listening intently, more intently than anyone has ever listened. The sun is warm, and my skin aches and sweats underneath my pink sweater. "I loved her," I say. "I really did." Joshua covers my hand with his. "Sometimes we fought. But I always loved her. She was beautiful, and she was brave. She was smart and loud and pure and brilliant. I still miss her," I tell him. He squeezes my hand, and his eyes reach out to me in a smile. "You know her," I tell him.

"Me?" he asks, his eyes turning now in confusion.

"Or you think you do," I tell him. "Everyone thinks they do. But no one really knows her, not the way I did." My face is turning wet, but it is not until Joshua reaches his thumbs up to wipe the tears away that I realize I am crying.

"Margie?" he says, wanting me to tell him more, wanting maybe to understand it. The sun beats down upon us, burning on my back, my shoulders.

I want to tell him everything, but my words, they are suddenly choking me, and there are so many tears that it is hard to keep on speaking.

Instead, I pull at my pink sweater, tugging it gently off. I free my right arm, revealing my pale and unmarked skin, and then I take a deep breath, and I free my left arm, the arm by which Joshua sits. I fold the sweater in my lap, and I close my eyes, listening to the sounds of the sea whispering in front of me. If I hold out my tongue, I think, I might be able to taste the salt.

Joshua's finger dances gently against my left forearm, tracing the *A,* then the numbers that follow, each one slowly, and I can hear the echo of them in my head.

"Margie." Joshua whispers my name.

After a while I open my eyes. I turn and I look at Joshua. I catch his gray-green eyes, and I hold on to them. "My name isn't Margie," I finally say. "It's Margot."

EPILOGUE

SOMETIMES NOW I STILL THINK ABOUT THAT FRIDAY *afternoon in April when I first learned about your movie. In my mind, that afternoon marks the beginning of the end of my hiding in America. Maybe because it was when I first began to understand that staying hidden forever, even here, even now, it is impossible.*

But do not think I blame you for this, Pim. Do not think I blame you for anything. The book, the movie, your new life in Switzerland . . . In one way, I should probably thank you. Had it not been for the movie, I might not have searched for Peter again, or met Bryda, or worked more closely with Joshua. Ilsa might not have figured out the truth about me, and in doing so, I might not have figured out the truth about myself. I am still not sure what happened that day on the train. But now, when I think about it, I realize that Ilsa is partly right. I do think my sister would want me to live. And not in hiding either. If I could ask her now, I believe she would say, much like Ilsa, that I very much deserve my American happiness. And that is what I am working toward now, Pim.

A month after Joshua buried his father, he officially left his position as lawyer at Rosenstein, Greenberg and Moscowitz. We packed up our desks at the same time as Shelby clung to her cigarette and pleaded with me not to leave her all alone, but then both of us, Shelby and I, we laughed a little, since we knew it would only be a matter of time until she was married and she would be leaving too. Shelby also finally asked Ron about the woman Peggy saw him with, and it turns out it was his secretary, helping him pick out Shelby's ring. So I am pleased that Shelby too really genuinely seems to have found her happiness. And even though we are no longer working together, we are still friends, and we sometimes find ourselves meeting for a drink after work.

In August, I completed my paralegal studies, and Joshua officially opened the doors of his new firm, which he simply calls Joshua S. Rosenstein, Attorney-at-Law. He contacted Bryda and Reisel and the others on our list, and since then, we have been working hard on their case. In September, we attracted the attention of Philadelphia magazine, and they did a write-up on Joshua, calling him a "pioneer of our time." I clipped the article, put it in a frame, and hung it up in our new office, which for now is only one tiny room with two large desks, just above Isaac's storefront. It is meant to be a studio apartment, I think, but for the time being, it suffices as our office space.

The article also has brought in some fresh cases. Not murderers, but generally Jewish people who need help, and who

*have come to understand that Joshua is a person they can trust.
Joshua has handled several divorces, one adoption, and also
helped a man sue another man who hit him with his car. Joshua
says this will be enough for us to keep our doors open for now
and continue work on our group litigation, which pleases us
both.*

*Most days, Joshua does not even wear a suit to work, but
casual pants and a starched, collared plaid shirt that almost
always brings out the handsomeness of his gray-green eyes. I go
to work without my sweater, except for now, when the weather
is turning cooler again, and a sweater has become a necessity—
not for hiding, but for warmth.*

*My Jewishness is no longer a secret in the city of Philadel-
phia. And if I am being honest with myself, I'm not sure why I
really kept it one for so long. Though I am sometimes still afraid
of anti-Semites, when I read the news now I make a point to
look for good things that happen to Jews in America. And there
are a lot: weddings, births, and even that very nice article about
a Jewish lawyer who is trying to help other Jews. I was lying to
myself, as much as I was lying to everyone else, I guess. My
Shabbat candle was more than a ritual. And so were my prayers.
In a way, the Nazis tried to erase our Jewishness. Then I tried to
erase my Jewishness too. But as Eduard once very wisely told
me, you are who you are. I understand now that hiding, it is not
really being alive. And I am, Pim. I'm alive.*

*Maybe I clung to Peter's words much more than I should've.
Who knows if Peter even meant them, or if they were just fairy
tale? But they were the only thing that made me feel safe, for so
very long. And there remained a secret strand of hope that if I*

did what Peter and I promised each other, he would still find me. Maybe you think that's silly, and I wonder if you have even known before now about me and Peter. If you found my diary, then you did, I suppose. But if the NSB destroyed it, or if it is still tucked away somewhere under the folds of my cot . . . well then, I expect a lot of this might surprise you. I hope it will not upset you.

I guess I should also tell you that everybody here in Philadelphia still calls me Margie Franklin. Even Joshua and Ilsa, who know there is more to me than that. I am *Margie Franklin* now, Pim. She is the woman I have become. Margot, she is the girl who only lives on as a character in the book.

Everything I have revealed to you here, I am telling you in confidence. I do not want the entire world to know me, or to think they know me. My sister, she can be the face of all the suffering, the one reminding everyone, still, now, that it cannot, must not, happen again. That we were real people. This is important, and I am glad her legacy lives on this way, whether her diary was stories, fantasies, reality. I do not know. Perhaps it does not even matter. But me—I do not want a book, or a movie, or even a play. I have a life, and what I want now most is to finally live it.

I hope you will understand my story, Pim. That you will understand why it has taken me so long to write you. I do not know if you will respond to me, but I hope you will. I would like very much for you to meet Joshua and Ilsa and Bertram too. Someday.

Quite often, I think about that line from my sister's book, where she said that even amid all the terrible things that were *happening to us, she still believed in the goodness of people. So do I, Pim. Brigitta, the nun, saved me. And Mother's friend Eduard took care of me in Frankfurt when I thought I had no one left. Ilsa and Bertram, they brought me to America, and loved me as if I were their family. Shelby has become my true American friend, and Joshua . . . Joshua has given me breath again.*

I hope that you too have continued to believe in the goodness of people, Pim. That you too are happy in your new life.

✣

I hear a knock at the door of my studio apartment, and I put my pen and the paper down. The papers form a long thick pile now, more than a diary, maybe even more than a book.

I gather the paper into a neater pile and put it all into the thick brown envelope, which I have already addressed to Switzerland. I seal it. And then I put it on the corner of my table. I will mail it. Soon. Maybe tomorrow. Maybe next week. Sometime—

I hear the knock at the door again, and I stand. "Just a minute," I call. I give Katze a quick pat on the head and pick up my small pink purse, which Shelby had been ecstatic to find in the exact pink shade of our bridesmaid's dresses.

I open the door, and Joshua stands there, his tall body arched in the frame. He wears a black suit with a starched white shirt and black tie. He holds his hands behind his back, but when he sees me, he pulls his arms around, and I see he is holding a small nosegay of pink roses in one hand. "For the bridesmaid," he says, smiling his uniquely Joshua smile, where his gray-green eyes dance across my face. Then he unfolds his other hand to reveal a small ball of twine. "For Mr. Katz," he says.

I laugh, and I take the twine and throw it in the direction of Katze, who is lying on the blue couch. He peeks his head up for a moment, then ignores both the twine and Joshua, and goes back to sleep.

I turn back to Joshua and take the flowers. "They're beautiful," I say, and I smile back at him. I hold them to my nose and inhale the sweet sharp scent. They too seem to match my dress exactly, which is a pink taffeta with long sleeves, which Shelby decided upon after I told her I was Jewish and showed her my tattoo. In typical Shelby fashion, she only shrugged, offered me a cigarette, and then told me not to worry at all about the dress. To her, my tattoo, my religion, it changed nothing between us. Though of course she might have flinched had I told her the rest. Worse, she might not have been able to keep it to herself. And that, I think, is the real reason that I hold my final secret close, and have told only Ilsa and Joshua.

"You ready?" Joshua asks now. I grab my coat off the chair, pull it over my shoulders, and then Joshua holds out his hand, across the doorway.

"I'm ready," I say. I take his hand and step out into the hallway. He gives my hand a squeeze, and he smiles one more time as he pushes open the front door to my building with his other hand.

We are still holding hands, even outside on Ludlow Street, then Eighteenth. As we walk we laugh and talk about the future, our breath frosting beautiful circles in the winter night.

AUTHOR'S NOTE

❧

THE FIRST TIME I READ *THE DIARY OF A YOUNG GIRL*, I WAS thirteen. As an American teenager in the early 1990s—even a Jewish one—I didn't think the book would have much to do with me. That is, until I read it. I was the same age as Anne was when she wrote the diary, a writer, a dreamer, Jewish— had I lived fifty years earlier in Europe, I might have been the one writing the diary in hiding. It was a terrifying thought.

Nearly twenty years later, I picked up the diary again, and this time, as I read it, I was struck by something entirely different. Anne Frank had an older sister, Margot, who also kept a diary in the annex. I realized I didn't really remember Margot from my earlier teenage reading of Anne's diary, but as an older sister myself, I was interested in what happened to her, in how her experience in the annex was different from Anne's, and what their sister relationship was like. So I set out to learn more about Margot, only to discover that virtually all that is known of her today is the little that Anne wrote within the pages of her diary. (Margot's diary, unlike Anne's, was never recovered after the war.) I began to wonder about the two sisters, both of whom were teenagers during the Holocaust, both Jews, both hiding in the annex, both keeping diaries. How is it that one sister and her diary have, in the aftermath, become an icon of the Holocaust, a symbol for a whole generation, while the other sister is today virtually unknown? And thus the idea for *Margot* was born.

Though this book is a work of fiction, and the Margot Frank/Margie Franklin within these pages is my own creation, I drew loosely from historical fact for some of the scenes and people surrounding the annex, as well as for Margot/Margie's character.

In July of 1942, sixteen-year-old Margot Frank received a call-up notice from the Germans to report to a forced-labor camp, and Otto Frank quickly took the family into hiding in the annex above his office at 263 Prinsengracht, sooner than he'd originally planned, in order to prevent Margot from going. The Frank family—Edith, Otto, Anne, and Margot—were soon joined by the van Pelses—Hermann, Auguste, and their son, Peter. Later they were also joined by a dentist, Fritz Pfeffer, and when he came to the annex, Margot left the room she shared with her sister to sleep in their parents' room while Anne shared a room with Mr. Pfeffer. Peter brought his cat, Mouschi, to the annex, while Margot and Anne were forced to leave their own cat, Moortje, behind.

As described by Anne in her diary, Margot was the older, quieter, more responsible sister. Anne often teased Margot, calling her a "paragon of virtue." Margot was highly intelligent, and used her time in the annex to further her studies. (Among many other things, Margot really did learn shorthand in the annex.) Anne also mentions the annex members' weights at one point in her diary, and Margot did weigh 132 pounds then, though there are also several mentions in the diary of Margot not eating enough.

Some episodes in the annex that Margie remembers here are also based on things Anne wrote about in her diary. For instance, Anne and Margot did lie cramped together in Anne's bed and read each other's diaries. Margot did listen in to a business meeting for her father while Anne fell asleep on the floor beside her, but Margie's memory of Otto praising Anne for her notes is fictional. The burglary Margie recounts in the annex also happened on several occasions, though Peter's coming to find Margot in the middle of the night is fictional.

One of the things I distinctly remembered from my earlier teenage reading of the diary was Anne's relationship with Peter. But rereading the diary many years later, I noticed that while Anne wrote of her own growing feelings for Peter, she also wrote and wondered about whether Margot might like him too. Which led me to also wonder: how might Margot have felt about Peter, and how might Peter have felt about her? Without Margot's diary, I'm not sure we'll ever know the true answers to those questions. In reality, I don't know how close they were, how much they liked each other, or if they did at all. The idea that they spent time together at night in Peter's room, that Peter told Margot they would be together after the war and go to Philadelphia, is all completely fictional. However, the idea that Peter would not want people to know he was Jewish after the war is based on what Anne wrote about him in her diary.

Margie Franklin refers to specifics from her sister's diary here, and I have tried to keep these things consistent with the actual diary, although I (and Margie) conveniently leave some pieces out. For instance, Anne does write that she is not in love with Peter at one point in her diary (though I, and Margie, leave out the part where later on she wonders if she might be).

The reality of Margot Frank's teenage life just before the family's move to the annex remains, for the most part, a mystery to me, and the majority of what I've included here is fictional. The Frank family really did live on the Merwedeplein, and Anne and Margot attended the Jewish Lyceum, where Margot did very well academically. However, Margot's first diary, *Maria,* and the boy named Johann are fictional. The scene where Margot is approached by the Green Police on the Prinsengracht shortly before she was called up did not, to the best of my knowledge, happen. Though I found a photograph of the Frank family at the beach in happier times, the scene here where Margie remembers her last beach vacation with Anne is fictional.

The inhabitants of the annex were found in hiding in August 1944, though I took fictional liberties with what they were doing in those last moments before they were discovered. They were taken to Westerbork in Holland, then, in September, they were transferred to Auschwitz in Poland, where the men and women were separated. Anne, Margot, and Edith were given tattoos, though the scene here that Margie remembers is fictional. Their exact tattoo numbers are not known today, but they are thought to have been between A-25060 and A-25271.

Though Anne and Margot were transported from Auschwitz to Bergen-Belsen in the fall of 1944, all the details here of Margot's escaping from the Nazis are entirely fictional. The real Margot Frank made it to Bergen-Belsen and succumbed to typhus there a few days before Anne in March of 1945. Both were buried in a mass grave. Peter van Pels died in Mauthausen in May of 1945, just before the camp was liberated.

Thus the characters and situations Margot/Margie encounters after she escapes the Nazis are all fictional. There was no Sister Brigitta, Eduard, or Ilsa, and no Judischausen synagogue. In Margie's Philadelphia world, all the characters, situations, and places are fictional with the exception of many of the street names and a few locations such as Fairmount Park, Reading Terminal Market, Robin's Books, John Wanamaker's, Levittown, and Margate, which are or were real places in and around the Philadelphia area.

The incidents of anti-Semitism that Margie describes in Philadelphia in the 1950s are historically accurate. In May of 1954, a flaming flare was nailed to a door accompanied by anti-Semitic language; in April of 1954, a gang of hoodlums was arrested for committing anti-Semitic attacks against Jewish kids; and in October 1953, a firebomb was thrown into a synagogue. However, I read about the incidents in the archives of the *Jewish Telegraphic Agency* (not in the *Inquirer,* as Margie does). The incident Margie mentions reading about of swastikas on synagogues in 1959 is not based on one specific incident in Philadelphia, but on several articles and accounts from that time period recording Jewish places being defiled with swastikas.

In reality, Otto Frank was the only one from the annex to have survived the concentration camps, and after he returned to Amsterdam and learned that his daughters were dead, Miep Gies gave him Anne's diary, which she had rescued from the annex. Anne's diary was originally published in Dutch in 1947, then in English in 1952. The book was followed by the play in 1955, and the American movie *The Diary of Anne Frank,* in 1959, which won three Oscars. Mr. Frank married Elfriede "Fritzi" Markovits Geiringer, and they settled in Switzerland.

While writing this book, I read countless books and articles, visited Web sites, and watched several movies in an attempt to glean everything I possibly could about Margot and the people of her world. I read and reread (and reread again!) *The Diary of a Young Girl,* both the definitive edition and the version that Margie would've read in 1959, as well as watched the 1959 movie that Margie talks about in the book. Additionally I read *Anne Frank: the Book, the Life, the Afterlife* by Francine Prose, and *Anne Frank Remembered: The Story of the Woman Who Helped to Hide the Frank Family* by Miep Gies and Alison Leslie Gold. (The epigraph quote about Margot came from "Afterword: My 100th Birthday" in Gies and Gold's book.) The United States Holocaust Memorial Museum Web site and the Anne Frank House Museum Web site were especially helpful. Any inaccuracies, mistakes, or fictionalizations within these pages—intentional or not—are entirely my own.

In the end, neither Margie Franklin nor I know what actually happened to Margot Frank's diary from the annex. What I do know is that what happened to these two sisters, their family, their friends, and so many other Jews is something that still terrifies, horrifies, and haunts me. And that, most of all, is why I wrote this book. In creating Margot/Margie here, I wanted to give back what was stolen from her, even if only in a fictional world: her voice, her life, her happy ending.

ACKNOWLEDGMENTS

An enormous thank-you to my agent, Jessica Regel, without whose encouragement and support, I'm entirely sure I never would've written this book. I am so grateful for her comments, ideas, and wisdom on countless drafts, as well as her continued unfailing belief in me and my work. I'm so lucky to have her in my corner, always! Thank you also to the amazing team at JVNLA, who truly are the best, especially Tara Hart, Laura Biagi, and Jennifer Weltz, to whom I am indebted for her invaluable early feedback.

I feel so incredibly fortunate that this book found its way into the very wise and capable hands of my editor at Riverhead Books, Laura Perciasepe. Her unparalleled enthusiasm for this story and her brilliant edits and insights have made her an absolute joy to work with. I am deeply grateful for her guidance and support, as well as that of the entire team at Riverhead, who gave this book a home and brought it through every step of the publication process in the best possible way, with extra thanks to publicists Leslie Schwartz, Craig Burke, Fiona Brown, and Meagan Brown. Thank you also to the team at Orlando for giving this book a home in the Netherlands, and especially Jacqueline Smit for her early insights.

I'm very grateful to have a network of friends and family who offer unlimited support. Thank you especially to Maureen

Lipinski and Laura Fitzgerald, whose encouragement kept me going in the early stages of writing this book; Monica Tufo, BFF extraordinaire; and Rachel Fogarty, the reason why I tell stories about sisters. Thank you to Ronna and Alan Cantor, my parents, who always encouraged me to follow my dreams and never give up. And an extra thank-you to my dad for helping with the Philadelphia details. Any mistakes here are mine, not his.

Thank you to my husband, Gregg Goldner, who always believes, listens, loves unconditionally, and insists I find the time to disappear into a fictional world. And to my children, who make all my stories worth telling, but most especially, this one.

Jillian Cantor has a BA in English from Penn State University and an MFA from the University of Arizona, where she was also a recipient of the national Jacob K. Javits Fellowship. The author of several books for teens and adults, she grew up in a suburb of Philadelphia. She currently lives in Arizona with her husband and two sons. Visit her online at www.jilliancantor.com.